FREE TO BE ME

MARY V. MACAULEY

Edited by
KIRSTEN REES

Cover Design: Julie Williams
Editor: Kirsten Rees | Book Editor & Author Coach Published by Rees Publishing
www.kirstenrees.co.uk

CONTENTS

Foreword   v

PART I

1. – A WORKING-CLASS LAD –   3
2. – THE JACOB JOHNSON LINEAGE –   14
3. – SADIE MCGEE –   22
4. – THE JOHNSON'S LINEAGE –   27
5. – LIFE IN THE NEW WORLD –   31
6. – THE YOUNG FOREIGNERS –   35
7. – TEATIME ENGLISH STYLE –   39
8. – A CHILD IS A BLESSING –   48
9. – ADAH –   54
10. – SAMANTHA DIES –   60
11. – ARISTOCRATIC HAWTHORN'S   63
    SEARCH FOR AN HEIR –
12. – AGE OF DISCOVERY –   68
13. – DANIEL HAWTHORN –   72
14. – LORD JOSEPH HAWTHORN –   76
15. – 1830 FINANCIAL DISASTER –   79
16. – KEEPING UP APPEARANCES –   80
17. – THE HAWTHORNS VISIT PERTH –   87
18. – THE FATAL ACCIDENT –   93
19. – ORPHANED & PENNILESS –   97
20. – MANNA FROM HEAVEN –   105
21. – THE HAWTHORN JOHNSON   109
    COOPERATIVE –
22. – A GUARDED ENCOUNTER –   115
23. – A NEW GENERATION: LET IT BE A   118
    BOY –
24. – NEW HOME FOR THE NEW BABY –   124

25. – THE JACK & SARA JOHNSON   128
  LINEAGE –
26. – NOT ANOTHER BOY –   132
27. – EVERYONE PULLING THEIR WEIGHT   134
  –
28. – A FLUTE AT ANY PRICE –   142
29. – FREEDOM –   149
30. – RIDING THE FREIGHT TRAIN   157
  NORTH –
31. – EPILOGUE –   163

PART II

32. – INNOCENT & IMMATURE –   167
33. – HOMELESS, PREGNANT, PENNILESS – 181
34. – MR. ROBERT NEWCOMB,   192
  PLANTATION OWNER –
35. – THE OLIVER FAMILY –   198
36. – MAIZE'S STORY: A NEW BEGINNING – 208
37. – THE ATTIC –   217
38. – MAIZE'S BATH –   229
39. – MAIZE'S DILEMMA –   233
40. – LOUISA AT THE PIANO –   237
41. – MAIZE AT THE PIANO –   240
42. – THE SINFUL EVENT REVEALED –   247
43. – PLANNING MAIZE'S ESCAPE –   253
44. – THE TERRIFYING ESCAPE –   256
45. – ARRIVAL AT THE BUS STATION –   259
46. – MABEL'S JOURNEY HOME –   265
47. – MAIZE ON THE BUS –   269
48. – A BRAND NEW WORLD –   275
49. – THE DEVASTATING NEWS –   285
50. – ENTERING THE HOUSE –   292
51. – MAIZE'S REFLECTIONS –   303
52. – A MATCH NOT MADE IN HEAVEN –   307

PART III

53. KENNETH'S REFLECTIONS   317
54. ALONE AGAIN   325

Afterword   329
Acknowledgments   331
About Mary V. Macauley   333

FOREWORD

Is there any better feeling in the world than being able to say, "I finally made it, I have arrived, I'm finally *FREE To Be Me* (no matter what your age)?"

As the daughter of author Mary Macauley, I felt compelled to share that I am so happy, honored, and proud to be able to write the Foreword for this book!

I'm thrilled to have had the honor and the privilege to be able to help my mother with this book.

At eighty-three years young at the time of publication, my mother, who's always been a trailblazer, having been one of two other women who started the very first domestic violence shelter in California, back in the late seventies, now has truly proven that AGE IS NOTHING BUT A NUMBER!

She's been writing the story for donkey's years, (as she says) and all I can say is that, although it was not written as a thriller, to me, it is an electrifying, suspenseful thriller!!!

This story had me literally sitting on the edge of my seat with tingles and goosebumps at every turn! All I could do was shake my head NON-STOP in wonder and disbelief. I constantly asked my mother (while in the middle of reading it) . . . "Where in the world do you get this stuff from?"

But believe me, it's not 'stuff ' - it's sheer genius!!

I told her more times than I can count, "I never knew you had this kind of talent! Where have you been keeping this creative brilliance buried?"

My mother's incredible, deep, soulful writing has been compared to authors such as the renowned Dr. Maya Angelou, to name a few.

Joyce King, Ph.D, Board President, Professor Of Education at Georgia State University after reading just five pages told my mother she would describe it in just two words . . . "Toni Morrison!"

I am honored and thrilled my mother is able to see her book in print. All she would love is just to know that other people enjoy her stories as much as she enjoys writing them and she would also hope she might inspire and remind other senior citizens to NEVER STOP CHASING YOUR DREAM! It's *never* too late!

I love you Mom and sooooo proud of you, and there's no question I got my talent for writing from you!

- Julie Williams

PART I

1

– A WORKING-CLASS LAD –

MALCOLM HAWTHORN, BELPER, ENGLAND

MALCOLM HAWTHORN
1790-1860

SAMANTHA HAWTHORN
1791-1855

MR. MALCOLM HAWTHORN AND SAMANTHA SHARP, THE woman who would become his bride, were born and raised in the small rural village of Belper in the middle of England. The young couple had known each other since childhood and were both raised by a single parent.

When Samantha was four years old, her mother died in childbirth. Her father never remarried and he raised his only child alone; he loved and cherished her.

Mr. Sharp was the headmaster of the local high school. Their lives were simple but pleasant. Likewise, Malcolm's mother, Mrs. Agnes Hawthorn was widowed when tragically his father died in a traffic accident. She was a ward sister at the local county hospital. At the end of her day shift, Agnes checked out and left the hospital. It was a bitter cold night, so cold the streets were covered with ice. She'd had a busy shift due to the bitter change in the weather.

There were several emergency room accidents, many of the patients were children due to them slipping on the ice. Eager to get home at the end of her long shift, she walked cautiously across the red road to the tramcar stop on the opposite side of the road. Agnes was looking forward to enjoying a hot cup of tea in front of the fire.

After reaching the tramcar stop, she heard nurse Kitty from her ward, calling after her.

"Sister," she called, slightly out of breath. "We just got a bike accident from Grey Lane an' I know you're -"

Ignoring the weather, Mrs. Hawthorn ran as fast as her legs could carry her back to the Emergency Room. When she rushed into the emergency area, Dr. Grey the E.R. specialist on duty, reached for her.

"Agnes," he said. "I am so very sorry ..."

But Agnes did not stop to listen, she ran straight into the only curtained-off cubical. Devastated at the sight of him, she threw herself on the bed where her dead husband was still.

Traffic had been light and he was familiar with the route, in fact, he would joke he could find his way home with his eyes closed. He was that familiar with it.

A witness shared that her husband hadn't anticipated the struggle of a huge lorry he encountered as the driver fought to prevent his vehicle from sliding across the ice.

The anxious driver panicked when he saw the faint light just ahead of him. He told the constable he attempted to swerve his truck to avoid hitting the moving light.

Later, she heard the driver's version of events. "I did my best officer, I didn't realize it was a bicycle until I collided with the bike and the unfortunate rider. It was the ice officer, that infernal black ice ..."

As a ward sister, Agnes was no stranger to death. Over the years, she had perfected a very sensitive approach to the heart broken survivors. Her approach was so serene and the effect eased the survivors' pain. And yet now, her own grief was uncontrollable so Dr. Grey had to sedate her.

In time, Agnes resigned herself to being a single mother. Although a young woman still, the thought of remarrying again, never entered her head. She adored her husband and considered herself blessed having had him in her life, even for a short time.

Agnes had a son to raise and she would do the very best she could to raise him right. Young Malcolm was her world. From a very early age, his parents had recognized and encouraged their son's enquiring mind, coupled with his sense of adventure.

From the moment of his birth, Malcolm was raised in a loving and secure home. He was a happy child, always learning more of what he loved, never letting the present define his future. And, from an early age, Malcolm knew his future would be bigger and brighter than the rural village he called home.

Malcolm was fascinated with botany while still a very young child. What caught his attention and began his life-long interest and love of gardening began when he was invited to his classmate, Barry Martin's eighth birthday party.

There were lots of homemade cakes, pies, blancmange, and the sweetest red strawberries. Barry bragged that his mother made everything herself, even the strawberries. Malcolm loved strawberries, especially strawberry jam, but he had never previously given much thought to the fruit he loved so much.

When he went to bed that night, he thought about strawberries and his mother spreading strawberry jam on his toast. He told his mother the next morning about the homegrown strawberries he had at Barry's party.

"And were they plump and sweet?" his mother asked, smiling at her only child.

"They were Ma, they were delicious."

"And did you have lots of cake?"

"Lots of cake, but his ma got the strawberries from their backyard! She planted them herself," he said incredulously.

"Yes, darling a lot of people grow vegetables and fruit in their gardens."

"Can I grow some strawberries in ours, Mom?"

Mrs. Hawthorn smiled at her ever-curious and eager child and ruffled his red, curly hair.

"You want us to grow strawberries in our backyard?

Staring at her little boy in amazement as he nodded excitedly; she said, "Well if that's what you want to do, I think you should go to the library and read all about starting a garden. Then we can have a chat with Mr. Simpson, the green grocer."

When he saw pictures of the tiny seeds, Malcolm was truly amazed and he wanted to know how food could grow from such teeny, weenie seeds.

Fascinated, he read on. When he discovered the soil in his garden was too fine to grow strawberries and so he would need to add sand to the soil, he knew exactly where to go.

One of his classmates, Danny James' father made bricks and he kept a big supply of sand in his backyard. So, he paid Mr. James a visit.

"Mr. James," said Malcolm when the man answered the door. "I want to grow strawberries and me ma said I need to add sand to the soil in our backyard. Your Danny said you have stacks of sand because you make bricks."

"Aye, that's right lad. An' just how much sand will you be needin'?"

"About a bucket full, me ma said, Sir."

"An' do ye have a bucket lad, 'cos the sand is free but I'll charge you rent for my bucket," he said, smiling.

"Me ma has two buckets," Malcolm said, smiling from ear-to-ear.

"Well then, boyo, you go an' fetch your ma's bucket an' I will fill it up for ya. But I'll want some of those strawberries come summertime, mind ya."

"Yes Sir, Mr. James. I promise, the biggest and the best."

Mr. James watched him run down the lane to his house.

Malcolm planted in April and by the end of June, he was amazed at the yield. He kept his promise and took a bowl full of plump red strawberries to Mr. James who was clearly surprised and delighted. He ruffled Malcolm's hair and thanked him for the gift.

Malcolm's mother made jam and preserves plus, they had fresh strawberries for several weeks. Now, Malcolm also loved sprouts and asked his mother if she would buy some seeds in late fall. He wanted to plant them before the frost set in.

Mrs. Hawthorn took her little boy to the local greengrocer and purchased a few packages of the tiny, black seeds. Malcolm was rather skeptical when he saw the size and color of the tiny seeds, but he followed the instructions to the letter.

He nurtured his very first winter crop, fighting all the time to rid himself of his doubtful thoughts. He did so well with his first yield, he had to give a lot of the sprouts away to neighbors and friends. The following year, he took over the entire back garden and planted several rows of his favorite vegetable.

"Malcolm, do you have any idea just how many sprouts this lot will yield?" his mother asked her industrious little boy.

"Aye, I do Ma."

"Well, what in God's name do you plan on doing with them?" she asked him, wide-eyed. "They're not strawberries, so I can't make jam out of sprouts."

"Well," he said, winking at his mother. "This time I'm going to sell them."

And he did. He could have sold more if he'd had them. Malcolm was chuffed. He spent two pennies for the seeds but he made thirty shillings.

While mates were kicking a ball or riding their bike, Malcolm was in the public library learning as much as he could about botany. What started as a child's doubtful experiment, in time, turned into a creative hobby and a profitable business venture for him.

He became a shrewd and profitable young man while still in his teens; depositing most of his profits into a savings account with the Bank of England.

In addition to his love of plants and agriculture, Malcolm was also an adventurous lad. He dreamed one day of sailing across the world, traveling to the Continent or America.

The local library was no stranger to Malcolm. Unlike most boys his age, the main librarian knew him from when he was just a little boy. His mother would meet him after school let out and walk him to their local library. She would leave him to browse and read his favorite books.

Three houses later, at the end of her shift, she would walk back to pick him up. He was seldom ready to leave. His mother would gently say, 'tomorrow is another day'.

Obediently but reluctantly he would leave, knowing he would return the following day. In the winter months when he was ten years old, Malcolm would walk to the library after school, promising his mother he would return home before it got dark.

Malcolm was an obedient son and he never let his mother down. By the time he turned fifteen, his constant dream was of immigrating to America.

With no desire to go to university, Malcolm left school when he was fifteen-years-old and got a job with a local farmer. His interest in agriculture became a passion and he continued to spend time in the local library researching soil composites and all aspects of enriching soil to produce a healthy crop.

The winter months were always slow and he could most often be found in the library reading or researching.

The librarian, Mrs. Wentworth had worked in the library for over forty years. She was very fond of Malcolm whom she had known since he was five-years-old and over the years she learned how keen he was to go to America.

So, when she spotted an advertisement one day, Mrs. Wentworth immediately knew he would be interested in it. She patted him on the shoulder and when he looked up at her, she put her index finger to her pursed lips and handed Malcolm the folded newspaper.

She tapped her finger on the ad. Had it been her own newspaper, she would have circled the ad for him, but it was the property of the library and under no circumstances would she deface library property.

It was an advertisement for a small plantation in America. Malcolm was over the moon with joy as he read the advertisement silently.

For Sale: Rain-damaged tobacco plantation.
Sole heir resides in a distant state.
Must sell, rich soil; house in need of repair but generously priced;
including many workers.
Please, contact my lawyer immediately,
Sincerely,
Robert Johnson

Overjoyed, Malcolm rushed home to share his delightful news with his mother. He had over the years said he wanted to travel to other countries and learn about agriculture on other lands and in other climates and as he grew older his desire had only grown stronger.

He had from time to time shared this dream with his mother but she paid little attention to his 'wistful daydreams'. She had no idea he was quite so serious, instead expecting he would soon marry the lovely Samantha.

She had long imagined they would settle in the village so that she and Samantha's father would delight in becoming grandparents one day.

Malcolm Hawthorn had not considered that his happiness would be one sided or his joy would bring instant sadness for his mother. He had, after all, shared this dream with his mother since he was a lad; this dream had stayed with him throughout his adolescence and youth.

When he had fallen in love with Samantha Sharp, the prettiest girl in his village; he had also shared his adventurist dream with her. Samantha was thrilled with her new fiancé's vision. For years, she had dreamed of escaping the tiny village, so remote from urban life.

Mrs. Hawthorn was devastated when her only child shared how serious he was about his dream to immigrate to America.

She knew of his passion and love of agriculture and he had from time to time mentioned he would love to travel to other countries.

However, she thought these were just youthful, adventurist dreams! Never in the world did she suspect or imagine his dream was to immigrate to America. The thought of no longer walking with him each Sunday morning to their parish church at the bottom of the hill, made her bottom lip quiver.

Nurse Hawthorn did all she could to quell her tears and keep her emotions in check. She held back her tears, feeling instantly alone and knowing if his dream came true there would be no one to console her.

Reginald Sharp, who was affectionately known to his mates as Reggie, was devoted to his only child, Samantha. He too was devastated when Malcolm shared his lifelong dream with him. Mr. Sharp did not want his daughter to leave him, to leave her home, her country, and to cross an ocean.

Reggie was torn emotionally; he liked and respected Malcolm very much. Still, Samantha was his only child and her going so far away would leave him all alone, and he knew it would break his heart. She was all he had.

One evening, over a drink in his local pub, he discussed it with oldest friend and drinking buddy Arthur.

"I knew him from when he was in nappies. An' I watched him grow into a fine young lad, well-mannered and respectful of everyone. He'll be a good husband of that, I have no doubt. It's just that America is so far away."

"Aye, it is that," said his friend. "But you can go over and visit them, and then visit their little ones when they arrive."

Mr. Sharp smiled warmly, but his heart was sad even though he knew Malcolm would make a fine husband and would take good care of his daughter.

Still, it broke his heart just the thought of her being so far away from home. After all, she had never been out of England, or Derbyshire, for that matter, let alone the British Isles.

Sam's father feared she was much too young to travel across the world to a new life; a life neither of them knew much, if anything, about.

Reggie admired and respected Malcolm. "He's a fine young man with a good head on his shoulders."

"He's an ambitious lad, I'm sure he'll take good care of your bonny lass," said Arthur.

"Of that, I have no doubt," Reggie replied sharply. "But she's only eighteen-years-old," he mumbled as he gestured to order two refills. "An' she's all I've got."

Hearing the sadness in his friend's voice gave Arthur pause to reflect. As he reached for his fresh drink, he said, "It's easy to speculate about so many things when you're young, in love, and have a head full of dreams weighing you down," he said.

"Aye, but they are young; their heads are in the clouds all full of dreams. But it's a long, long way to go, to realize your dream," Mr. Sharp said softly.

However, young Mr. Hawthorn was not only determined, he was persuasive too and promised Reginald Sharp that as soon as he made his fortune he would bring or send his wife back to England every couple of years, and in time her father and Malcolm's mother would cross the ocean to visit them in their new home. Or, better still, he added, "They decide to make America their new home too."

Malcolm had read many articles on the thriving opportunities for hard working, self-starters in America. He studied long and hard, especially the agricultural reports. He was well informed and learned of opportunities abound in the new world.

Samantha pleaded with her father relentlessly and he was torn emotionally. After all, she was all he had in the world.

However, when he realized just how much his daughter loved Malcolm, he consented. Albeit reluctantly, fearing his only child would lose the love of her life if he refused to give her hand in marriage.

Mr. Sharp finally gave in to his daughter's constant pleading and also agreed to lend his new son-in-law the money to go to America and purchase the farmland he saw advertised.

It was with a heavy heart when Mr. Sharp gave his blessing and approval, for Malcolm Hawthorn to marry Samantha.

– THE JACOB JOHNSON LINEAGE –

MACON GEORGIA, USA

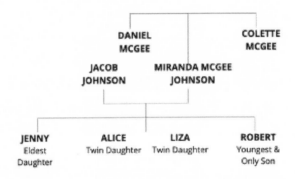

MR. JACOB JOHNSON FELL HEAD OVER HEELS IN LOVE WITH THE beautiful Miranda McGee, with her green eyes and golden hair reflecting her rich, Irish heritage. As the only surviving child of Daniel and Colette McGee, she was adored by her parents.

She was just a toddler when her young parents immigrated to America. The McGees were shrewd and wealthy landowners. They each came from very large families in Ireland and hoped to have many children themselves.

Alas, it was not to be. Miranda was their only surviving child; several infants were either stillborn or died in infancy.

Jacob Johnson was a poorly paid schoolteacher whose first love was carpentry. His father was a master carpenter and taught his son the trade. Jacob loved carpentry; he helped his father build their home and many of the pieces of furniture in his father's home.

Jacob had aspirations of opening his own school, to teach the skill of carpentry to other boys. However, when he fell in love with Miranda, her father convinced him to take a job with him as his accountant.

Mr. O'Grady liked Jacob and when he realized his daughter was in love with him, he convinced Jacob he would need a better paying job in order to provide his only child with the comforts she was born into. Jacob accepted the position and six months later, he married Miranda with her parent's blessings.

On the first anniversary of their wedding, a beautiful golden- haired baby girl was born. The happy couple was delighted with their first child. One year later, she gave birth to twin daughters.

Over the next four years, there was a series of miscarriages and still born pregnancies. Miranda was weak, there was very little time for her body to heal and regain her strength before she was pregnant again.

Days before their baby boy - the desired son and heir - was born, Miranda's father died in a hunting accident. Miranda's mother Colette was in Ireland at the time, taking care of her own mother who was recovering from a stroke.

When word reached Colette about her husband, she was devastated and consumed with grief. But as the only remaining child to survive more than one epidemic, she was both morally and duty bound to remain with her poorly mother.

She was deeply traumatized at the thought of not attending the funeral and burial of her beloved husband.

The decision on whether to remain in Ireland weighed heavily on her. She decided to speak with Mother Superior at the Sisters of Mercy's convent and nursing home.

Colette made this request knowing full well she would not arrive in time to witness the burial of her darling Danny, but she felt compelled to reduce the thousands of miles separating her from her one and only life-long love.

Mother Superior agreed to accommodate her mother until Colette returned at a designated time. Colette contacted her solicitor and her bank manager to purchase her Ocean Liner ticket for a private berth and to make regular payments to the convent home where her mother was convalescing.

Before retiring for the night, Colette instructed her mother's housekeeper to prepare a hearty breakfast and to wake her in the morning at 7:30 on the nose.

Molly had, as instructed, prepared a hearty breakfast the following morning, for the long ride to the North Sea where her mistress would sail across the ocean to America.

Molly knocked softly on Colette's bedroom door in the morning as requested. When there was no response to her knock, she knocked again and called her name several times. Feeling a little agitated, knowing the breakfast she had cooked was now getting cold, she started to walk away when she heard the alarm clock buzz.

Relieved, she waited for a few seconds, but when she did not hear any movement, she knocked again, but was not sure if her knocks would be heard over the loud buzz of the alarm clock which was still buzzing. Molly banged really hard on the door and rattled the doorknob, but there was still no response. Frustrated she began to walk away, then she decided on second thought to open the bedroom door and poke her head inside.

"Madam!" she called softly, but when there was no response, she called out louder.

"Madam, it's just turned seven thirty and, and ..." Gradually, Molly approached the bed and she screamed at the top of her voice; Madam was dead.

Molly and a few school friends of Colette's attended the funeral.

Forever prone to fantasy and superstition, Molly informed those who attended the Wake, "I would swear on me own mother's grave I heard Daniel himself, calling to his beloved wife from the grave. I, an' not just once mind ya. Sure, and didn't he love her that much? Well, it's their wee lass I feel sorry for, her bein' with child an' all. May God have mercy on her and her babi."

She then crossed herself several times.

Dr. Brian Davis, the McGee's family doctor forbade Miranda to attend her father's funeral, he said she was far too weak and he insisted on complete bed rest. She was very weak but she insisted, after all, she was the only family member and felt compelled to attend. She adored her papa.

Her husband asked Annie, who was his wife's personal maid, to stay close to his wife while she attended her father's funeral. Annie's baby boy was just three weeks older than Miranda's son.

This would be the first of two devastating tragedies Miranda would have to suffer through in as many days. As the only surviving child of her parents, Miranda was their grief-stricken heir.

She inherited their entire estate, which was vast. The 8,000 acre plantation, which consisted primarily of cotton, was a thriving enterprise. In addition to the cotton, there were several acres of corn, pecans and a wide variety of livestock plus a significant number of slaves who worked the land.

Three weeks after losing both of her parents and still very weak from the lengthy and painful delivery, Miranda was too fragile to fight for her own life.

Devastated, her heart-broken husband buried his beautiful, grieving wife. Miranda could not survive her broken heart, even the joy of finally giving birth to their much-wanted son, could not ease her painful loss.

Fear engulfed Jacob, and he became a skeptic and extremely superstitious. He feared there was a curse on him and his family. His greatest fear was losing his baby boy, his son and heir. He turned to Annie who was nursing her month-old baby boy. He asked her to nurse his son, along with her own baby boy.

Annie Johnson was more than happy to accommodate the desperate and grieving father who offered to pay her. But Annie rejected his offer of compensation, instead asking for a larger cabin so the two baby boys could have some room to grow once they began to crawl.

Jacob Johnson was so relieved, he accommodated her many subsequent requests. Almost a dozen years later, Jacob married a much younger woman. His new wife, Isabella, he soon learned was vain, self-centered, and had very expensive tastes. So along with his three teenage daughters from his first marriage, his millinery and fancy-attire budget had skyrocketed.

Several storms over the next few years had seriously damaged his crops. Many fields were left fallow and a series of diseases killed some of his livestock. To keep his head above water, reluctantly Jacob had to sell portions of his land. Still in an insolvent state, he was also forced to auction off some of his livestock.

Mr. Johnson did not see himself as a scrooge by any means; but, was often heard mumbling about his new wife's expensive taste. He was constantly overheard saying, 'It seems like my money just flies out the window.'

Each year, he had to sell off more and more acreage in order to keep up with his household expenses. In addition to Isabella's vanity, her outrageously expensive taste, he soon discovered she was more hard hearted than he had previously realized.

In less than a year, Mr. Johnson knew he was over his head in serious debt. However, his sexual passion dictated his actions which included the heinous and drastic decision he made.

There developed a growing tension, throughout the slaves' quarters which spread rapidly. The able-bodied men and women did all they could to stay busy.

However, with so much of the land they used to work no longer belonging to the current owners; many more of them were being sold, along with each parcel of land.

Each evening when the remaining families lay their heads down, on their own pallet, with their children in tow, became a blessing. All they could do was hope and pray their family, sons, daughters, husbands or wives would not be sold.

Fear was forever evident, on the faces and minds of slaves on the plantation, when rumors spread about extensive financial issues or diminishing profits.

Mr. Johnson blamed his new wife. He was heard saying, "She cared less about the enormous debt from the wedding and then the honeymoon. It was Isabella who insisted on staying at the newly built hotel, the best Miami had to offer. My wife is to blame for all these catastrophes."

Selling half of his animals provided some modicum of relief; Mr. Johnson had no idea his new wife was such a spendthrift.

But he was in love with the woman half his age and he was bound to please her, especially when she withheld certain marital favors to get what she wanted. The last purchase she made was a very expensive, four-seater Surrey with a fringed canapé on top.

In order to keep his daughter's and his wife's dress and millinery bills paid, still unable to keep his debts in check and his creditors at bay; Mr. McGee decided on a third auction. This auction included some animals and small parcels of land.

The auctioning of slaves was not an unfamiliar sight on plantations in the South and although most families were forever vigilant; doing all that they could, to escape being selected for the auction block.

They would become extra cautious whenever there were rumors of extensive and outstanding bills, or when the bank manager made an uninvited visit to the owner's residence.

The enslaved adults were not unfamiliar with the consequences of their 'master's' financial indebtedness.

There would be lots of shouting and floods of tears being spilled after expensive purchases were made. Consequently, slaves, both outside and inside of those palatial homes, remained invisible to the occupants; even when serious financial discussions took place.

Word soon spread throughout the quarters. So, the entire compound was acutely aware of the tension experienced by the owner; especially if it had been a financially poor year.

The next auction, which was not for land, or cattle, would

be the last auction on his plantation. This kind were despicable, cold hearted, and contemptible.

It inflicted agonizing pain on each victim and all members of their family, not least because it often meant being separated from the members of the family. That decision was made and carried out, without giving a thought to the devastation his cruel act would have on the families being destroyed; the heartbroken parents and their petrified children.

This heart wrenching and agonizing pain, which these families experienced, was suffered mostly in silence. As they stood stoic, choking on their tears, while they watched their beloved husband, children, wife, or parents being auctioned off to God knows who.

This agonizing pain was also devastating for the remaining slaves as it was for the devastated family members. Throughout the slaves' quarters, there was a sea of stoic expressions on the faces of the emotionally silent and powerless family members.

3

– SADIE MCGEE –

SPRING 1808

SADIE JOHNSON WAS THE LAST CHILD BORN ON THE JOHNSON plantation. Her parents Henry and Hannah, a devoted couple since they were teenagers, had jumped the broom a decade earlier.

They had three handsome and lively sons already. Hannah loved her boys as much as her husband did, but deep down she wanted a baby girl. So, when she discovered seven years later that she was pregnant again, she was happily surprised and prayed that this pregnancy would produce a baby girl.

Nine months later, their prayers were answered; Henry and Hanna were ecstatic with joy; they finally had a beautiful baby daughter. The entire community joined the family, as it was their custom to celebrate the joy that this baby girl bestowed on her devoted parents.

Two weeks later, however, the shared joy and happiness that everyone experienced; almost instantly and without any warning, turned into a devastating and heart wrenching tragedy. In less than a year, little Sadie would be orphaned.

When the young Hawthorn couple purchased the rundown property; sight unseen, Sadie was the only surviving member of her biological family still living on the land.

She was told much later that she had three brothers, Timmy, Tommy, and Tucker. However, this orphaned little girl had no recollection of her birth family; what few memories she had of her parents, were told to her, as if in a story.

So, vague in fact, she didn't know if the memories were her own or memories of what she had been told many times as a small child.

Sadie, whose birth had brought so much joy and happiness to her parents, a sister to her three handsome brothers had completed their happy family. Sadly, this baby girl would have no knowledge of the absolute delight, excitement, and overwhelming joy and happiness that her parents shared with their community upon her birth.

However within weeks of her birth, the bottom of her family's world collapsed. Sadie's three brothers were snatched from the 'pen' they had been placed in, along with several other able-bodied young men and boys.

Snatched and sold together. Selling the brothers together was the only humane act that the seller insisted on.

The cruelty of the auction consumed the happy family, ripping them apart. Destroying them and the joyous excitement this new born baby created was instantly crushed with such a deep sadness; an excruciating heartache, with uncontrollable grief.

The absence of visible emotions and heart wrenching pain, engulfed the father of his three young sons just knowing how devastated his wife was.

Powerlessness consumed him; as he stood stoic as she

gripped his hand tightly in the presence of the reality of the ultimate evil and hopeless sin unfolding before their eyes.

A powerlessness that would rip at his own heart and also the tender heart of his beloved wife, knowing full well, and to their detriment, that there was not one, single thing they could do to prevent the excruciating evil unfolding before their eyes.

And so, the grieving, heartbroken mother held back her tears and her sobs, painfully aware that the man she loved could do nothing to prevent it. Hannah knew her husband would not be sold. She also knew that should he try to intervene. Even with a simple plea, the overseer would respond with brutal and anticipated pleasure.

Denis, the illiterate, scrawny man, considered 'poor white trash' all of his life; a small man with the body of a frail teenager. The scrawny little male; inferior in stature and strength; took great pleasure in whipping slaves, often twice his size; until their skin split open with all of their old wounds.

The heart-breaking sorrow and deep distress at being powerless to intervene, was often vacant on the faces of parents, partners and the children, sold or left behind to mourn the loss of kinfolk.

This cruel and emotional trauma consumed Hannah, causing her milk to dry up. Heartbroken, she took to her bed as the deepening depression overwhelmed her. Henry grieved with his wife over the loss of their three sons. Devastated and painfully distraught, he also feared for their new born baby girl, so he went in search of a wet nurse.

His neighbor, Tom Johnson told him that Miss Maggie's daughter Lula Mae just had a healthy girl baby. Henry was grateful for the information and prayed he would get help for his infant daughter. So, without telling his distressed wife, he paid the family a visit.

He first asked permission of the girl's mother; Maggie Johnson was the cook for the owner's household. And after commiserating with him over the loss of his sons and the emotional state that his wife was in, she invited him to kneel-down with her and pray for his son's, his wife and his brand-new baby daughter.

Henry was deeply moved by the sincerity of the woman's prayers and he wept. With Maggie's blessings, she and her daughter agreed to nurse his infant daughter every day until she could feed from a bottle.

Sadie was still being nursed by Lula Mae when her mother died 'of no known causes' according to the doctor's notes on the death certificate. Henry knew full well, what had caused his loving wife's premature death.

Henry adored his wife, and he felt powerless to ease her grief; she had refused to eat. It devastated him, as he watched his adoring wife, waste away. Henry grieved until his own premature death which followed shortly after.

Sadie's parents were still in their teens, when they 'jumped the broom' as was the custom, in their quarters. They were very young and deeply in love. Henry and Hanna's devotion to each other was the envy of the entire compound.

Years later, when the boys were approaching pre-adolescence, their parents were often seen walking hand in hand on warm summer evenings along the lake; from time to time they would fish for Red Snapper.

Henry was often seen pushing his wife on the swing he built when she first announced she was pregnant the first time, almost a dozen years ago.

When Hanna had announced to her husband less than a year earlier that she was again pregnant; they were both surprised but delighted. Their wish for a girl was granted, however, the tragedy that followed was unimaginably cruel.

He was overcome with grief and lethargy intensified his sorrow with his wife's unexpected death. Henry's once enormous appetite waned and sleep was the perpetual stranger that eluded him.

Outside of his window, the shadows from the huge Oak trees that swayed to and fro on his bedroom wall, that rhythmic motion that once relaxed and soothed him, now tormented him. He could find no solace in the beauty that once calmed him.

"Why!" he cried out to God; in anger. "All that I ever loved for more than half of my life, taken away from me. Tell me Lord, what sin did I commit, that You should punish us so?"

In his grieving anger, he cursed at God and all of His angels. He was a desolate and broken man who died of a broken heart, just three months after his wife passed away.

As an orphaned child, Sadie grew up being cared for by no one specifically. However, the remaining families in that community chipped in to care for the now orphaned toddler.

All her basic physical needs were taken care of, she never went to bed dirty or hungry, but she never had a bed to call her own. However, each of the women in the compound, made sure Sadie was fed and had a place to sleep each night.

During the first two years of her life, Sadie never knew from one day to the next which pallet would be hers for the night or whose table she would sit at for supper. She was a lonely child and often pined for the family she was deprived of.

4

– THE JOHNSON'S LINEAGE –

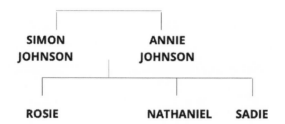

SIMON JOHNSON   ANNIE JOHNSON

ROSIE   NATHANIEL   SADIE

Nathaniel Johnson's family was one of the oldest family's living on the Johnson's plantation; yes, that is where their last name came from. Old Mr. Johnson renamed all the slaves Johnson. It was little Nate's mother, Annie who finally provided a permanent place at her table for Sadie, the orphaned toddler. Annie and her husband Simon, made room for Sadie's pallet in her daughter Rosie's sleeping quarters for the orphaned child and they raised the baby girl as if she was their own daughter.

Several years earlier, Nathaniel and Mr. Johnson's only son Robert had been raised, for the first four years of their life, pretty much together. They were nursed and nurtured by Annie.

She bathed them together and they slept together in the same crib. As toddlers, they were inseparable. Even after young Robert moved permanently into his father's house, the boys spent many hours each day together. Robert was happy to have a playmate his own age; they would go fishing together, swim in the lake and climb trees.

As the only boy, flanked by three older sisters he was seldom seen at home; his only playmate was Nathaniel. Whenever he fell or hurt himself, he would run to Annie to take care of him.

When the boys turned twelve, Mr. Johnson Sr. taught his son and his friend Nathaniel carpentry skills. Robert wasn't very keen, but Nathaniel's father, Simon who was a self-taught carpenter was very pleased for his son and encouraged him to learn all that he could.

Years later, father and son worked on projects together, sharing their skills and knowledge. It was often rumored that the main reason this particular Johnson family was not torn apart or sold as chattel was due to the early care that Annie provided for the land owner's infant son and the sustaining friendship Robert had with Nathaniel.

Robert's father was a zealous carpenter and he looked forward to the time when he would teach his son and his playmate Nathaniel the art and skill of carpentry. Alas this was not to be. His only son showed very little interest in this craft and was soon bored. Mr. Johnson, however, was extremely impressed with Nathaniel's keen interest and delight in learning the new skills.

The landowner was disappointed that his son showed very little interest in what he considered to be one of the oldest professions. The skills he learned were passed down from his father and his grandfather.

Mr. Johnson hoped and expected that there would be a fourth generation of creative carpenters. Alas, this was not to be. Robert's passion was in sports.

However, Robert's father was delighted that Nathaniel shared his love of carpentry, was a quick learner and over the years, they worked on many projects together.

Nathaniel was distraught by the loss of his father; his mother had died earlier that year from a bout of influenza. Emotionally bereft, Nathaniel built a coffin in which to bury his father in the same grave where his mother's remains rested.

Jimmy worked day and night along with Nathaniel to erect as many coffins as they could to bury the dead. There were only a handful of survivors so Nathaniel decided to take charge.

He consulted with Jimmy who approved of his plan to move all of the survivors into the big house. Everyone stayed in the least damaged portion of the house, until the storm was over and the saturated land began to wither and dry.

Mr. Johnson's son, Robert was up north in Ohio visiting friends. He heard about the impending storm but was unable to acquire suitable transportation to take him back home.

When he did eventually return to his father's plantation, it was in shambles; almost everything had been destroyed. It was common knowledge that Robert Johnson, the sole survivor and heir detested farming and had no interest in holding on to the now-dilapidated plantation.

Seeing the state of the place only solidified his distaste for life on a farm. As the sole heir to his father's estate, he immediately contacted his father's insurance broker and was compensated for the damages to the plantation and also collected his father's life insurance.

Prior to leaving the south forever, Robert instructed his attorney to immediately place as many advertisements 'to sell, as is' in as many publications and as soon as possible.

Robert walked away, a very wealthy and conscience-free young man. He headed up north where he invested in a furniture manufacturing company.

5

– LIFE IN THE NEW WORLD –

MALCOLM'S FIRST, SEEMINGLY INSIGNIFICANT INVESTMENT WAS a reasonable sized farm surrounded by much larger farms, he learned that some neighboring plantations once belonged to the deceased owner of his current holding. On the farm he purchased stood the remnants of a once grand house; the dilapidated structure was in dire need of repair.

Fortunately, it was summertime when he arrived with his bride. The newlyweds took great delight in camping out on their own land.

Malcolm gave Jimmy – the only remaining white man on the property - a set of blueprints he had sketched out for the remodeling of the main house. Jimmy was impressed but at the same time overwhelmed, so he asked his new boss if he could bring Nathaniel on board.

Mr. Hawthorn agreed, given the information Jimmy shared with him regarding Nathaniel's carpentry skills. After looking at the plans, Mr. Hawthorn put Nathaniel in charge of the total refurbishment.

He and Jimmy plus a few farm laborers worked to rebuild the ram shackled house and by late autumn, the new owners had a substantial and sturdy roof over their heads. The new windows and shutters were crafted and installed by Nathaniel. The rebuilt hearth with its cast iron ovens in the kitchen was large enough to heat up the whole house in the wintertime while baking several pies, a turkey and a ham, all at the same time.

The morning room, which welcomed the early morning sun in spring and summer through the glass paneled French doors, adjoined the rear sitting room which overlooked the back garden. There were five bedrooms, all of them large, plus the master bedroom wing which was huge compared to what they had been used to in England. Nathaniel knocked down walls in order to refurbish most rooms beyond their former glory.

Malcolm and Samantha were more than satisfied; clearly Nathaniel had gone beyond the owner's expectations. Work on the house, which was now more than twice its original size, would continue throughout the year. The newlyweds were delighted with the transformation, so far, which was more than halfway completed.

Work would continue on the rear of the house, weather permitting. Autumn was slowly moving into winter and the new owners were looking forward to their new and comfortable home being completed before winter set in. They had heard that winters in the south east of the country were often very harsh.

Over the years, the Hawthorns continued to expand their estate and their investment holdings. Malcolm was only interested in purchasing adjoining farms. He was informed that some of the smaller farms were once a part of his estate.

Quite often such properties included field hands and kitchen staff, in addition to the domestic and farm animals. Consequently, their land acquisition increased and he was eventually able to repay all of his debts to his father-in-law.

As he diversified, his rich crops increased, boosting his wealth fivefold. He was proud of his accomplishments and hoped in time that his father-in-law would cross the ocean to see for himself. Alas, that was not to be.

Samantha and Malcolm Hawthorn were totally opposed to slavery. However, with each land purchase that Malcolm made over the following years; there were generally slaves who resided on the property included in each sale. From the very beginning the Hawthorns made it clear that they denounced slavery and if the people who were a part of the sales contract wished to leave, they could. However, none of them had any money as they were never paid a wage.

Malcolm agreed to pay them a living wage if they agreed to stay on and work for six months. After all, the Hawthorns were at a loss as to how they could manage the newly acquired properties given its size and scope. Attracted by this offer and seeing that this new 'owner' was a decent man, many of the families remained. Some, however, chose to leave in search of other family members that had been sold to other plantation owners. And one young man, who went in search of his sweetheart, while the remaining workers stayed on with the Hawthorns.

Malcolm was advised when he took ownership of his new plantation to hire a manager to oversee the work done in the fields, 'since he was a novice in this area of the local agriculture and managing laborers'.

He was informed that all of the survivors of the destructive storm were slave. He was also informed that he would need more workers and an overseer would be the best person to choose the best field workers.

The overseers or manager of the estate he purchased had either perished in the storm or absconded before the destruction was complete. In years, past, Nathaniel's father Simon and Jimmy, an aging white worker were semiskilled in carpentry and would occasionally work on projects together.

After old man Johnson taught Nathaniel the skills of carpentry, Jimmy would engage him or ask his opinion on a job that he found difficult to complete.

Years before the storm which took Simon's life, he and Jimmy had forged a lasting friendship based on mutual respect that would last many decades. Both men liked to fish in their spare time but their main passion was carpentry. Jimmy who was self-taught and he shared his limited knowledge with Simon who preferred carpentry to working in the fields; between them both they were able to manage most tasks. Nathaniel had been trained first as a youth by his father and Jimmy, then by Mr. Johnson, the former landowner who recognized the boy's interest in this trade.

While still working for Mr. Johnson the overseer, Adam Davis constantly refused to free up Nathaniel whenever Jimmy needed his help. Jimmy, who was an indentured servant, didn't like Davis so he would go directly to the owner and obtain written permission to engage Nathaniel whenever Jimmy needed him to complete a new job. Many of the jobs were too big for Jimmy or too difficult; he was suffering from arthritis, so holding a hammer for any length of time caused him great pain. Later as Mr. Johnson's plantation continued to deteriorate and long before the devastating storm, Adam Davis was among the first of the paid workers to abandon ship.

Both Jimmy and Simon were happy to see him go.

6

– THE YOUNG FOREIGNERS –

THE YOUNG HAWTHORNS WERE FOREIGNERS TO THIS PART OF the world. They were outsiders and totally unseasoned to the lifestyle, which dominated this part of the world.

It took several years before they were deemed as a 'well-respected and a socially accepted couple'. Their open distain for slavery put a huge wedge between themselves and the established slave-holding society of prosperous plantation owners.

"Old sins cast long shadows," he told his wife. "We could never be friends with any of our neighbors."

Malcolm was a creative and shrewd businessman; he was also a very hard working landowner who came from humble beginnings; he valued hard work and loyalty irrespective of who the worker was.

Eventually, however, as their land acquisition and crops significantly increased, they were deemed respectable by their neighboring peers and finally invited into 'southern society'.

The young couple was admired by everyone who knew

them, including his many workers who they refused to have them referred to as slaves by anyone. He paid them a fair wage for the work they did on his properties.

At the end of each year, he presented his employees with a deserving bonus for their loyalty and hard work. For those who wished to move on in search of relatives who had been removed or sold by the previous owners, he wished them well on their search; and a job for them should they return.

Both Malcolm and his wife Samantha were raised as an only child and all throughout their childhood they wished for siblings or a cousin to play and share secrets with.

And so, they were also outraged and horrified when listening to the many stories of children or siblings from the estate having been sold and sent away.

Shortly after they'd settled into their completed home, Samantha found herself with idle hands so she decided to work in the kitchen with Adah, the cook and housekeeper.

Being so far from home, Samantha and her husband missed some of the comfort foods that they were raised on. Malcolm loved Cornish pasties and Samantha missed the fruit scones her dad used to make for her.

Martha was Adah's only surviving child still with her; she was fifteen-years-old. Adah's two sons and her oldest daughter were sold years ago, by an earlier landowner.

Adah and her only remaining child were very close, and she was training Martha to be her assistant in the kitchen. She was a warm-hearted young woman, a quick learner and eager to please.

It was Martha's job to keep stock of the food supplies. Each morning, she would go into the garden or greenhouse to pick whatever vegetables were in season, plus eggs from one of the small hen houses that Samuel built for Samantha.

Martha collected freshly laid eggs and fed the animals. There were ducks in the pond, chickens and roosters in the yard or the hen house and swarms of rabbits. Food was plentiful for everyone.

The Hawthorns were completely comfortable in their refurbished home and whenever Malcolm had to go away on a trip, he would hurry home to his wife and the home they both loved.

On the second day of one of her husband's early-on business trips, Samantha decided to engage both mother and daughter to help her create a typical English meal for him when he returned. Martha was a sharp girl with a quick mind, as Samantha soon discovered while helping out in the kitchen.

When he returned from trip, tired and hungry, he devoured the Cornish pasties that Samantha prepared and the roasted garlic sprouts Martha added as a side dish, but what he raved on and on about was the fruit scones.

Samantha told him she had taught Martha how to make them and was pleasantly surprised when she tasted her first batch.

"They practically melted in me mouth," she said amazed. "She watched me make them just once, yesterday and today she made them on her own. Our Martha has the magic touch."

"Aye, that she does, these are even better than me mam's and she's been makin' them for donkeys years. Wait till I tell her."

They both laughed and agreed that from now on Martha was in charge of making the English scones.

As teenagers in England when they were courting, evening walks in the woods was one of the things they enjoyed.

The typography in the area where they now called home

was vastly different, however, they both enjoyed taking walks in the evenings often spotting a rare bird or beast, sometimes they would stop at a favorite spot and read or fish in the small lake.

They totally enjoyed each other's company. It took five years before they were totally accepted by the various social groups, not that they were eager to be acknowledged.

Once the invitations were forthcoming the couple was very selective as to whose invitations they accepted. Many of the invitations were to join a hunting lodge but Malcolm was opposed to the killing of animals just for the sport of it.

Samantha had a more difficult time rejecting her invitations, although they were in her opinion mundane.

The social gatherings included sewing circles, flower arrangements, piano recitals, and high teas hosted by several of the more established families, none of which held much interest for Samantha.

She enjoyed reading, painting and taking walks, often on her own. But she did attend one or two, just to show that she was not a British snob.

7

– TEATIME ENGLISH STYLE –

SEVERAL MONTHS LATER WHEN SPRING WAS IN THE AIR, IT WAS Samantha's turn to have the 'ladies' over for lunch. Samantha discovered another talent of Martha's was her ability to play heavenly music on her flute.

When Samantha first heard the lilting notes, she was up in her bedroom; the melodic sounds were coming from the garden; delighted with the melody.

Delighted with the sound, she looked out of her window. When she saw that it was Martha walking toward the salad garden, she opened the window wide and she watched the young girl as she walked with ease while playing the sweetest music effortlessly. When she reached the greenhouse, she stopped playing and put the flute into her apron pocket then proceeded to gather the vegetables needed for the fresh salad.

As soon as Samantha finished dressing, she ran down the stairs and into the kitchen.

"Martha!" she called; she was out of breath and her voice was louder than she intended it to be.

Martha turned suddenly, at Samantha's raised voice. "Ma'am!" she said in a voice louder than she had anticipated.

"Oh, my dear girl, it was not my intention to startle you," she said panting. "I just heard you playing the most heavenly music in the garden. It was so beautiful; it clearly took my breath away. I had no idea my dear child that you had such a talent. Why have you been hiding it when it brings such pleasure to the listener?"

Martha lowered her head shyly so Samantha changed the subject, vowing to herself to bring it up again later and gently coax the girl to play again.

Samantha told her husband she was not looking forward to an upcoming social that she felt compelled to attend.

"If this group is anything like the gossiping circle I attended last month, I'd just as soon stay 'ome an' wash me 'air. I am truly of the opinion that this is a group of the idle, lazy and jaded, rich, women who make up the exclusive membership of this so-called elite ladies country club. Don't you think?"

"But they can't all have pea-sized brains," he said laughing as he patted his wife on her shoulder, and as he walked away he said, with a chuckle. "Aye and 'tis your civic duty, my dear."

She could still hear him laughing after he closed the drawing room door, Samantha called out to him. "Civic duty, me eye."

Two months later, it was Samantha's turn to host the 'Women's Social Circle', which in her opinion was a complete waste of time.

Having attended more than one of these events, she knew she would soon become bored with the silly, idle, gossip. And of course, the gossip was both idle and boring. So when she caught Martha's eye, the girl brought over the silver tray containing the crystal decanter and eight sherry glasses. However, after the sherry was served, the tiresome gossip continued.

Samantha was bored with the trivial gossip, so she changed the focus. One of the less verbal women was wearing a very stylish hat. It was lavender with purple and white tiny flowers just visible under the pale grey veil.

Samantha was genuinely impressed with the style and color combination and she complimented the women.

"Mrs. Chambers, that is a very pretty hat, surely you did not purchase it locally; or have you been to New York since last we met?"

"No dear, my maid made it for me."

"Your maid! Surely not, Oh my goodness, you have a maid with that much talent, but surely a hat as stylish and as beautiful as that, belongs in a New York or an international millinery shop, or magazine, oh my goodness," she said, delighted, both by the hat and the creator of it.

"My, my, Mrs. Chambers what a wonderful talent, and right in your own home, how fortunate you are. Surely, having the skill to design such a fashionable item as that, she could open up her own millinery shop. Don't you agree Mrs. Proctor?"

The wearer of the hat smiled in agreement but said nothing as she looked beyond Samantha in the direction of Mrs. Molly Proctor, the president of 'the Women's Circle'. Mrs. Hawthorn turned her head to look directly at Mrs. Proctor.

"Don't you think Amanda's hat is a beautifully crafted design? I'm sure you could not find anything finer in the smartest of millinery shops in Atlanta or even New York.."

Getting no response from Mrs. Proctor, she turned back to

the hat-wearer. "Do you think she would design one for me? Maybe if we all ordered one, she could open up her own shop here in little old Macon?

Why I'm sure that the rich ladies would come from New York just to have a hat designed by your good lady. What is her name?" Samantha asked, reaching for a piece of paper and a pencil. "I would love for her to design a hat for me, maybe more than one. My goodness, such a talent."

"Well, yes, it is rather eh different," the president said, as she raised her lace trimmed handkerchief to the corner of her mouth, "but you must know my dear, that even though some of them may have a skill such as that …"

She waved her handkerchief dismissively, in the direction of the hat wearer, "well my dear, they are, in the first place, very rare and of course, lack the intellect to amount to, well anything. After all my dear, and you will soon learn, that, well, they really are nothing but, well, but what they are."

"Oh! I see. And just what are 'they?'" Samantha asked her most vocal guest, using her softest and most enquiring voice, while looking perplexed.

The club president was quick to respond to the hostess in her most reassuring, authoritative voice.

"Why, well, they're, just, well, what I mean to say is that, well you know as well as I do Samantha dear, that they, well, they're Negros. They can't learn much and aren't really fit for anything much, as you will soon see.

Well, what I mean to say my dear is that they are, after all, just slaves my dear," she said clearing her voice and checking that all eyes were on her as she spoke. "Not one of them will ever amount to anything and it will do you and your husband well, to understand this my dear.

After all, you are both new to this life; to our way of life. In time you will learn, and you will thank me for the advice that I give to you freely."

Samantha smiled, not at Mrs. Proctor but at Martha. "My dear, Mrs. Proctor," she said, using her most conciliatory voice. "I know you are much older than me and I suppose that makes you much wiser."

Mrs. Proctor glanced at the other women and smiled in agreement.

"However, if what you say is true then I have no business being here."

"But why, my dear, what on earth do you mean? You have every right to be here, living in this grand house and with all of your grand finery, how could anyone look at you, and all of your finery and think that you are, well I mean to say -"

"Well according to me sixth form teacher," Samantha cut in "and every teacher after her, 'I was a good for nuthin'," she said reverting back to her 'less than proper working-class East Midlands mother tongue.'

"But why would anyone say such a horrid thing about you? "Why you must have been a lovely child," chimed in Mrs Chambers.

"Not according to my second-grade teacher, Miss Whealan was her name; she said 'because I had no mother and lived alone with my father who doted on me too much, I would amount to nuthin'.

So, you see my dear, we all make mistakes and misjudge innocent people based on their position in life. I could no more be responsible for not having a mother than Amanda's hat maker is responsible for being enslaved."

The room fell quiet, a time for reflection Samantha hoped, as she picked up her glass of Sherry and dramatically threw her head back and drained the last of it as if it was a dram of Scotch whisky.

She was, after all, a working-class girl who had never outgrown her roots even though she had moved three-thousand miles away from them.

She and her husband were new to this country and the expected and accepted way of living. They were outsiders, considered gentry and of course they did live well, but there was nothing pretentious about her or her husband. Both came from working class stock.

Samantha broke the silence by asking everyone to bow their heads in prayer before the refreshments were served.

Martha wheeled in the elegant mahogany and glass serving cart. On the top tier was the silver teapot, milk jug, sugar bowl plus a gold rimmed tea service for six. The second-tier held two cake servers with freshly made fruit scones, a china container of homemade strawberry jam and another container of homemade clotted cream.

Before showing the ladies the art of dressing their scones, Samantha said, "Thank you dear, you can do that other thing after I serve tea."

Martha nodded and walked out of the drawing room. Samantha noticed a disapproving frown on Molly Proctor's face as she repositioned herself on the blue velvet wing chair.

"Are you all right Mrs. Proctor?" Samantha asked her most vocal guest.

"Well my dear, it is not for me to tell you how you run your own house …"

"Oh dear, do I hear a 'but' coming?" Samantha said, smiling at the woman.

"Well my dear," Molly said, wearing a condescending look, "you are still very young and, of course, I don't know what the culture is like in England, but here in America, we reframe from personal pleasantries when ordering our slaves; they need to know their place and act like ... like, well my dear to be forewarned is to be, well mm, well-armed.

Well, that's what my husband says, it's not as if they are going to amount to anything now is it? They are after all just slaves and in my opinion, they should be grateful.

After all, we do take care of them. Oh! This looks heavenly; shall I say grace?" And without waiting for a response she bowed her head and said grace.

After they had done so, Samantha took great pride and pleasure as she demonstrated to the group the correct way to eat and enjoy high tea English style. She poured the tea then demonstrated for her guests how to hold their cup and saucer. The women were delighted, some giggled.

Molly was the first of the group to bite into her scone and as the taste reached her pallet, she had to restrain herself from speaking with her mouth full.

Amanda was the first to speak since she only took a nibble. Whereas Molly it seemed, was trying to consume the entire scone.

"They are as light as a feather," Amanda said, "they almost melt in your mouth; what did you say they are called?"

"How on earth can you make them so light?" Molly cut in, wiping some jam from her mouth with the linen napkin. "It must be the flour; do you import it from England?"

The women were all nodding in agreement; they also wanted to know if Samantha would be willing to share with them the recipe.

At that moment, Martha began to play the sweetest music the women had ever heard played on a flute. She was in the next room so they had no idea who was playing the music.

The room fell silent as they listened to the sweet melodious sounds wafting over them.

After all the scones had been consumed and the second pot of tea had been served, the women congratulated Samantha on one of the nicest gatherings they had ever experienced.

Still praising both the high tea and the beautiful music, Samantha promised to tell them her secret before they returned home. So, as the ladies drained the last of the tea and engaged themselves in idle chatter, Samantha rang her tiny gold bell and Martha appeared to collect the dishes.

As she made her way around the room collecting the used dishes and placing them on the serving cart, Samantha stood up and walked over to the white marble fireplace, coughed softly to get their collected attention, then she said: "Ladies I think your applause would be most welcomed by the hands that made those delicious scones and, played that beautiful music, don't you agree."

Their hostess extended her hand as she spoke in the direction of Martha who was arranging the used china dishes on the serving cart. The women were amazed and speechless.

All five women looked at Martha in shock. Molly picked up her hat and bag and was ready to leave, however, the remainder of Samantha's guests gave a huge round of applause.

Three of the women walked over to Martha who now had tears in her eyes and patted her on her shoulder. "Thank you for everything,' said one."You are truly a very talented young girl," said the other.

As they walked out of the room and into the hall leading to the front door, the women were smiling. They hugged Samantha and thanked her for the tea, the music and the lesson. Molly, who was obviously irritated by those last comments, had walked out of the house in a huff. She was already sitting in the front coach. She waved a swift goodbye, but refused to look in the direction of the house, no doubt suspecting that Martha was standing in the open doorway along with the hostess, Mrs. Samantha Hawthorn, as her coach pulled off in silence.

As the door closed on the second coach, the women gleefully talked about the delightful experiences they encountered at the young English woman's home.

Later, when Samantha shared the events of her first hosting experience with her husband, she gloated on how she subtly put Mrs. Molly Proctor in her place.

8

– A CHILD IS A BLESSING –

SEVERAL YEARS LATER, NATHANIEL MARRIED THE GIRL HIS parents had raised. He was several years older than Sadie, all though that didn't matter to the orphaned teenager. Sadie knew she had three older brothers and that they had all been sold just weeks after she was born and that Nathaniel's parents raised her.

Since she had been adopted by them, she had been raised in his loving family. Nathaniel's only sibling was his sister Rosie who was several years younger than him. He always wanted brothers, especially when his playmate Robert went away to school.

Nathaniel and his wife hoped to have a big family. Although Sadie had no memory of her brothers, based on what she had heard all of her young life, it was very clear she was born into a very happy and loving family.

The story of the swing was told to her at an early age, and as she grew older, she was often found sitting on the love filled swing that her daddy made for her momma. She never knew her family but was often seen sitting and crying on her mother's swing.

When the new couple moved into their refurbished cabin, they both fell on their knees and prayed they would fill their new home with lots of babies. It was not to be.

Sadie had several miscarriages and still-born births during the first six years of their married life. Finally, their first healthy child was born; a strapping, baby boy. They named him Jack and the whole community joined in the celebration; Jimmy included.

Only three years later, Sadie died giving birth to their second living child. However, this infant was very frail and within hours of his mother's final breaths, their infant died. A devoutly religious man, Nathaniel was overcome with grief.

Jimmy was there at Nathaniel's side mourning the death of mother and baby. Nate feared God must have been punishing him for some committed sin. Yet, he couldn't think of anything so outrageous to have angered God so much; that he would take his beloved Sadie from him.

Nathaniel was a pious Christian, a God-fearing man; he was also a deacon in his church. Jack's father grieved for many years after his wife and baby boy died. He never remarried.

In order to carry out his duties, the grieving father needed someone to look after his motherless child who by then, was just three years old.

He asked Mr. Hawthorn if his sister Rosie and her young daughter Beth, the scullery maid could keep an eye on little Jack while he was working. Mr. Hawthorn agreed, somewhat reluctantly; having never had a child of his own.

He agreed the little boy could spend his days in the big house where his relatives could keep an eye on the child, as long as the child's presence did not interfere with their duties.

As it happened, Samantha Hawthorn, who was often bored; having so much time on her hands was drawn to the child and his constant inquiries.

She became besotted with the little boy who ended up spending far more time with her than with his aunt. Samantha looked forward to him being dropped off each morning, always ready with something new for the little boy to discover. She could often be seen lying next to him after she put him down on her bed for his afternoon nap.

Samantha taught him how to read, ride a pony, and swim in the lake - so much of her time was devoted to caring for him. His father very happy with the time and attention Mrs. Hawthorn dedicated to his son.

He would smile to himself whenever he saw the two walking in the fields or sitting by the pond fishing. He was also very happy with his child's progress, as he developed new skills like riding the pony unaided, catching his first fish, or recognizing several flowers by name.

Samantha was delighted with Jack's progress and she often bragged to her husband and Nathaniel just how bright little Jack was.

Jack had just turned four when Samantha made the decision to visit her father. She told her husband she would like to take little the little boy with her to England.

"That's fine with me dear, but he is Nathaniel's child and he might not want to be away from his only child for the four months you plan to be gone."

Samantha's husband, had for a while feared his wife was growing far too attached to the child. Knowing how much she wanted a child of their own, he hadn't had the heart to voice his thoughts.

Now, however, he thought taking the little boy to England

was a bold move. He was sure Nathaniel would refuse her request if he knew how long they would be away.

Several weeks went by and Samantha hadn't mentioned her trip to England to Nathaniel so he assumed she had put the idea to rest.

When Nathaniel returned to the big house to collect his son, at the end of his workday, he was always happy to see his little boy sitting in a winged chair next to Samantha, reading from a large book she held for him.

Nathaniel appreciated all the time his boss's wife spent with his son and it was quite clear that they were genuinely fond of each other.

One day soon after, Samantha told Nathaniel of her plans to visit her father. She paused only momentarily before revealing her hope to take little Jack with her. Malcolm was taken aback his wife had gone ahead with her request. His thick, bushy brows arched amusingly; knowing Nathaniel would discourage such an undertaking. And yet, the man's expression did not reveal his objection.

In fact, Nate thought it would be a great experience for his son and initially, he said yes. He recognized how fond they were of each other and the bond that had developed between them in a very short time. Knowing how persistently curious his son was about everything new he saw, heard, smelled, and touched, he also appreciated the education his son was getting from his boss's wife.

Malcolm, on the other hand, feared his wife was becoming too attached to the boy and when he told Nathaniel how long the visit would take both there and back; Nathaniel changed his mind. He had heard of New England, which was in the north, but had no way of knowing just how far away England was. When he calculated how long it would take just to reach

Boston, where they would sail from, not to mention the weeks it took to cross the ocean, to reach England and then having to travel for two days by coach to reach her father's home; he realized it would be months before they could return to Georgia.

Nathaniel rescinded his consent. He told his boss's wife that he could not be without his son for such a long time.

Samantha was clearly upset when Nathaniel changed his mind, but she also understood. She knew she would not want to be separated for several months - if she had had her own child - and that Nate could not be away from his little boy when Samantha finally sailed to England.

From that day forward, little Jack was a constant shadow behind either his father or Mr. Jimmy. Both men became his role models in what would later become his own passionate trade.

The Hawthorns were a devoted couple and among the many interests they had in common, reading was a favorite pastime, they often shared the same books.

Malcolm continued his fascination with botany and it consumed most of his time over the years. Samantha developed a keen interest in gardening, she was very fond of flowers and there was at least one vase in each room filled with the flowers she and often her husband had cultivated or nursed together.

Malcolm kept his promise to his father-in-law; and Samantha returned to England to visit her father every two or three years until his death, sixteen years after they immigrated to America. She had just turned thirty-four when the news reached her, informing her that her father had died suddenly. His death devastated her.

It was her father's wish to be buried next to his wife; and

his wishes were obeyed thanks to his solicitor. By the time the news of her father's death reached Samantha in America, her father was already buried. She was quite naturally distressed and mourned his loss but it was more than that.

The tuberculosis epidemic which had taken the lives of her extended family members, several years earlier, left her with the responsibility to keep the blood line going in her parent's ancient clan.

Samantha was consumed with grief over the loss of her father and the fact that she still did not have a child of her own. She was tormented with the sad realization that her family's long and ancient Saxon line would end with her death, if she was unable to have a child of her own.

9

– ADAH –

Adah, the Hawthorn's housekeeper had suffered from bronchitis ever since she arrived in America, a country she could never call her true home.

She was just thirteen years old when she was snatched by a giant of a ghost-faced monster. Her mother had sent her out to the garden, to gather up some yam for their first meal of the day. Adah loved yam, especially when they were baked over hot coals, and served with honey. She had thought it was one of her brothers trying to frighten her, as they often did. And so, she had not attempted to struggle out of the coarse sack. Instead remaining silent, allowing them to carry her back to the house.

It was only when she heard strange voices, not in her tongue, that she realized it was not her brothers trying to scare her. Instantly, she realized she had become the victim of the dreaded fear.

For the past several months, Adah had overheard the elders talk about such things with her father and uncles whenever they held council in her home. She and her brothers had been warned not to venture beyond their compound unaccompanied by adults. 'These were troubling times,' she often heard the adults say.

After being carried over a man's hard shoulder, she was placed into a vehicle that instantly sped off. The journey in the vehicle was extremely long.

After some time, she felt very sleepy but was too afraid to close her eyes. When at last it stopped, after what seemed like many hours in that bumpy vehicle; she could smell the ocean and a deeper fear consumed her.

It was too dark to see, even after the stinking sack had been removed from her body; but she knew instinctively, it was pointless to struggle. Now her eyes were free, she could see the stars above so she knew it was night time.

Afraid now, she attempted to struggle as she was guided up steep, narrow stairs and when her bare feet touched solid ground, then realized she was standing on the river's edge. The frightened child could see nothing, but was overwhelmed by a strong, foul smell.

She heard moaning sounds coming from many directions and was deathly afraid. And as her eyes began to adjust to the darkness, she was too afraid to move from the stairs.

Pushed through a dark doorway and down into the depths of something that wasn't quite still. She had no idea where she was only that she was deep in the bowels of a damp and musty prison. In addition to being cold, hungry, and frightened, Adah was unbearably sick for the next few days.

The terrified and lonely child survived the horrendous ocean journey, unlike many of the captured who died and were thrown overboard. Their burial was on the ocean floor.

Each time the ship docked many stolen people came and

went. She learned much later that the ship which captured her sailed to several ports in Europe, England and the Caribbean, before it docked in America.

The petrified child had no idea just how many young people were captured with her. So many of the captured spoke in different languages, but the one thing they all had in common was that they were all black and deathly afraid.

Finally, after too many days and nights at sea, the ship reached shore and was anchored in an unfamiliar land. The bright sunlight burned her eyes but she was relieved to finally breathe in fresh air.

There were many Africans captured and brought to this new country. She had not spoken a single word since her capture; however, she soon comprehended the meaning of the new language there. Words she had heard repeated often, and by many voices.

Adah was eighteen when she was sold for the second time. This innocent young girl's life was far from easy, still a child, when captured; she had many masters and was expected to work like an adult. She had been ravaged several times by as many men, old and young; but the fragile girl was unaware of her condition.

It was not until she arrived in America, that she realized she was with child. She was very young and naïve and so when her period stopped, she blamed it on the stress and fear that consumed her. She knew nothing of the 'birds and bees' but was obviously pregnant when she arrived.

Adah was among the very few captured who was able to keep her baby. Still in her early teens, she feared being a mother, she had had no training. But as time passed while she was in captivity, she reflected on the loving care she had received from adoring mother.

And in time, she was grateful to have her own child to love and fortunate her health did not interfere with raising her beloved, baby girl. Adah named her baby daughter Martha, after her own beloved mother.

The chest cold and repetitive cough she had developed while imprisoned in the filthy, stuffy, bowels of that prison boat; that stinking vehicle, which took her from her loving family and happy home, was the beginning of a respiratory condition she suffered each year, especially in the winter months.

When she arrived in America, the first thing Adah did was search for plants. She was determined to find a cure for her troubled chest.

She was fortunate enough to find plants and herbs; identified by other captured Africans that she was able to use whenever her condition flared up. They were not as potent as those she had depended on at home but they did suffice for short periods of time.

Some coughing attacks were stronger than others. It seemed the older she got, each attack became more serious.

Her greatest fear was that she would die before seeing Martha married to a decent man; a good man who would protect and take care of her. As the years went by, she was just thankful she had not passed on her ailment to her daughter.

Six months after Martha celebrated her eighteenth birthday, Adah took ill again. Unfortunately, her usual bouts of bronchitis did not clear up and eventually it developed into pneumonia. Sadly, the curing remedy she had developed over the years, failed to clear up her lungs.

This final bout was in the dead of winter. Martha nursed her mother as best she could but everything she tried failed. She wanted to send for the local doctor, but Adah adamantly refused to see him. She didn't trust the white man's medicine.

Martha was devastated when her mother died several days later. She adored her mother, and there had not been one day in her life she had not seen her mother to talk, laugh, and eat with her.

Often on very cold nights, she would get into bed with her mother, and they would cuddle together to stay warm. Martha was now consumed with sadness, loneliness and she grieved the loss of her mother for many years. Now she completely alone and her days seemed to be so much longer.

Several weeks after the death of her mother, Samantha came to speak with Martha. Martha had been a youngster when the Hamiltons bought the rundown property.

Her mother, who was bought by the previous owner, often told Martha that Mr. Hamilton and his wife were 'decent people who had heart and real blood in their veins.'

Martha was very fond of Samantha; she didn't make the staff feel little, like so many other house staff she knew, who hated their bosses or masters as they were made to call them. And Martha liked her accent.

"I wanted to ask if you would like to assume your mother's role as housekeeper? I'm confident you could fill your mother's shoes," asked Samatha gently.

Martha told Samantha she would like to think about it; then she asked the lady of the house, "Who will replace me?" Martha said she needed to know before she accepted the position of 'housekeeper'.

"My mother's job was not easy, she had a lot of responsibilities every day and without me assisting her, well, this is a big house and there are many duties to be carried out every day."

"Yes, Martha I am well aware of that and don't think I don't know how hard your mother worked, and you, as her constant helper to keep this house running in tip top shape.

So, do you think Daisy is ready to move up from scullery maid to parlor maid? You know those duties and you did a fine job assisting your mother, God rest her soul. Do you think Daisy is ready, with some coaching or training from us?"

Martha didn't have to think about it, she had in fact, anticipated this promotion would be offered to her by Mrs. Hawthorn, and that she would accept it. Daisy would be happy to move from scullery maid to parlor maid, even if only for a short time.

While her mother had been laid up, Martha had begun to do more and more of her mother's chores; she had already instructed Daisy to take over some of her own daily duties.

Martha had already been preparing to relieve her mother of some of her duties once she was well enough to return to work but now she was to step into her shoes.

10

– SAMANTHA DIES –

TEN YEARS AFTER MARTHA BECAME THE HOUSEKEEPER, AN epidemic of whooping cough swept the south. Both children and adults were affected by the killer infection, which took Samantha's life, ending the twenty-eight-years of a blissful marriage she had enjoyed with her devoted husband.

Her death left Malcolm a broken man. He adored his wife; she was only forty-six-years-old when she died.

Samantha was his lifelong friend and devoted partner. When she died, he grieved for several years after her death. The one regret throughout their lives was that they never had a child; this fact seemed more of a burden to Samantha than it did to Malcolm.

However, with the untimely death of his beloved wife, he began to brood openly; not only over the loss of his life-long partner and beloved wife, but the realization of not having an heir hit him hard.

For the first time, on a deeply conscious level, he pondered. Lonely and weary, he was now painfully aware that the empire he had built with love with sweat and years of toil, may revert to the state of wreck and ruin it was when he first found it all those years ago.

The stark reality, that he was totally alone, now penetrated his psyche on a much deeper level, an emotional level. Each day, his grief deepened into a great depression.

Finally, when he did consciously, accept the fact that there was no living relative on either side of their family. There was no heir to inherit the fortune he had amassed. He was often heard saying out loud; 'all of this and all for nothing, my sweat and toil and all for naught'.

Depression and loneliness consumed him and he brooded for many years after his wife's death, and as his sadness deepened, his interest in the land, in the house, and in life itself began to deteriorate.

His favored room in the house had always been the library, a room he now seldom entered. His daily rides across the plains of his estate ceased and he seldom, if ever went into the stables.

He had no appetite, despite the efforts of the kitchen staff to prepare his favorite meals. It was obvious he was losing weight; all of his clothes hung loosely on his diminished frame.

While Mr. Hamilton continued to grieve over the death of his wife, many attempts were made by Martha to coax him into eating.

'Just a few bites,' she would say. 'Or look, I cooked your favorite.' But after retrieving his untouched plate, she knew she had failed once more to entice him to eat.

Martha did worry about him but she felt her hands were tied. She often pondered whether she should send for his doctor.

However, the last time she took it upon herself to send for

his doctor, Mr. Hawthorn's wrath came down on her and the whole household like a thunderstorm. Martha knew he was pining over the loss of his beloved wife.

Over the years, Martha had developed an affection for Samantha and she was deeply saddened by her early death, especially so soon after her own mother's death.

Martha was now the person in charge of the entire household. She missed and loved her mother and her mistress, both of whom encouraged her and praised her for the work she did, keeping the house running smoothly and efficiently, plus her great cooking skills.

11

– ARISTOCRATIC HAWTHORN'S SEARCH
FOR AN HEIR –

SEVERAL MONTHS AFTER THE SAD EVENT, MALCOLM INFORMED
Mr. Gray, his solicitor in England of his wife's passing. After
expressing his sincere condolences for his client's loss, Mr.
Grey urged the wealthy landowner, 'to identify a possible
beneficiary, in the event of his untimely death'.

It was clear to Malcolm that he knew of no living relative;
he came from a very small family in the village of Belper in
the Midlands, a rather insular sheep-rearing village. His
mother was an only child, as was his father who had died
when Malcolm was just five years old. There were no relatives
he knew of on his father's side.

As he searched his memory of that time so long ago; he
remembered seeing a lot of strange people at his father's
funeral, although he was never introduced to any of them.
They were many adults and he was just a small lad. He had
asked his mother about the visitors; so many strange people in
his little house.

As Malcolm reflected, he remembered the way his mother

responded; she put her index finger to her pursed lips. Much later he remembered her saying, 'besides my little boy, he's all I have left'. He also remembered hearing her crying in her room long after the last relative or visitor had left. Whenever he asked questions he was told to 'be still' or 'not now darling'.

Three months later, his mother packed up their clothes and they moved down to Cornwall to visit a friend of his mother's. They were school-mates and had always kept in touch. Aunt Lydia; that was her name, had a cottage on the coast of Cornwall.

And over those next few years, they had spent three or four weeks there, every year for their summer holidays to visit with Aunt Lydia. He knew she wasn't a real auntie but a very close friend of his mother's from childhood.

Malcolm was fifteen when Aunt Lydia died. He remembered his mother being very sad, he was sad too because he enjoyed his summer holidays in Cornwall.

On reflection, he realized he liked it better in Cornwall; the weather was so much nicer there. How strange he thought, that my sadness should bring forth so many good and happy childhood memories.

"Perhaps," he heard himself saying out loud, "I should go back to England for a visit. It has been many years."

Two years after he buried his beloved Samantha, Malcolm returned to England, a sad and empty man. His wife had meant the world to him and he was lost without her. He was not an old man but after conferring with Mr. Herbert Gray, his solicitor, he agreed it was time to seek out an heir to his vast property.

Mr. Gray suggested a clandestine search through the vast ledgers at Somerset House in London; the headquarters of all recorded births, deaths, and marriages in the United

Kingdom. He said there could be some distant relative he may never have been aware of.

Weary and anxious to return to America, he gave in to his solicitor's suggestion. Malcolm was lonely, drained of energy and sunlight, he needed to be surrounded by all that was familiar to him.

He felt out of step in England; so much had changed during his decades of absence and he needed the warmth of the southern sun to heal his physical aches and pains.

Malcolm also longed for the familiar surroundings and pleasant smells of his much-loved home, where so many years of happy and loving memories were etched into the canvas that he and his beloved Samantha had created.

He was not looking forward to the return journey across the Atlantic Ocean in mid-November as he knew it would be bitter cold. Although he did not consider himself an antisocial person, he was not drawn to socializing with strangers.

He decided to take all of his meals in his personal dining room in his first class cabin. Thus avoiding the bitter cold traveling back and forth to his cabin and having to mingle with the snooty first class passengers who swanked too much, in his opinion, about their opulence and wealth.

Nine months later, Mr. Malcolm Hawthorn received a cable from his solicitor in London. He was in no hurry to open up the cable; he knew the outcome of his solicitors search. Each of his parents was an 'only child' so he knew what the conclusion of the timely and costly search would be.

'Just another waste of my money,' he was heard saying several times, especially in the evening after he had consumed his favorite drinks.

So, he was shocked and totally in denial when the following cable arrived:

30th day of September 1830

My dear Sir,
It is with much delight that I can inform you that our inquiries were not in
vain. After a lengthy and extensive search throughout the British Isle, we
have at last located a blood relative.
Sadly, he was left an orphan less than one year ago, when his parents
tragically met death during an outrageous storm in Scotland. We will
inform him forthwith, pending your approval of my extensive report.

Most sincerely,
Herbert Grey Esq.

An heir had been found. Mr. Joseph Hawthorn III, the only living but very distant male relative; a struggling artist down on his luck.

The confused recipient could not believe the news, that he was to inherit a vast estate in Georgia. All of the documentation, according to Sir Herbert Grey, had been verified by researchers at St. Catherine's House in the City of London.

However, when news of this reached Mr. Malcolm Hawthorn, he was not in the least bit pleased; in fact, he was extremely angry. He felt betrayed and to some extent misrepresented, to the point of mounting anger.

"Who is this young whippersnapper?" he said. "And why haven't I heard of him before now? I'm not going to let some stranger, a young scallywag come over here and just take over all that I have built over the years, the cheek of it."

Enraged and bitter, Malcolm wrote a cable to send to his solicitor first thing in the morning demanding further proof.

You're my solicitor and I demand to know who this imposter is. I demand
to know why I have never heard of him.
I might be old but I still have me wits about me.
If need be, I will take the next ocean liner and see for myself.

Sincerely,

Malcolm Hawthorn

Malcolm could feel his temperature rise as his anger accelerated. He told his housekeeper that he wasn't hungry then walked down to the wine cellar to retrieve a bottle of his favorite port.

He stepped into the dining room, he opened the china cabinet, and removed a crystal wine glass. With the glass in one hand and a bottled of his English Port in the other, he then proceeded towards the spiral staircase.

Upon entering his room, he closed the door and sat in his favorite chair; remembering fondly that it was the loveseat he had designed for himself and his beloved wife, Samantha, who left him too soon.

They would sit together at the end of each day, sip on a glass of port or brandy and gaze out of the picture window, counting the stars or watching the sun fade into night. He sat alone now, reminiscing; allowing his mind to drift, to remember and wonder.

The cable was never sent; in fact, it was several months before it was eventually discovered. Malcolm had used it as a marker in the book he had placed on the nightstand next to his bed.

Eventually it was found by the estate's new owner, one hot and muggy night when Joey Hawthorn went looking for a book to read because it was too darn hot to sleep.

12

– AGE OF DISCOVERY –

HALF A CENTURY EARLIER, LIVED LORD JOSEPH HAWTHORN. A man of great wealth, tall and lean with a full head of thick hair, once auburn and now silver.

Almost sixty-years of age, he was ruggedly handsome, well liked and admired by his peers and staff, both professional and domestic. This admiration was reciprocal. Joseph Hawthorn was a gentleman in all regards. He was highly respected and he adored his wife, Lady Sybil.

His only downfall was his insatiable gambling. Half of the dozen or so horses in his stables were racehorses; many of them purchased after winning impressive national and international races.

Lord Joseph was proud of the winning thoroughbreds in his stables. Gambling was the favor that ran through his veins.

He often engaged in fox hunting on his estate and for this momentous birthday. Lady Sybil had presented her husband with a brand new mare for his sixtieth birthday. Lord Hawthorn was thrilled and eager to try out his new horse.

On its maiden fox hunt, the mare was frightened by an adder, a domestic unaggressive snake. Joseph was thrown to the ground as the mare reared up her hind legs in fright. Lord Hawthorn was taken by complete surprise and he struck his lower back on a sharp wooden tree stump as he fell.

His injuries were severe and he was rushed to The Royal Infirmary hospital; but sadly he never fully recovered from a deep puncture wound to his lower spine which left him paralyzed from his waist down.

The severed nerves would leave him paralyzed forever. His adoring wife Sybil was devastated; knowing the gift she gave in love would destroy his quality of life.

The couple had only one child, his name was Daniel. Lady Sybil Hawthorn doted on him; her son and heir to his father's estate and title. Her reputation as a great pianist was well known and with little persuasion from her husband, Sybil had often entertained his dinner guests.

He had always encouraged her by having two baby grand pianos set up in the music room; one was ivory, the other ebony and they sat back to back.

Late at night, she could often be heard, albeit softly, playing some of her favorite sonatas. However, as accomplished as she was, Lady Sybil Hawthorn never played in public and only ever in their home.

She also inspired her son Daniel, when he was quite young, she recognized his interest and his keen ability to recognize significant keys and after some persuasion, his father agreed to a private piano tutor for the boy.

The piano became Daniel's passion in life and he confided in his mother that he would aim for a career as a concert pianist.

This pleased Lady Sybil, no end. Daniel chose music as his

major when he enrolled in Cambridge he read archaeology as his minor. Cambridge was his father's and grandfather's Alma Mata and he was proud to carry on the tradition. At the end of his third year, he was excited to go to Egypt on an archaeological dig.

The week before departing for Egypt, his mother developed a cold; she knew Daniel would be concerned and would possibly postpone his trip and she wanted him to follow his dream. So at her request, the state of her health was kept from him.

"It is, after all," she told her staff, "just a summer cold".

Sybil Hawthorn was sixty-three-years-old; she was otherwise a strong, sturdy woman. Tall and lean in stature and as part of her daily exercise she rode her stallion, Ebony each morning at 6:30 and every evening after dinner.

She was a strong and determined woman who ran the estate with a firm hand; she was well respected by all of her staff and the many merchants she had to deal with on a weekly basis.

Her doctor was not surprised when she made a complete recovery within five days. One week later, however, when she retired for her afternoon nap, Lady Hawthorn died peacefully in her sleep. Even her doctor was shocked.

Daniel was devastated when he received the wire informing him that his beloved mother had died in her sleep and just one day before his birthday. His grief was inconsolable.

Sybil was a great birthday celebrator and plans were afoot to celebrate her son's twenty fifth birthday. She had been so looking forward to hosting a grand birthday party on the vast lawn for her son's special day on his return from Egypt. Sadly, that was not to be. The grand gathering to celebrate her son's birthday, was instead gathered for her funeral.

Daniel was halfway across the world when the shattering news of his mother's death reached him. Overwhelmed with grief, he immediately booked passage back to England. He knew, however, that by the time he reached home, two weeks later his beloved mother was already interred in the family mausoleum.

Daniel was so distraught, his beautiful mother dead and his father confined to a wheelchair. He was totally overwhelmed with sadness, so much so, that he had to postpone his final year at Cambridge. He adored his parents and mourned his mother's demise for many years.

13

– DANIEL HAWTHORN –

DANIEL HAWTHORN HAD RETURNED TO UNIVERSITY TO complete his studies one year after his beloved mother died. He cherished his mother who inspired and encouraged him to play the piano. Three years later, he graduated with a first honors degree in music.

He was happy knowing that his adoring mother would be proud of him and his many accomplishments.

Professor Daniel Joseph Hawthorn, PhD. was an accomplished pianist and an aspiring composer. He was the head of the music department at Liverpool University where he taught classical piano full-time. He was also the alternate conductor at The Liverpool Philharmonic.

It helped knowing that his beloved mama would be very pleased as she looked down on him from heaven.

His name and reputation as a first-class pianist stood him in good stead and so, he had several very promising students from some of the most affluent families in the district.

Rachel Martin was orphaned at age six. She was the sole survivor of the influenza epidemic that wiped out her entire family and the lives of over two hundred people of all ages who resided in the same village of Aigburth which was on the outskirts of Liverpool.

Having been baptized a Catholic, she was sent to Mount Carmel convent and raised by the Carmelite nuns.

Her mother was an aspiring landscape artist and was just beginning to make a name in the art world when the influenza epidemic took her life.

Rachel had just turned eighteen when she graduated with honors. She won a scholarship to Liverpool University where she majored in art and minored in music.

Rachel enrolled in the same cello class as her best friend Linda Strong who was studying violin. After a few weeks, however, Rachel decided the base was not a fitting instrument for her.

"I find it far too awkward and much too heavy for my liking. Next, I will attempt the piano," she told her friend Linda.

And that is what she did. Rachel enrolled in Dr. Daniel Hamilton's piano class which is where they met. Rachel liked the piano, but her true passion was visual art, especially landscapes and yet she kept up the lessons.

Daniel was several years older than Rachel and he was besotted with her. She was lively, curious, and possessed a passion for life.

Daniel had never met anyone like her; she was witty, charming and always greeted people with a smile. Within a few months, they had fallen in love.

The couple honeymooned in Venice, Paris, and the Rhine Valley. When they returned to England, Daniel took his young bride to his family home, Berkley Hall.

Rachel loved the opulence of the grand estate and the spectacular views. She was flabbergasted by its splendor and felt certain she could paint for months and never run out of new scenery.

Rachel Hawthorn specialized in landscapes; she loved to paint and she would travel to various isolated country scenes in order to stretch her talent and skills as an artist. Her husband lovingly provided her with an assortment of canvases.

Over the years, many of her paintings were purchased by close friends and admirers. Her paintings were not of the quality that significant galleries would hang or list in their catalogues, but she lived in hope.

Given that the current title holder of their home had only one heir, it was expected that the newlyweds would produce the next male heir to inherit all that they owned.

However, Rachel was only just beginning to make a name for herself in the world, as an up and coming landscape artist. So she prayed that this first pregnancy would produce a baby boy; the much wanted and needed Hawthorn heir.

Rachel did not enjoy being pregnant, she hated the side effects, the morning sickness, the swelling of her ankles and the invasive, embarrassing examinations.

But she knew it was her duty to produce a male child. The family was anxious for an heir to inherit the Hawthorn title and estate.

When Lord Joseph Hawthorn learned that his son and daughter-in-law were expecting their first child, just eight months after they were married; he was overjoyed to hear there would be an heir to the estate.

The Hawthorns had resided on their vast estate for centuries, the manor house sat on hundreds of acres of rolling hills in Soften Park, an affluent district in Liverpool. Their highly elevated estate was dotted each spring with sheep and baby lambs.

For centuries, the Hawthorns were considered gentry. Daniel's parents, grandparents and great grandparents were born on their estate in Liverpool, England in the district of Sefton.

He hoped this first child would be a son and the natural heir to the family's vast fortune. With the child's arrival imminent, Lord Hawthorn commissioned the finest London architect to design and build a state-of-the-art house for his son Daniel, his bride Rachel, and the anticipated heir to the Hawthorn dynasty.

Joseph Hawthorn III, or Joey, as his mother would affectionately call him, was the only child of Daniel and his wife Rachel and named after his grandfather.

14

– LORD JOSEPH HAWTHORN –

YEARS LATER, SPECULATION SWELLED WORLDWIDE AND investors were extolling the wealth gained by British explorers and seamen when they returned home to England, with tales of exotic places.

Merchants brought back spices and dyes from India; gold, diamonds, cocoa, and palm oil from Africa; silk and tea from China; and cotton and tobacco from the America's. These items were in extremely short supply because of the expense to ship costs; only the very wealthy could afford them.

It was said that all of the items were available in abundance and with enough investors these rare but highly desirable items could be shipped from foreign lands to Britain for a reduced price.

It was rumored that considerable profits could be made from funding an expedition to one or more continents. It was also widely speculated that hundreds of British merchants were eagerly awaiting delivery of such goods. People with means were tempted by news of these new and rare finds.

So many of his peers at the gentleman's club, the club that his father commissioned over forty years earlier were constantly bragging about their great investments and how well they had paid off.

Lord Joseph Hawthorn was as eager as most people in his class to increase the legacy they would leave for their heirs. He invested heavily. Unfortunately, his speculations yielded far less than he anticipated. After five years of yoyo speculative investing, he had more losses than yield.

His accountant, Mr. Reginald Swift began cautioning his client. He received several cables informing him that his many unpaid overdrafts would eventually lead to bankruptcy. Unfortunately, these warnings were ignored.

In his desire to leave a healthy legacy for his son and grandson, Lord Joseph got carried away. He became increasingly inflicted with the gambling disease, losing far more than he gained.

Finally, his accountant urged him as forcefully as he could to cease his investing before losing the family home and young Joey's university endowment.

However, Lord Joseph Hawthorn was resolute; he refused to hear that his financial affairs were in such dire straits. He was a hefty gambler, perpetually in a state of denial, so he continued to ignore the warnings from his accountant for several years.

Unable to dissuade him of his reckless speculations and diminishing fortune, Mr. Swift decided to make an appointment with his esteemed client. Knowing full well that Lord Joseph would continue to reject his repeated warnings, he tried another tactic.

In an effort to strengthen his concerns, he arranged for his client's solicitor and bank manager to accompany him on what he hoped would become the final visit in this matter. Mr. Swift hoped that a face to face confrontation with the three of them would do the trick.

The sight of these esteemed gentlemen in his home for reasons other than social intercourse made quite an impression on their host.

Lord Joseph finally acquiesced to the seriousness of his foolish speculations. He was devastated when he heard he was practically bankrupt. Even though his accountant and his solicitor had written to him several times cautioning him, he refused to heed their many warnings.

When Lord Joseph read the figures, when he saw the steady decline in both assets and profits, he was devastated. At last, he comprehended and realized what a fool he had been; that his wealth had significantly declined, save for his grandson's university endowment. He was virtually penniless.

Lord Joseph Hawthorn succumbed to a great depression and within weeks, his declining health took its toll. His physician was called and he recommended complete bed rest.

Among the many prescriptions he wrote, he included a strong sleeping tonic in order to facilitate the total bed rest that he demanded. Sadly, within two weeks of taking to his bed, the patriarch of Berkeley Manor died of heart failure.

The manor went into receivership, along with the valuable furnishing and paintings. The public was soon made aware of the state of the esteemed family's finances, his heir's prestigious standing in their community slyly diminish considerably.

Daniel and Rachel were devastated as they acquiesced to the sad state of affairs, although through no fault of their own, they feared there would be humiliating and financial repercussions.

15

– 1830 FINANCIAL DISASTER –

WHEN LORD JOSEPH HAWTHORN DIED; HIS ONLY SON AND HEIR Daniel should have inherited the family's estate, which included the manor house where the young Hawthorns lived when they first wed.

A home that was doomed to become the last remnant of his family's estate.

The young Hawthorns were, at least, established both professionally and socially even without his family legacy.

Daniel and Rachel Hamilton lived a very comfortable life in the house Lord Joseph had had built for them once news of an heir was announced.

Their house had been among the first homes that had more than one inside bathroom. They had a live-in housekeeper and a daily scullery maid, neither of whom had to seek outside employment.

Prior to Lord Hawthorn's death, they were a very happy couple and they entertained lavishly.

16

– KEEPING UP APPEARANCES –

With the financial downfall and the societal humiliation that ensued, the Hawthorns did all that they could to hold up their heads as they attempted to keep up appearances.

Daniel felt the brunt of the demise financially. He gradually lost all his more prestigious students and his wife was having difficulty selling her paintings.

Prior to Joey's enrollment at Cambridge, his parents had to sell the family estate to pay off many of his grandfather's outstanding debts.

The family had no idea that Lord Joseph had invested so much money; most of it borrowed from banks and some from unsavory lenders. Fortunately, their son's tuition and boarding fees at the university had been secured.

Berkeley Hall was auctioned off, which included all the magnificent grounds, most of the furnishings, plus many of the paintings.

Daniel and his now very distraught wife Rachel were, in

private, devastated. However, they tried to make light of the catastrophe, which they feared would ultimately put a blight on the good Hawthorn name. After the sale of Berkeley Hall, their circle of friends began to diminish.

They were completely distraught when they found out that they would also have to sell their 'state-of-the-art home'. However, in order to become completely debt free, they would pay off all outstanding debts, including the death duty taxes.

Their financial situation was rapidly deteriorating. "Is there no end to this madness?" Rachel cried on the day that yet another summons arrived via their solicitor.

"My home," she cried, as she walked from one room to another, tears streaming down her cheeks. "Must it too, go under the hammer."

Her husband put his arms around her his wife in an effort to soothe her distress. Financial stress was such an abomination to them, so much had been handed to them most of their lives.

Even Rachel, although she was not to the manor born, she was the sole survivor of her family, and while they were not rich, financially she had very little to concern herself about.

However, she did have rather extravagant taste and her inheritance was all but spent when she married Daniel.

Desperation, coupled with despair and to some extent shame, forced them to take a serious look at the situation they found themselves in, albeit no fault of their own.

In an attempt to 'save face' and ward off societal gossip they looked for a less affluent village to purchase a modest cottage. They wanted to live in Cambridgeshire, in order to be close to where Joey would be studying for the next four years.

Once they had settled into their modest village home which was considerably smaller and far less opulent in all respects than their former, custom-built home, Rachel invited some friends to tea at the quaint little village tea shop.

After warm greetings and friendly hugs, Rachel was eager to find out what her friends had been doing since the last time they met while still living in the manor house. Rachel felt compelled to inform her friends about the dramatic change in residences.

"With Joey so far away," she informed her guests, "we decided to purchase a home, closer to Cambridge, given that we seldom saw him at all last year.

This village is so much closer to his college and so quaint, don't you think? So, I'm sure he will come home more on weekends and occasionally during the week."

The waitress arrived at their table and Rachel ordered tea and cream scones for each of her guests.

"My goodness the youth of today," she said, "are so much more independent than when we were, at their age. Don't you think?"

She waited for a comment or two, but her guests remained silent.

"We scarcely saw him during his first year, he was so far away," she continued. "We, well I, wanted to be closer so that he could visit us more often."

Rachel realized she was being redundant when two of her guests looked at each other and held their gaze for longer than was usual.

Clearing her throat, she continued talking as the waitress placed a double server in the center of the table. The top tray had two dishes, one contained the clotted cream, the other was filled with fresh strawberry jam, and the bottom dish contained freshly baked scones. Rachel decided to pour tea for her friends, from the Royal Dolton china teapot.

"And besides," she continued, as she reached to pour a second cup; "as beautiful as the house my father-in-law had built for us; it was far too large for the two of us she." She sighed. "Yes, a house that large needed the patter of many little feet, don't you think?"

Her friends smiled softly in skeptical agreement.

"It can be terribly lonely when one's only child leaves the nest."

In addition to the village house being considerably smaller than the opulent home her father-in-law had built for them; the flow of daylight was dismally limited.

Rachel chose two of the rear rooms with south facing windows as her studio. Quite naturally, everything was considerably smaller than she had been used to at their previous home, including the windows.

No longer being in the position to pay for what she required, Rachel bartered with the local mason to make significant changes to the rear of the house to allow more natural light to flow into the room she had designated as her new studio.

She instructed the mason to demolish the exterior wall of the house and install floor to ceiling windows to facilitate her need for more natural light. In exchange, for the work she commissioned, she agreed to paint a portrait in oils of the builder's wife and his daughter.

Rachel had a vast supply of oils and canvases in various sizes and she had a burning desire to complete at least twenty canvases and arrange an open-house at one of the local galleries.

She hoped that with the completion of her works, galleries from far and near would display her landscapes, seascapes and portraits. She longed for her paintings to be respected and ultimately collected. No longer in society, the Hawthorns found their middle class lifestyle depressingly boring.

Most piano instructors in the area were very well established and there were no vacancies at any of the neighboring public schools for a piano instructor.

Daniel Hawthorn, PhD advertised in the local newspaper, for students requiring private music lessons, after no response to his advertisement, he advertised further afield.

Sadly, however, nothing was forthcoming. Consequently, his ego was severely damaged and he became overtly idle. As lethargy set in, his drinking increased and his nightly Port, was often consumed to excess.

Several months later, Rachel was in tears as she confided in her childhood friend Linda, who had come to visit. Both girls were orphaned as children and raised in the Carmelite convent, their beds next to each other in the sixteen-bed dormitory.

Afraid and lonely, they immediately became best friends. They were like sisters and remained very close all the way through to college and beyond.

Linda was visiting her great aunt who lived in the next village, just a short distance from where the Hawthorns now lived. Before returning home, she paid a visit to her old school chum.

After their affectionate greeting and some idle chatter. Rachel confided in her old friend.

"More than anything," she said through muffled tears, "I so long to be recognized and respected as a landscape artist, not for myself you understand, but for Daniel. I fear this is the only way we will be accepted once more and welcomed back into society.

He has been drinking quite heavily, and I fear he has lost

all interest in music. I am certain, it is because he is depressed. He was devastated when his grandmother's baby grand pianos had to go under the auctioneer's hammer; he treasured them so," Rachel said, wiping her eyes.

"You know, of course, that his family have been in high society for generations and he feels the heavy weight of failure bearing down on his shoulders. He fears he has nothing to leave his son. I do so hope you understand, my dear.

I love my husband with all my heart ... I, I just fear he is drinking more each day and heading towards a great depression."

Linda patted her friend's hand reassuringly.

"I fully understand my dear," she said, "but I am sure his situation is nothing more than a slight setback. Your husband is a fine musician and in time his talents will be recognized and required once more. Keep praying my dear friend and I am sure all will be well in the not too distant future."

Linda's eyes were now brimming with genuine tears, ready to fall. She smiled reassuringly while speaking, then she held her friend's hand. Rachel could sense her compassion, her genuine sorrow and that meant the world to her.

Joey was only mildly aware of the pressures on his family and the decline in their social standing in the community. He was constantly assured that his education and financial needs would always be met.

As an artist, he had a rather bohemian outlook on life; art was his passion and he thought of little else. Days after he completed his first year at Cambridge; he took the overnight train to Perth, Scotland. He had been invited to spend a month with a fellow classmate whose family lived in the highlands.

Joey and his friend Duncan were avid outdoorsmen.

Duncan was studying bird migration and Joey, like his mother, was inspired by the beauty of Britain's various landscapes.

Joey fell in love with the rugged landscapes, the mountains, and the seascapes of Scotland. After his first visit to the highlands, he informed his parents by post that he wanted to live and paint in Scotland. His father was angry and adamantly objected.

"What rot," he said to his wife after reading his son's letter. "The Hawthorn men for the last five generations have all been educated at Cambridge, and each one graduated with honors; it is our tradition and I will not hear of him breaking that tradition.

He can paint anywhere, anytime and besides England is just as beautiful as Scotland. No, I will not hear of it," he told his wife. "I will not hear of such rubbish. I am totally opposed. Move to Scotland and give up his studies at Cambridge, nonsense. You're his mother; make him come to his senses."

However, Rachel admired her son's work and she understood his passion. It took some doing but she was finally able, after weeks of coaxing, to persuade her husband to let their son move to the place which had captured his heart.

17

– THE HAWTHORNS VISIT PERTH –

Almost two years after Joey left England to reside in Scotland, his parents decided to surprise him with a visit.

Joey corresponded with his mother, frequently espousing the beauty of the various landscapes especially in rugged isolated areas.

Rachel was thrilled at the idea of painting brand new land and possibly seascapes. It took her some time to persuade her husband to agree to the trip, but he finally gave in, albeit reluctantly. They decided to wait until mid-Spring when the worst of the winter would be over with.

"Scotland is a long way from here, my dear. God only knows how many times we will have to change trains; it can't be done in a day; you do know that."

"Yes darling, I do know that," Rachel replied with a tiresome sigh, "but I want to go, it's been almost two years since we last saw our son. I am so excited, as is he. I'm sure it will be fun and we need to get away from here, plus the fresh mountain air will do us both the world of good."

Rachel was extremely happy as she began to carefully pack up her canvases, paints and easel. She also packed two Mohair blankets.

They decided to take the late afternoon train, from Cambridge to London's Paddington station; it was less expensive than the morning train and this way they could have breakfast at home, saving on the expense of having to purchase an extra meal.

They had a ninety-minute wait for the train to Scotland, so Daniel took advantage of the layover. He asked a porter where the closest wine merchant was. The porter gave him directions, which, as it turned out, it was quite close to the station.

Before leaving for the wine merchant's shop, however, Daniel found a vacant seat, close to the fire in the first-class waiting room, for Rachel to sit on while he went in search of alcohol. He returned to the station in plenty of time with one bottle of gin and two bottles of port.

"It's going to be a long journey, my dear," he said. "Gin is quite costly on these long-distance trains."

They had to change trains three times. It was an arduous journey. However, despite the inconvenience of having to change trains so many times, Rachel thoroughly enjoyed the train journey, whereas Daniel huffed and puffed each time they had to make a train change.

Once they transferred on their connecting train and were settled in their seats each time, Daniel was usually fast asleep and didn't want to be bothered. Whereas, Rachel saw so many beautiful sights and wanted to stop and paint them all.

Throughout the journey, she kept her eyes glued to the windows marveling at the magnificent views that passed them by. Daniel spent most of his waking hours in the train's pub drinking gin and tonic or port. They dined together for lunch and dinner. Daniel ordered a bottle of wine with each meal and then after dinner he had at least three glasses of port.

Later in the evening after Rachel had retired for the evening, she heard her husband open up another bottle of spirits; she didn't know what it was and she decided not to confront him. Daniel slept off and on during the day and very little each night.

Rachel feared his consumption of alcohol had gotten out of hand but she would not complain. She did all that she could to control her disdain. Not wanting to make a scene in public, for fear of souring the atmosphere and besides, she was delighted to be on her way to see her only child.

Finally, they arrived at Perth train station; they hired a porter to carry their luggage to the railway hotel where they checked in. They had expected to see Joey upon arrival and were disappointed when they checked in; the concierge handed them the cable that Joey had sent the previous day informing his parent.

It read:

"I will see you in a couple of days, engaged on a project in Dundee.
Delighted you decided to visit.
Can't wait to see you both, I have worked out a glorious itinerary, that is guaranteed to knock your socks off.
See you both for dinner on Wednesday."

They were both, understandably, upset but too fatigued to ponder over their disappointment, by the time they checked in and were taken to their suite.

The room was delightful, spacious, and warm. Rachel particularly enjoyed the view of the lake, sheep, and the rolling hills beyond the fields of heather.

After a welcomed night's sleep in a very comfortable bed, the couple awoke well rested. They rose to what promised to be a beautiful sunny day.

After they had eaten a healthy Scottish breakfast of porridge, haggis, and kippers, the couple decided to explore the highlands on their own. The hotel manager was very helpful, providing them with a map and verbal directions to several scenic areas. He then walked the couple to the stables where they hired a single-horse carriage.

They planned to take their time and stop at various sites. The concierge ordered a packed lunch for them to take along.

They meandered through so many beautiful areas and it was difficult to decide where to stop. It was late morning and the sun was in full bloom, they were not in a hurry and were content to have the horse trot aimlessly down country lanes.

After about an hour of sightseeing, Rachel spotted a scene that was appealing to her.

"Oh, darling let us stop here, this is a heavenly spot, and we can have our lunch here."

Daniel was happy to oblige and after helping his excited wife out of the carriage, he began to unload her portable easel, canvases, folding chair and sketch pads. He followed her instructions as to where she wanted to sit while Rachel set the table so they could have their picnic lunch.

As usual, Daniel was content to sip his port while engaging his wife in pleasant, if not idle conversation. It was a lovely day, and occasionally, she would throw him a kiss and say what a good sport he was to indulge her.

On the second day of her painting excursion, they rode for about an hour until they found 'another perfect spot'. Daniel finished setting up his wife's easel and folding chair, he was rather tired after steering the carriage up the steep hillside.

The horse he thought; was more like a mule, stubborn and slow to climb the hill. He took a moment to fill his lungs with the crystal clear, air of the mountainous terrain. Finally, he began to relax after drinking his first snifter of Cognac.

Daniel didn't have a care in the world, or so it seemed. He had just poured a second glass of his favorite drink when they both heard the first roar of thunder. It boomed in the distance.

Rachel called to her husband who was sitting some distance away between her and the carriage. She pointed up to the sky, a note of disappointment in her voice.

"Darling! Look!"

But Daniel was content where he was and he dismissed the sound as being miles away, "probably on the other side, just south of the "Pennine Chain," he assured his wife.

However, thirty minutes or so after that first roar of thunder, the weather suddenly took a bad turn. The clear blue sky had suddenly turned gray, so they had to rush to collect Rachel's equipment and run to the carriage for cover

Rachel suggested they wait out the shower as she called it; however, Daniel wanted to get back on the road.

"But darling, we are only an hour outside of the city," Rachel pleaded.

But Daniel was adamant; he wanted to get back to the hotel. He wanted to rest up before Joey arrived.

"Please," his wife protested. "We've only just arrived. I'm sure this is just a summer shower that will soon pass and besides it's still early, we have all day. Joey will not be there until this evening."

While sitting in the buggy, they argued, but Daniel held the reigns and was determined to move forward. The rain was extremely heavy making visibility a strain. As Daniel urged the horse to move forward, the horse whinnied high and long under each thrashing of the whip and the rain did not give up. Rachel reminded her husband that he was unfamiliar with the area and perhaps he should heed the mare. But Daniel, stubborn and inebriated, insisted he knew what he was doing.

"This stupid beast is not going to rule me," he yelled. "I know this is how to get down to the lower level, this stupid beast is just stubborn. I'll show him who's in control."

The sky had lost its luster and the dark, pregnant clouds began to overshadow the once idealistic terrain. Daniel was determined to master the beast in a direction the horse clearly did not want to go.

It was obvious to Rachel that Daniel had consumed far too much port and was clearly not able to steady the horse. It reared up its hind legs in protestation, but her husband was just as determined as the animal.

It was raining heavily and the sky had suddenly turned black, as the huge thunderous clouds turned the afternoon into night. Daniel was incapable of seeing what the horse could see and he pushed on aggressively. Rachel and her husband were unaware that they had come to the cliff 's edge.

According to the coroner's report, death was instantaneous for all three.

The hotelier was perplexed as to why the horse led the couple off the edge of the cliff, given that this horse knew the terrain as well, if not better than any man.

18

– THE FATAL ACCIDENT –

At seven o'clock, as promised, Joey arrived at the hotel with a bouquet of flowers for his mother and a cigar for his father. The desk clerk told him that his parents had gone out earlier that day. "Given that the weather took a bad turn, they must have taken shelter along the way," he said.

Joey waited until half past ten, by then he was quite concerned. The maître d suggested they may have stopped over at one of the tiny inns.

"I'm sure they will be here bright and early in the morning. You may take their gifts up to their room, in fact, if you wish to occupy their room you may do so, after all your parents have paid for the room. Now won't that be a nice surprise to open their door and see you sleeping in their bed, ha, ha, don't you think?"

It was storming out, so Joey decided to take up the maître d's suggestion; he had cycled to the hotel on his bike and was sure to get a good soaking under the continuous downpour. Joey had a restful night's sleep in his parents' suite.

When they did not return the following day, the manager of the hotel contacted the local constabulary to report the missing couple along with one of the hotel's horses and buggies.

Two days later, the local constable while walking his beat spotted a carriage and horse at the foot of a hill. On closer inspection, he discovered the bodies of a fashionably dressed man and woman.

Based on the clothing the corpses were wearing, the constable deduced that the bodies were not local.

The duty sergeant contacted the hotels and inns in the area to find out if the corpses were registered in the nearby villages. It was the job of the first sergeant on duty to locate a next of kin.

There was nothing on their person to indicate where they were staying. Fortunately, because the manager of the main hotel in the village had made a missing persons inquiry two days before the tragic discovery, the duty sergeant did not have far to go.

Joey was devastated, naturally and silently he blamed himself for not being available when his parents first arrived. He also blamed himself for the way he espoused the local topography, knowing that his mother would be enthralled and eager to visit such sites.

Mr. McGregor, the hotel manager insisted Joey stay on for another day so that he could compose himself and take whatever time he needed to collect his parents' belongings and take care of any legal matters. Joey was extremely grateful.

Not wanting to impose on the generosity of the hotel manager, Joey took pains to pack up his parent's belongings; then he crammed all of his belongings into his holdall.

The journey back to England was a daunting experience and for the first time in his life he felt desperately alone.

Strange he thought, *'I have been on my own and away from my parents for the past four years but I never felt alone. I suppose I always knew or felt that they would be there if or when I needed them. I always knew they were only a postcard or a train ride away'*.

The funeral was very private with just a handful of old and faithful friends attending. Mr. Hargrove, his parent's lawyer along with a few new friends from the village and a couple of old friends from Liverpool attended the private service.

Linda attended the funeral with her husband, she could not stop crying. A couple of Rachel's school friends paid their respect, as did the cook and scullery maid from their former home.

"We always liked your mam and dad," said the cook. "They always treated us decent."

Rosie, the scullery maid smiled in agreement. After a few heartfelt condolences, Joey returned to the family home in Cambridge.

Lying on his bed that night he felt desolate, he was truly all alone in the world; and while he mourned the loss of his parents, dismay and uncertainty overwhelmed him.

He found he was unable to rid his mind of the nagging thoughts that seemed to overpower him like; what to do now with his desperate and lonely life.

Should I at least stay in this house they bought just to be close to me? Should I return to Cambridge which is what my father wanted? Should I give up my dream of becoming a landscape painter? Perhaps, I should give up painting altogether.

He was his parents' only child and the heir to their estate, so everything they owned was bequeathed to him in their joint will; still he was at a loss as to what he should do.

He could sell everything and move up to Scotland. But this was their home, the home they bought so that they could be close to him while attending university; he felt an obligation to keep the house and remain in the village.

However, apart from the small house that was free of debt and a dozen or so of his mother's paintings, he had very little to sustain himself with if he wished to continue painting.

Joey was very tired, but sleep refused to interrupt his thoughts.

19

– ORPHANED & PENNILESS –

IN THE DAYS AFTER JOEY BURIED HIS PARENTS, HE DECIDED TO try and pursue employment but he soon realized he either had too much education for some jobs and not enough for others. Depression continued to overwhelm him; he was at a loss as to what he should do. He considered renting out the house and returning to Scotland. However, several days later he received a letter from Mr. Hargrove requesting a meeting.

The tone of the letter was cordial, if not friendly:

Dear Joey,
I hope this letter finds you as well as can be expected under such sad circumstances.
There are a few matters I need to discuss with you; I have an open space in my diary on Wednesday at 2 pm. However, if that is not a convenient time, please stop by to reschedule a mutually convenient time with my secretary.
With fond regards
Mr. Hargrove, Attorney at Law

Two days later, without any hesitation, Joey kept the two o'clock appointment. He rather liked the old man and was grateful that he had attended his parents' funeral. He was after all; a well-respected professional who basically took charge of the attendees, interacting with everyone and casually putting people at ease.

After shaking hands, Mr. Hargrove invited Joey to have a seat across from him. "I hate to add to the distress you are already experiencing sonny boy but needs must. I'm afraid, dear me." He took in a deep sigh. "I'm afraid I have some rather disturbing news to share with you laddie; and I'm afraid there's no easy way to say it."

Joey could feel his stomach tightening up. "What is it Mr. Hargrove? What could be worse than my parents dying so tragically?"

"Aye lad, I was myself devastated."

The meeting, though delicately presented left Joey quite ill at ease. He could feel the color draining from his face while his intestines began knotting up.

Mr. Hargrove rang for his assistant to fetch a glass of water. "Come immediately into my office," he told his secretary. He then rushed over to the boy and began to rub the back of his hand. Mr. Hargrove took the glass of cold water from his secretary and helped Joey sip the cold liquid.

Joey was devastated to learn from his family's lawyer that he would have to sell the house to pay back taxes, death taxes, as well as several smaller bills for paint, canvases, and his father's outstanding brandy, port, and tobacco bill. All of which was quite substantial. He was astounded to learn that his parents had purchased items on credit and worse yet, they had failed to pay off their debt.

This was so out of character for his parents who, he

thought, prided themselves on their honesty and determination to live within their means.

Joey Hawthorn was the last remaining member of a once wealthy aristocratic family, where money was freely available throughout his life. His situation now was dismal, he was an impoverished orphan with no one to turn to for help, and he prayed desperately for guidance.

In an effort to preserve his parent's good name, Joey had no alternative but to pay off their debt in full. The only assets he had were his mother's piano and a few of her paintings.

It pained him to sell the house, not that he was attached to it, and in fact, he had spent less than one month all told in the house, since his parents moved into it.

So much of his sadness was in realizing how much he meant to them and how selfish it was of him to spend every holiday abroad, except for Christmas. He did have Christmas dinner with them and the odd weekend. But most of his free time was spent on scenic excursions while residing at university.

He really felt wretched when he thought about the sacrifices his parents made to be closer to him during his first few years at Cambridge. He realized in that very moment he had made very little effort to see them.

While waiting for the estate agent to find a buyer, Joey began selling off his mother's paintings, then he sold his father's collection of leather-bound classics.

Joey experienced real melancholy when it came time to sell his father's grand piano, which was among the first items to be sold. It had not been new like the ones his grandmother had once owned in their beautiful home on their estate but it was beloved by his father.

His nostalgia engulfed him when he sold the huge hand-carved desk that Joey would hide under when running away from his nanny or mother. He smiled thinking about those happy days.

"So many memories." He sighed. "So long ago!" he said out loud, and then he inhaled deeply. "Time to move on," he said with a sigh.

It took several weeks to completely sell everything from rare books to fine china crystal and Irish linens. It was Joey's aim to clear his father's good name as quickly as possible, so he did not haggle over prices even though he knew he was selling most items for far less than they were worth.

With what little money there was left over from the sale of the house and after all the debts and taxes had been paid in full, there was not much left for him to live on.

Once the house was sold, he rented a small room in the village, and as his money was slowly dwindling away, he considered returning to Scotland for a while to visit with his friend Duncan.

His once regal family had died shamefully destitute. And so, without any warning, as a starving artist and through no fault of his own; he'd experienced loneliness, anxiety, hunger and fear.

When he realized just how dire his situation was; he could see no solution to amend his circumstances - he needed help. Given his present, despicable and humiliating circumstances; he feared he would die of starvation in that dismal attic room. He was consumed with both hunger and depression.

Just then, his landlady called up to him at the top of her voice in order to reach him in the attic.

"Hey sonny boy, there's a letter for you, but I don't think it's a job; 'cos it's from your solicitor."

"Not another one," he said out loud. Devastated and disheartened, he walked heavily down the four flights of stairs.

"I hope it's good news this time," she said.

She patted his arm and handed Joey the official letter. He thanked her with a half-smile then reluctantly put the letter in his coat pocket. He fingered it several times as he slowly walked back up the stairs; he just couldn't face any more bad news.

"Dear God! What now?" Joey said out loud; when he entered his room, then he flopped into the only chair in his attic room.

He took a deep breath; his stomach was in knots, he had no idea what was in this letter but he was too nervous to open it. With no one to turn to for help, he felt totally alone. He stood up and reluctantly removed the letter from his pocket and read the contents.

The letter contained just two lines:

Dear Joey,
Please come to my office at your earliest convenience. I have an urgent
matter to discuss with you.
With fond regards,
Mr. Hargrove, Attorney at Law

Feeling as though he had the weight of the world on his shoulders, he walked over to his shabby little bed and climbed into it, pulling the covers up over his head. Several hours later he woke up, wondering what time it was; he was hungry.

His feeling of being overwhelmed however did not evaporate while he slept and he knew he would have to take some action, after all, Joey Hawthorn was a gentleman, impoverished though he may be. Noblesse oblige dictated he face the music, no matter how damaging or painful it might be.

He was extremely cold and very hungry, unable to recall the last decent meal he'd eaten. Suddenly, he was consumed with a deep depression. He was sure it was predicated on the fear of the unknown. Joey had no one to turn to for support or help or advice. He was penniless and all alone in the world.

He thought of his parents and as he did, he wondered if it was his fate to join them. Feeling weary and hungry, having not eaten one morsel of food in days; not even the dried-up crust of a day-old loaf of bread.

His depression overwhelmed him and he took to his bed, which was not fit for the mice he heard scurrying at night.

He closed his eyes effortlessly, allowing sleep to consume him. He knew full well that he would starve to death without remorse, believing it was his fate to join his parents.

Then, as he closed his eyes allowing fate to take control, effortlessly, he began to doze; then as if being pricked by a sharp object, he thought of his one dear friend, Duncan.

Joey opened his eyes and instantly reflected on the happy times he had enjoyed with his school mate and how much he enjoyed conversing with his gracious family up in the highlands of Scotland.

He reflected on how very happy he was whenever he visited his old school chum; and how genuinely happy Duncan and his family were to have him as their guest.

Infused with this new and pleasant thought, Joey sat up suddenly in his bed, as if he had been jolted out of a bad dream. He wrapped the patchwork quilt around himself, then slipping his feet into his well-worn slipper he scurried hastily across the small room.

Joey sat at the tiny desk and removed the notepad, ink pen, and the bottle of royal blue ink from the drawer.

Once he was sitting in a comfortable position, he dipped his quill into the inkwell and began composing a letter to his old classmate.

The words did not come easily and he crumpled up several pages before he managed to collect his thoughts and write a compelling letter.

It was a pleading letter to be sure, but his hopeless situation necessitated a desperate, if not radical solution. Weak and somewhat nervous, it took several attempts to construct his begging letter; because that is what it was.

He was all alone in the world; penniless, hungry, and soon to be homeless. As he reflected on his many visits, he recalled the happy and stimulating times he experienced, both as an artist and in the many conversations they had engaged in.

I have such fond memories of my visits with you my old chum, he thought and he smiled as he reflected on those happy times. After several attempts, he finally composed his 'begging letter'.

Dear Duncan,

It is with a heavy heart that I attempt to compose this letter. I fear I am at my wits end and with nowhere to turn. I have just received another cable from my parents' solicitor. He has requested an audience with me, yet again and at my earliest convenience.

I have been besieged with debtors and have no idea just how much more debt I may be compelled to pay.

To say that I am shocked at the amount of debt my parents accumulated, would be an understatement.

Reluctantly, I sold the last of my mother's paintings last week. I am truly amazed at how selfish people are, paying pennies on the pound for some very valuable pieces. I am truly overwhelmed. I have no job prospects and my depression is consuming me.

Would you be so kind, as to invite an old-school chum, to escape this madness for which I had no role in creating?
How I long to experience the beauty of rural Scotland once more; to paint and breath the exquisite air.
I need to walk through the highlands, smell the heather, converse with friends, and sleep in a comfortable bed.
I look forward to hearing from you at your earliest convenience, even if your answer is in the negative; which I pray it will not.

Most sincerely,
Your friend Joey

20

– MANNA FROM HEAVEN –

At twenty-two-years of age, Mr. Joseph Hawthorn III recently orphaned; penniless and hungry, began praying.

that his friend Duncan would come to his rescue. After sealing up the letter he had carefully written to his friend, he placed his last penny postage stamp on the sealed envelope and returned to his bed.

He awakened to a bright sunny morning and was eager to go out and post the letter to his friend.

With his hand still firmly holding the doorknob, he felt his stomach churning and he felt faint. *Dear God! What now?* he thought.

He leaned against the door frame to steady his body, fearing his knees would buckle under him while descending the four flights of stairs. His legs felt like jelly and he could hear the heavy pounding of his heart. Joey realized it was hunger causing him to lose his balance. He had not eaten in days.

After collecting the solicitor letter from his landlady, it had taken him almost two days to gather the courage to respond.

However, having made the decision to meet with Mr. Hargrove, the weak and destitute lad climbed down the four steep flights of stairs and nervously walked into the town center. When he reached number 48 Market Square, he paused outside and inhaled deeply.

Still fingering the letter to Duncan in his pocket, which he planned to post right after the meeting with his parents' solicitor, Joey gingerly pulled at the cord to ring the highly polished brass bell.

Mr. Davis, his solicitor's clerk opened the door and greeted him warmly. "Hargrove is expecting you Sir, please follow me." Mr. Davis tapped on the huge mahogany door and the voice inside said: "Enter!"

Joey had barely released Hargrove's enthusiastic handshake and sat down before the man shared the good news. Words eluded him as he attempted to describe the overwhelming sense of shock; joy and elation he experienced.

The news was stupendous, he could not believe his ears. He was stunned, speechless and at the same time ecstatic. When he learned of his incredible inheritance and from an absolute stranger, he was truly dumbfounded.

He apparently had the same last name of a wealthy Englishman, but he hadn't a clue as to who his benefactor was. This inheritance, however, was over three thousand miles away and across one of the world's five oceans.

This inheritance was a huge plantation in the southern portion of America. Included in the documents, Joey received from his father's solicitor was a first-class ticket on a steamship to New York.

He was told that he would be met by a representative of Mr. Malcolm Hawthorn's American lawyers. Hargrove assured him it was legitimate and he should make arrangements to travel soon.

Standing up, a little unsteady on his feet but now from the shock rather than the hunger, he thanked his parents' solicitor for all he had done for them and now for him. When Joey walked out of the solicitor's office, he felt like he was walking on air.

"I'm free, he said aloud. "Truly free to do whatever I want to do. I am free of debt; I am free to paint; I am truly free to be me."

However, by the time, he returned to the boarding house, young Joey had a new set of knots in his stomach, when he read that the land was in need of extensive care as was the once, most impressive house due to damaging storms.

Joseph Hawthorn Esquire had no way of knowing what state the land was in. He was to be the landowner of several hundreds of acres in America.

Miraculously, he had inherited a huge estate and he was finally free of the financial strain that had been plaguing him for months. In his mind, land meant money and money meant freedom.

Given that Joey had no idea just what a 'plantation' was, let alone how to run one, he spent hours in the library researching the various commodities produced on southern plantations.

He was mildly interested but finally concluded that this was not anything he would be interested in. He would, however, put this visit to good use.

He decided he would sell the land and live off the proceeds; after all he was no farmer.

And so, he crumpled up the original letter to Duncan and started anew.

'I will use the ocean liner ticket to visit the property,' he wrote to his friend Duncan in a wire; 'just think of it, a brand new territory, new landscapes to paint; I shall put this visit to maximum use and paint landscapes that few people in Britain will have ever seen.'

Joey was extremely excited about the prospects of painting new horizons and exhibiting, the never before scenes from across the world in England's finest galleries.

This upper class young man had no idea how to run a cotton or tobacco plantation, in fact, he was quite ignorant when it came to anything agricultural. So very different from his unknown benefactor who shared the same last name.

21

– THE HAWTHORN JOHNSON COOPERATIVE –

ON THE MORNING OF JOEY'S FIRST VISIT TO THE PROPERTY, HE met Jimmy Reilly, who in his estimation looked more like 'Father Christmas' than an estate manager. The man had a long white beard, piercing blue eyes, and his enormous belly that hung heavily over the rope that kept his trousers from sliding down.

Joey estimated that Jimmy - as he was affectionately called by everyone - must have been at least eighty-years-old. They each extended a hand in greeting and when Jimmy smiled, he revealed the absence of several teeth. Joey was taken aback; he had never seen a grown person without a full set of teeth.

Jimmy had harnessed his wagon in front of the hotel where Joey and his lawyer spent the night. The American lawyer, Mr. Cedric Parker met Joey at the dock when he had arrived the previous day. Joey was fascinated as they rode through the many little towns on the way to his inheritance. It all looked so picturesque, he thought and he longed to paint so much of what he saw.

Several hours later, they finally arrived and Mr. Reilly took the two men on a tour of the vast estate that Joey had just inherited.

The new owner was far from impressed; in fact, he was horrified to say the least when he saw the condition of the place. He had never seen a plantation but he didn't think this rundown, overgrown wasteland was worth holding onto. And besides it was vast; too vast to imagine being able to do anything with it, young Joey was sure.

Then when he saw the condition of the dilapidated living quarters where the 'workers' lived, he was appalled. Joey knew very little about slaves other than the occasional mention in one or two books he perused in the library after he learned of his inheritance.

"How is it possible that human beings can live like this?" he asked, incredulously.

And as if seeing the state of this rundown, almost forgotten land through fresh eyes; Jimmy shrugged his shoulders as he patted the mare's rump.

Still disgusted, the new owner took no delight in what he saw. As Jimmy continued to maneuver Joey and his lawyer around the perimeter of the plantation, he pointed out from a great distance the main house. Joey was repulsed when he saw the state of ill repair that the huge house had fallen into.

Oh! No, this is not for me, he thought.

Jimmy explained, "During the last few years of the previous owner's life, he was consumed with grief when his beloved wife died. He lost interest in everything; then about a year later the whole state just about flooded, the damage to buildings, crops land and animals was … well, it clear wiped out just about everything.

Windows, doors, roofs, you name it sonny, just about

nothing was left standin', an' the master was still grievin'. He didn't seem to notice the state of the place, we all did our best, but well that was the storm to end all storms. It's a mess, I know, but we figure with a new owner we might get to fixin' things up a bit."

"A bit!" Joey said, holding back how he really felt. "It's going to take a lot more than a bit. I don't know where to start, do you? Oh I guess not, otherwise you would have done something about it."

"Now see here sonny, don't take that attitude with me-"

"Well now, who else can I blame? You said you were the overseer, so once you oversaw the damage, my God man, common sense should dictate …"

"What! What was that …?"

"Never mind, never mind," Joey said wearily. "Just tell me there is a decent room in the house for me to sleep in tonight."

Frustrated, depressed, and angry, he reaffirmed in his mind that he would sell 'the wreckage'.

This is huge responsibility and I know nothing of farming, or of taking care of so many dependent people, he thought.

After the tour, Mr. Parker asked Joey what he thought of his inheritance. Joey was surprised to see that the lawyer was serious and he swallowed hard. Joey took Mr. Parker's arm and walked him away from Jimmy.

"I need to consult with my attorney," he called over his shoulder to Jimmy.

Seeing the expression on Joey's face, Mr. Parker reminded the new owner of the failsafe clause in the will. The clause prevented selling the estate, under penalty of extreme taxation. The disclaimer depressed the artist no end and he wanted to run and hide.

Finally, he resigned himself to the enormous nightmare

that lay before him, albeit with deep regret. He was informed that all of the slaves had been released by the previous owners many years before and recently many of the paid staff had left too. They just up an' left the place after their boss died, Jimmy told him.

"I be's the only white person left." And as old as he was, he was left in charge of everything. He was the oldest, semi-retired, semi-illiterate overseer, who like the handful of staff that remained had no place else to go.

Joey thought, *How incredible, that the likes of this toothless, illiterate, old man could be left in charge of hundreds of acres of land, not to mention the families living on the land. My God; as old as he is; putting him in charge of everything.*

It just didn't make sense to Joey. Apparently, this was a major concern for the attorneys until the designated owner could take charge.

To say that Joey was depressed would be an under-statement; he was exhausted and extremely overwhelmed with everything. He asked Jimmy to take him and Mr. Parker back to the inn where they had both lodged the night before.

"Come for me at 8am, I will clear up my bill and eat a hearty breakfast before I leave, given that I have no idea where or when I shall eat my next meal. And right now, I need solitude in order to think."

The inn was obviously a tradesman's inn, not the type young Joey had been used to when traveling in Britain. The bed linen was obviously not fresh and so as weary as he was, Joey had to contend with a loud spoken angry manager who very reluctantly provided him with fresh linen, although Joey had to make up his own bed.

"I thought I had been blessed," he said quietly to himself, "but now I think I may have been cursed."

He was obviously more exhausted than he'd realized and when he did finally wake up, he was starving; his last meal was more than twenty-four hours earlier. Annoyed with himself for sleeping so late, he rushed down the stairs to have breakfast.

"Breakfast stopped an hour ago, an' I'm settin' up for the lunch crowd now," said the barmaid.

Feeling weak and overwhelmed he staggered and fell into a chair. "Please," he said, "I haven't eaten in two days; I will take anything, a piece of toast and an egg. Please," he said again with emphasis.

The barmaid, who doubled as a waitress, was obviously moved by his desperate state. She told him to go back to his room and she would bring him a tray.

Joey was more than grateful and he told her so. About thirty minutes or so later, the girl knocked on his door.

"Yes," he said still groggy from oversleeping.

"I brung you some vittles, Sir," she said.

He invited her to enter and she crossed the tiny room and laid the tray down for him.

"I made these myself, just like my mamma taught me to," she said with pride while wearing a big smile.

He looked at the dish and said, "It's a bit early for mashed potatoes, but I'm so hungry I could eat a cow right now. Thank you very much".

"You is welcome, Sir," she said as she turned around and left him to enjoy her cooking.

Joey was so hungry he scooped up a spoonful of what he saw as roughly mashed potatoes, the butter was still melting in the center of the pile. He instantly spat out the mouthful he had scooped up. "What in God's name is this?" he said and began to examine the grainy substance.

When he returned the empty plate, he asked the barmaid

what the food was called. She smiled and said with pride, "Them's grits, Sir. My great gra-mar showed me how to cook them, did you like them?"

"Well, that is the first time I tasted them ... Oh, I see my driver is here. Goodbye to you and thank you for letting me sleep in so late."

It was almost noon when Jimmy arrived at the inn, in a hired buggy. Both men rode most of the way, back to the plantation, in silence; which took several hours.

Jimmy still annoyed with the boy, was lost for words and Joey, was deep in thought; finally realizing that he was virtually trapped and having no clue as to how a plantation should be run, he finally broke the silence and spoke to the toothless overseer.

Jimmy informed his new boss, that the Johnson family had been on the plantation longer than any other family, longer than him even. He also told Joey that the Johnsons were a hard-working family and that he was lucky they decided to stay.

He said that Nate Johnson knew everything there was to know about the plantation, because Mr. Hawthorn and his wife depended on Nate, to bring this plantation back to its former glory, when they bought it. And, that they depended on him when they first started buying small holdings one at a time.

"Nate Johnson's only child, Jack was as good a carpenter as himself and his daddy. God rest his soul, 'twas the storm that took old Nate."

22

– A GUARDED ENCOUNTER –

When Joey learned from Jimmy about Jack's skills and his talent as a carpenter, he felt relieved; he desperately needed to have his lodgings repaired so he wanted to meet this carpenter immediately. After seeing just how vast the state was, he asked Jimmy where he could find him.

"He was mending fences in the paddock beyond the cotton field over yonder; when I last saw him. I'll send for him."

"No, never mind, just take me over there, I need to see his work."

"Now! Sir?" Jimmy asked. He was tired after the long journey and he wanted to take a nap.

"Yes! Now," came Joey's sharp reply.

Jimmy sighed deeply and shook his head. He then sent a small boy over to the stables to fetch the two-seated wagon. His opposite, Jack Johnson, the son and grandson of slaves came from a vastly different social, cultural, racial, and financial background; and from two different parts of the world. Their worlds, separated not only by an ocean, but by wealth, class, reverend, respect, admiration, and to some extent language. However, in time, both young, parentless men would lean on each other for support, mutual admiration, gratitude, and respect.

When they finally arrived at the area where Jack was working; the two men found Jack on his knees nailing in the lower rung of the broken fence.

Hearing the wagon pull up, he looked sideways to see it, but kept on working. However, when Jimmy called out his name, Jack turned to face him and when he did, he saw the two white men walking towards him. He knew Jimmy from childhood and he relaxed, then glancing wider, he took in the second man's measure.

These two young men were of similar height and same age. These similarities, however, in no way reflected on who these two young men were, or where they had come from. One had clearly been raised as a gentleman, lived the life of a privileged child into young adulthood as he sat tall now in the wagon.

Joey had always moved with confidence. He'd had an enviable education and never been in want of anything. A positive, highly lucrative future had been ahead of him, most certainly assured.

Yet now, his situation was worrying and he could see no way out of his current situation. Last night, he had prayed desperately for a solution.

Jack began to rise as Joey stepped down from the wagon; the young Englishman walked over with a smile of gratitude on his face and his right hand outstretched.

The two men were eye to eye, one black the other white, both men were about six-feet tall. Each with a mound of hair on their head, one, deep auburn and the other, jet black.

The carpenter looked serious, not knowing what to expect; but Joey's blue eyes sparkled and when he smiled, a dimple appeared in his left cheek.

Surprised, Jack returned the smile revealing a single dimple in his left cheek. Jimmy introduced the two men, Joey extended his hand. Jack wiped his right hand down the side of his pant leg first.

Simultaneously, they reached out as if checking the strength of their opposite's upper arm. Jimmy watched from a distance and smiled inwardly.

23

– A NEW GENERATION: LET IT BE A BOY –

THE ANTICIPATED BIRTH OF THESE TWO YOUNG MEN, TWENTY-two years earlier, by their expectant parents, was filled with emotions and love.

From the moment of their awaited birth each set of parents were filled with joy. For both couples, this would be their first child; and for both, a son they had wished for. Both babies were born in the same month of the same year but that is where the similarities ended.

The difference between those two babies was wider than the oceans that once separated them. Like the distance between Antarctica and the Sahara Desert; like the Irish linen and Chinese silk compared to the rubber and burlap that their mothers lay on, on that momentous day.

Joseph Hawthorn III, known as 'Joey', was born in a private wing of St. Thomas' hospital in London, England; his bed draped in silk and Irish linen.

In attendance were his parents' family doctor, Sir Michel Wentworth; his mother's midwife, Regina Martin; the ward sister, Maggie Dempsey; and three of her senior nurses. Specific attention was given to every detail. Brahms' lullaby played softly in the background.

After the birth of Joey; heir to centuries old fortune and titles, the infant was taken away to be bathed and dressed before being presented to his parents. Champagne was served to the attending staff.

For Rachel, it was important, necessary even, to produce a son and heir. Had her first child been a daughter, she would have had to repeat the agonizing and humiliating process all over again, until a son and heir was born.

Far around the world, Jack's birth was nowhere near as opulent. However, his birth, which was his parent's fourth attempt, was equally if not more eagerly and emotionally anticipated.

When his mother Sadie announced she was going into labor, she was made to lay on a pile of straw which had been covered with burlap. On top of that a rubber mat, then a cotton sheet had been placed under Sadie's buttocks.

There were only two women in attendance, one was Annie Mae or 'Big Momma' as she was affectionately called; she was the oldest woman in the compound. Her twenty-five-year-old granddaughter Bella assisted with the delivery. Big Momma had delivered dozens of babies over the forty-odd years she had been enslaved on that plantation.

In Sadie's case, this was her fourth attempt to give birth to a healthy baby. The prior three attempts, her baby died within a few days of its birth or it was still born.

This time the baby was a strong and healthy male child and destined to survive. His mother, however, was very weak. Annie Mae did all that she could but she was unable to stop the hemorrhaging. Sadie died three days after giving birth to her first child, her only living son. But Sadie had died happy; she had finally given her beloved husband the son he always wanted.

Of all the people, over all the years who lived on the plantation, even before the Hamiltons bought it, Jimmy developed a fondness for Jack. As a toddler, he would follow his father and Jimmy around. Little Jack would carry the odd tool or fetch water for them. Jimmy never married so he had no family of his own. As the years went by, he watched the toddler as he grew and eventually mature into a talented and responsible young man. Jimmy's respect for the young man and his talents as a craftsman continued to grow.

Jack learned many skills from Jimmy and his dad, long before his father died in the storm. As young Jack matured, he showed a keen interest in the creative aspects of carpentry and in time, a mutual respect developed between Jimmy and his apprentice.

Before Jack's father Nate died in the storm, he and Jimmy taught the boy all that they knew about carpentry. They both recognized how artistic he was and they eventually gave him free reign.

Now, Jimmy was tired; he had arthritis in both knees and in his thumb and forefinger on both hands. He was eager to retire and wanted nothing more than to remain in his little cabin and fish every day in the river for his supper. He was very happy to see that there was a good spirit between Jack and the new owner.

"I understand you are a fine carpenter." The young white man said to the young Black man.

Jack replied. "Yes I am a skilled carpenter, trained by Jimmy here and my daddy who was trained by his daddy an' with each generation, we gets better."

"Yes, well I am very glad to hear that Jack, because I have need for a good carpenter to restore my house; put it back together, if you will. Can you do that Jack? Can you restore that old ramshackle of a building to its former glory?"

Jack removed his cap and with hat in hand, he scratched his densely thick hair.

"Well now, that's gona be a big job, and it's gona take a lot of time and a lot more sweat."

"Yes, I'm aware of that, Joey said rather irritably, "but Jimmy said you are capable and talented enough to take on the task, is that true?"

"Oh, it be true alright," Jack said, wiping the sweat from his brow on the back his bare arm.

"Good. Then I would like you to come with me and take a walk through the big house and tell me what you will need to make it livable."

The two young men walked through two fields before they could see what was left of the once fashionable and stylish house. Joey was aware now that his predecessor Malcolm had restored the crumbling house when he first arrived from England with his bride.

Stopping in a field, a visible distance from the house looking over the brambles and tumbleweeds and felled trees, the two men stood shoulder to shoulder and gazed at the structure that was once the envy of most landowners for miles around.

The ruins that were in its day, a grand three story house, but through years of neglect and decay plus devastating storms, the once elegant structure, was now sadly close to ruin, at least in Joey's eyes.

"As you can see," Joey said, "The house is barely livable,

except for a few of the rooms on the second floor. The roof looks good but I don't know if there is any running water."

"Well," said Jack pointing just to the left of the house. "That there is a well."

"Yes, said Joey," but I meant inside running water, both hot and cold."

"Well you gon need a plumber for that."

"So, you don't do plumbing?" Joey asked disappointedly.

"Maybe," Jack said removing his hat and scratching his hair that had been flattened down by it. "But I do have jobs to do here, lots of jobs so …"

"Jack!' Joey cut him off. "You see the state of this house, now as a carpenter I'm sure you will take great pride in bringing it back to its original glory. All of your other jobs can wait. My house takes priority; after all, I am the landowner …"

"An' I guess, slave owner by the sound of it …"

"Now look here Jack, I am the landowner but I lay no claim to being a slave owner. I really do need a place to lay my head at night, don't you agree?" Jack grinned.

The new owner consulted with Jack as to how they should begin the lengthy and possibly very expensive process of restoring the house to its original beauty, as near as possible that is.

Jack, who was secretly thrilled at the prospect of restoring what was left of the grand and enviable structure, informed Joey that there was an abundance of abandoned fallen trees on one of the furthest fields which also belonged to his estate.

He also told the new owner that with the right tools, he could use many of the huge oak and pine trees that had fallen years ago.

"Give me the right tools and I will rebuild or restore

everything to the way it was when my daddy helped restore it for your predecessor; the first Mr. Hawthorn many years ago."

This was music to Joey's ears and he gave Jack carte blanche to purchase whatever tools or materials he needed.

Before leaving for one of his painting excursions, Joey spent some time consulting with Jimmy while they walked through a range of fields to sort out the various agricultural commodities.

24

– NEW HOME FOR THE NEW BABY –

JACK HAD RECENTLY MARRIED SARA; THE GIRL LEFT ORPHANED by her devastated parents, after their three young sons were sold. The young couple was very much in love and excited at being pregnant and anxiously awaiting their first baby. So, when Jack saw how pleased the new owner was with the improvements during the first six months of restoration, he decided to ask him if he could use some of the left-over lumber to build a nice little place for them.

Joey agreed so long as it did not interfere with the work he was doing on his own house. "Use whatever you need, as long as my restorations don't suffer."

He told Jack any hours he put into restoring his own house would be during his own free time. Jack worked all day on the three-story main house which was beginning to take shape. However, before sun up he would work on his own little house, and after a full day's work refurbishing the big house, he would put in as much time as he could on his own house in the evening.

It took some time for Mr. Hawthorn to settle in and own the plantation as his home and his property, but it would have taken much longer if he had not given Jack carte blanch.

Joey often went away for long periods of time leaving the running of his plantation in the hands of Jimmy who was very close to retirement.

Jimmy was having more and more difficulty doing his job because he suffered from chronic arthritis which had plagued him for years, but more recently it was taking a greater hold on him. He was in his sixties when he began breaking in a new manager.

No one knew where Joey went; he was a stranger after all, in a country he knew very little about. Before leaving for one of his trips he would consult with Jack - in front of Jimmy, and Mr. Winters who would soon replace Jimmy.

He gave distinct orders. "Jack is to continue building, and under no circumstances is he to be pulled from the extensive work that still has to be done on my house. He is to continue to be exempt from work in the fields."

When Joey Hawthorn returned to his estate, after a long and fruitful absence, he had high praise for the work accomplished. Jack had captured the essence of the original style of his new home and he smiled in delight, completely satisfied. He certainly proved himself to be a very fine carpenter.

"First class," Joey told his friends, "and like any fine artist, the man takes great pride in his work."

Joey was also impressed and amazed at how quaint the little house Jack had built for himself and his wife. So much so, that he began referring to him as his 'carpenter' whenever he spoke about the excellent work created on his property. As an artist, he admired and respected the work of other artists and craftsmen. He also hated the ram-shackled buildings that permeated his estate; he told Jack that they were 'a blight on the otherwise beautiful landscape and that it depressed him each time he returned home.'

"I want all these shacks torn down, one at a time and I want you Jack to rebuild each and every one. When I look over my land, my estate, my plantation if you will, I want to see beauty in every direction."

Over the years, Jack won the respect and admiration of Joey Hawthorn. Joey finally began to take pride in his inheritance and felt proud when he looked over his landscape, which Jack had over the years transformed it into an enviable site to behold. Guests on the estate looked forward to their periodic visits which often lasted several days.

Eventually, Joey had a very successful plantation, he had a hardworking manager who replaced Jimmy plus a small number of well paid staff to run the plantation.

At the end of each season, he hired day workers to pick or plant along with the few families who still resided on his property.

In time, Joey fell in love with the vast and colorful terrains and on his long excursion from home; he found new and delightful scenes to paint. He enjoyed painting both small cameos and huge landscapes, the likes of which had never been seen in England.

The only drawback for Joey, was the intolerable heat in the summertime. He found the summers in Georgia unbearably hot, so he made annual lengthy trips back to England where he invested in a gallery in which he hung and sold all his painting. During his visits to Britain, he would travel up to Perth to see his old friend Duncan.

On his third trip to Perth, Joey declared his growing

attraction for his friend's younger sister Muriel. A romance ensued and Duncan was delighted.

He was honored with the distinction of being his good friend's best man. Joey took his bride Muriel back to America and there they raised a family of four healthy children on his now very successful plantation.

25

– THE JACK & SARA JOHNSON LINEAGE –

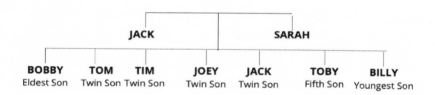

			JACK		SARAH		
BOBBY	**TOM**	**TIM**	**JOEY**	**JACK**	**TOBY**	**BILLY**
Eldest Son	Twin Son	Twin Son	Twin Son	Twin Son	Fifth Son	Youngest Son

JACK'S WIFE SARA WAS ALSO DELIGHTED WITH THE improvements made to their own home. Everything in it had been crafted with love by her talented husband. She had worked very hard to make her house a home they could be proud of. She loved her husband and wanted to fill their home with lots of love and many children.

She was twenty when she had her first miscarriage, they were both devastated. One year later, she had a still born baby and that was followed several months later by another miscarriage. One and a half years later, she announced that she was pregnant again. Jack insisted she take life easy.

"No more lifting and no more scrubbing on your knees, an' I want you to rest, rest, and rest. I'm gone come home in the day an' I better not catch you doin' any work, cos we gone have a healthy baby this time."

Eight months later, Sara gave birth to a healthy baby boy who they named him Bobby. Three years later, she gave birth to twin boys who were named Tom after Sara's father, and Tim after her uncle.

Jack was an only child and had often longed for a brother to play with, so he was thrilled at having three sons. They were proud, loving parents and they doted on their sons.

Three years later, they had another set of twin boys, they named Joey and Jack, soon followed by another boy they called Toby. They had hoped this time for a baby girl, but it was not to be.

The Johnsons now had five little boys and they considered themselves to be well blessed. Jack was very proud of his healthy sons. He often wished that his father Nate would have lived long enough to see all his grandsons; he knew he would be proud.

As his family grew, Jack informed Joey that he had outgrown his four-room house. Joey invited him to help himself to any lumber he needed to extend the house. Jack also added a front porch which was the width of the house. The family loved the front porch where they often ate their meals, especially in the summertime.

Several years earlier, Sara and Jack had resigned themselves to be content with the five boys but deep down they had longed for a baby girl. However, life went on and they were as happy a family as they could be under the circumstances, certainly better off than most of their neighbors.

Quite by accident, ten years later, the Jacksons had created their own cottage industry. It began when Sara realized that she was pregnant again.

They were both shocked and surprised, given that their youngest child Toby had just turned nine. Sara Johnson had stopped having her monthlies and she believed she was heading prematurely into menopause.

The cradle Jack made for his first baby; almost twenty years earlier had accommodated all of their sons. Several years earlier, it had been used for firewood; after Sara told Jack that there would be no more babies.

At the time, they were disappointed, knowing that their wish for a baby girl would not be granted. And so, both parents were shocked but extremely excited at this news.

"Sure would be nice if this one's a girl." Sara confided in her husband, they had wanted a daughter with each pregnancy after the first set of twins.

"I surely do hope so," said Jack, "maybe this time we be lucky."

"Me, too," said Sara, "but in case it might be another boy we should name this baby Billy, that way it won't matter if it be a boy or a girl."

"Well, ah guess ah needs to make a new crib for the new baby."

"I recon," said Sara reaching up to kiss her husband.

It was late spring and the nights were long and warm, most evenings the Johnson family would eat their evening meal on the porch that Jack built years earlier.

After they finished their meal, Sara would clean off the table, also built by Jack and the family would relax and read their bible or re-tell favorite bible stories.

Jack enjoyed working with his hands and as their sons had

grown, he encouraged them to help him. Now that a new baby was on the way, Jack began working on the new cradle. There was plenty of lumber from all of the felled trees which had been removed, and the cleared land made ready for the new tobacco crop.

Jack's neighbors liked his work and after he finished making a rocking chair for Sara, he was asked to make one for his neighbor's wife who was also pregnant.

Other neighboring folks gave him orders for chairs, cradles, and rocking chairs. Jack's family could be found every evening busy sawing logs or smoothing out strips of wood, hammering nails or painting.

The generations of Johnsons had lived and worked on that plantation for well over one-hundred years, long before the young Malcolm Hawthorn and his wife Samantha had bought it. They worked together as a family and were able to supplement their earnings.

26

– NOT ANOTHER BOY –

BILLY WAS BORN TEN YEARS AFTER THE LAST BABY BOY WAS born and this birth was complicated. Sara was much older when this unexpected baby was conceived and born. Her body was wrecked with years of hard work, constantly bending and toiling day in and day out for the past twenty-five-years. She never complained.

This pregnancy took its toll on her frail body. But she did survive. Jack feared he would lose his beloved wife and best friend with this last pregnancy, so after Billy was born, Jack took it upon himself to speak with Mr. Winters, the new manager. He told him that his wife was still very weak after his last child was born and now that his youngest boy who was ten years old and had been working in the fields alongside his parents and older brothers for over a year and can now pull his weight.

"I'll give her three months to get back her strength and, in the meantime, if the boy can work as fast as Sara did then, well, we'll have this talk again then," Andrews said.

Jack was relieved and thankful, he also knew that in three months Toby would be pulling his weight. Billy was a big baby, a demanding child with a healthy appetite and he was constantly hungry.

His mother feared she was incapable of satisfying his hunger, so after three months of feeling drained each day from his constant nursing, she decided to give him the bottle.

Eventually, he seemed satisfied. At least his demand for food diminished, he still cried a lot but not because he was hungry. Sara was at home with Billy all day long and she looked forward to the evening when her husband and little men - as she called her sons - returned home at the end of each day.

All of her men would arrive home, hungry every evening and looking forward to a great home cooked meal in which Sara took great pleasure cooking for them.

A freshly baked apple or a pecan pie usually followed and on balmy nights the family would eat outside, quenching their thirst with a pitcher of sweet tea Sara made for those hot sweltering nights.

The Johnson family had been well established for several years and news of this child's impending birth was a great surprise to all the family members, mother and father included.

Had this baby been a girl the child would have been a welcomed addition to the fold, but with six sons already they took everything in their stride! No fan fair, no great celebration.

27

– EVERYONE PULLING THEIR WEIGHT –

AT THE AGE OF FIVE, BILLY WAS STILL TOO YOUNG TO WORK IN the fields alongside his parents and older brothers, but he was not allowed to be idle either. As young as he was he had a job to perform and he did so willingly. He was still a small boy when he first started working in the fields of cotton, corn or, tobacco, depending on the season, all of which dwarfed him.

It was while he worked in the fields, craving attention from his family that Billy first heard the music 'over yonder,' cascading from a handcrafted flute created by a very old man.

He soon discovered that Bubba was his name and he had worked all of his life in these fields. At least one-hundred years Billy was certain, but as old as he was and even with his diminishing eyesight, he still had a job to do, six days a week. He had worked on this and other plantations, all of his life.

Now that he was old, he did not have to work as hard as the younger men and women, although he was still expected to do his share.

Billy was the 'water boy' and would do anything in those

days to win the attention, let alone affection, of his parents and older brothers. The cotton field where his family all worked was just one square acre but to Billy, it seemed as big and wide as an ocean.

Billy would have to walk along all four sides of the acre; in the middle of each side there was a huge barrel of fresh cold water, a ladle hooked onto the side. It was Billy's job to dip the empty ladle into the barrel and pour the water into two buckets. There were two buckets on either side of the acre.

When he was first assigned the job, he was too small to reach the top of the barrel and he would have to stand on a step ladder in order to fill the ladle. Each bucket had a handle on it and a ladle was hooked onto the side.

Billy would rotate filling the buckets on the two sides of the field that he was responsible for. Bubba took care of the other two sides. This way the field hands never had to go too far from where they were working to replenish themselves with a drink of cold water.

When he was ten years old, he would take the half full containers of water into the field to the pickers and return with the empty bucket. By the time he walked along the north and west parameters, taking the buckets of water into the field to the hot and thirsty pickers, it was time to start all over again. Billy did his job willingly and with pride.

Bubba's job was to make sure that there was enough water for the pickers all day long. He worked on the opposite side of the acreage from Billy. When the workers stopped to eat their midday meal, Bubba poured water for them from the barrels and whenever he had time, he played his music, all of which he composed himself.

Being self-taught and unable to read or write, his music

was of his own making and it was the most melodious sound to the ears of young Billy, the water boy.

As a child, Billy liked his job, even though, by the end of the day, he was too tired to walk all the way home. One of his big brothers would have to carry him, usually straight to bed.

However, as he grew older, he took no pleasure in his boring job and he began to resent the work he had to do. His father told him that if he didn't do his job right, he would be moved into the fields to pick, which would be much harder. So, he had to decide if he wanted a harder job or to keep his boring job. He decided on the latter.

As a very small boy, Billy grew up feeling that he didn't really belong to the family he lived with. They all seemed so close; they had worked together for years, long before he was born. He would listen as they shared stories and laugh out loud at something they all seemed to know about while Billy always felt like he belonged somewhere else.

He was always craving attention from this family that he lived with, he seldom received it and he never felt like he belonged.

Even as a little boy, he had always felt as if he was in the way. He often wondered if maybe they found him or rescued him from somewhere, like drowning or perhaps his real parents were sold and he was left behind because he was still a baby.

He was sure he did not belong with the people who called themselves family and he was becoming increasingly unhappy with each miserable and boring day. It seemed the harder he tried to please this family, the less interested they were in him. He often wished he had a younger brother but instead he felt lonely, cast aside; like an afterthought.

Over the years there were several incidents that caused

young Billy to silently question his true relationship to this family that he lived with. On one particular occasion, he observed an interaction that penetrated his young heart to its core. It was a scene that he remembered well, because it made a permanent indentation on his heart. He was just five years old, but decades later, the memory and the pain were just as vivid.

Whenever there was a plantation celebration, in the quarters, a christening, a wedding or a funeral, everyone took part. Those festive occasions always called for a community-wide celebration; with lots of lively music, dancing, and lots of great food to eat. It seemed everyone contributed to the happy feast.

On the more somber occasions, when it was a death or a search for a run-away-slave, there was a roar of wailing, sorrowful moaning and an abundance of tears being shed.

On this particular occasion, Lula Mae, had given birth to twins, a boy and a girl, a double reason to celebrate. Lula Mae and her husband Larry already had an eight-year-old daughter named Molly plus a five-year-old son, named David. Billy was the same age as David and the boys often played together. On this joyous occasion, the boys were playing catch.

When David's father called his son's name, young David dropped the ball and went running over to his father's, outstretched arms. His dad swung him around and around as the delighted child cried out in glee. Curious, little Billy followed his playmate with his eyes and when he heard the squeals of laughter and delight his friend made and the love his father showed his son; little Billy just looked on longingly.

After a few minutes of observing the joy his young friend experienced, he averted his eyes and when he did, he found his father staring at him.

Billy picked up the ball and began to kick the gravel beneath his feet. His father walked towards a group of men and faded into the crowd. Having seen for the first-time what love looked like between a little boy and his dad, young Billy longed for it all the more.

Seeing the sadness in the little boy's eyes each time Bubba saw the child, he would ask him from time to time, "Is you ailin' boy, 'cos most every time I sees you, you look like you carryin' the world on your shoulders. Is you sure ain't nothin' botherin' you boy?"

Billy would always shrug his shoulders. "I'm fine old man, I just wants to learn how to make music like you Mr. Bubba."

Billy liked listening to the music the old man played on his flute and he wanted to play music too. Because of the music he played and the personal joy Billy observed, the old man became his role model. In young Billy's eyes, Bubba was free. The boy was young and had no concept of how much hard work or how many years it took for Bubba to earn this distorted sense of 'freedom.'

He was free of hard labor but he was still dependent on the plantation owner for the roof over his head. Bubba had a small strip of land and he grew most of the food he ate.

Over the years he had developed a green thumb, so even if the fish were not biting and the rabbits remained in their hollows, he had plenty of food growing in his backyard.

He had no child to call him Pa; he was born on the plantation and had over his lifetime belonged to many masters. He knew he would die there alone, and it saddened him that there would be no kin to mourn his passing.

Having no family, at least none that he could recall, Bubba often envied those families who lived and worked together on the land, or in the 'Big House'.

So it was perplexing to him, as to why young Billy always appeared to be so alone and always looked so unhappy; less connected physically from the warm and close knit family that young Billy lived with and he assumed was born into.

He did from time to time attempt to inquire about how sad and lonely he almost always seemed to be. But the boy would just shrug his shoulders.

For years, while still a little boy, young Billy would sneak over in the evening, after dinner to Bubba's cabin to listen to the music he loved.

When Bubba realized that Mr. Johnson's youngest son was as passionate about making music as he obviously was, he fashioned a flute for the boy. He explained that this was just a 'po' man's flute'.

He told him about the pawnshop up in Macon where he could buy a 'real' flute after he saved up enough money to buy one.

"So, start saving all the pennies you spend on gumdrops an' such. An' by the time you is ready, you gon' have enough to buy you a used flute," he told Billy.

As a small child, Billy appeared to be overburdened with life. It was as if he was in the midst of a struggle, one he was unable to rid himself of. One might describe him as joyless, even in his childhood; he seldom smiled and his frown was perpetual.

His bad moods often simmered to the point of boiling. Even when the air was sweet, the nights cool and silent, he still could find no peace in either.

Billy dreamed of the day when he would walk away from the place, he had lived all of his life, he longed to be free, to be himself and when he did he knew he would make music just like Mr. Bubba. The old man had become his role model.

Bubba lived alone, but he was not lonely. From childhood, Billy was drawn to him. Young Billy liked hanging around him even when he was not playing his flute.

He enjoyed the stories that Bubba told him. Billy didn't always understand these stories, but he hung around the old man because he talked to him and he looked at him when he talked to him. Bubba made Billy feel like he was real, that he was seen. He never felt that way when he was with his family.

His parents would talk and laugh together, even his brothers who were very close, seemed to be oblivious of him. They would call him shrimp or pip-squeak, then they would laugh together.

Even when their mother would say, "Now you boys stop that teasing and get on with your work"....it didn't sound sincere. All of his brothers were, of course, much older than he was. They all seemed to talk over his head and about him even in front of him, but seldom did they ever talk to him.

He could not remember ever being asked a question. Oh, they told him to do things, but they never took the time to show him how to do the things they did and they seemed to do so many things together.

Bubba however, was like a grandfather to him, he always had time for the boy, and he even showed him how to use a carving knife to carve faces and other things out of fallen tree branches. He took the time to show Billy how to hold the wood and the knife so that he would not cut himself.

"I don't want your folks comin' after me 'cos I cut their baby boy," he said, as he instructed the boy.

Billy knew in his heart that that would never happen. He simply said, "Ain't no fear in that ol' man." And he left it at that.

Billy had just turned seven years old and as usual, after

supper he would meander over to Bubba's place, which was some distance away. One evening, as it was getting late, Mr. Bubba suggested Billy should head home.

"Your folks gonna be lookin' for you boy, an' I don't want them mad at me for keeping their youngster out after dark."

"Don't you worry 'bout that old man, 'cos that ain't gonna happen," Billy said, looking down at the ground while he kicked up the dirt. But Billy said 'good night' and headed on home anyway.

As he approached his parent's compound, he heard his name spoken in conversation. Billy stood still and froze in his tracks.

"You the one who suggested the name, Sara," his father said laughing.

"Uh arr!" she replied with emphasis, "We both agreed to call him Billy. Just in case it was another boy, this way we wouldn't have to find a new name." They both laughed.

"Well it's a good thing we did Sara, cos it turned out to be another boy, gosh darn it." And they laughed again.

Hearing this, Billy wanted to run away as far as he could, but he knew he had nowhere to go. So, he took in a deep breath and began walking backwards.

After several backward steps, he began to whistle as he walked as casually as he could into his family's compound, all the while he put on a brave face and held back his tears until he fell down on his bed.

He reckoned he must have cried himself to sleep that night, because when he woke up in the middle of the night, he still had his day clothes on.

The memory and pain of that conversation reverberated in his head for many years to come.

28

– A FLUTE AT ANY PRICE –

HENRY BROWN, THE ONLY SON OF A CLOSE ACQUAINTANCE OF the Johnson family, was also raised in rural Macon.

His father bought a small farm after years of scrimping and saving and he worked it with pride, sometimes with the help of Mr. Johnson's sons, as they were close neighbors.

As a young man Henry migrated to New York, his father wanted his only child to get a first-class college education but after two semesters, he found it too cold in the winter-time and too crowded in the summertime so he moved back to the south.

He was soon tired of rural living and wanted a livelier city to settle into. Having tasted the fast and lively life in the big city of New York, he knew he could not live in the rural south.

Henry enjoyed the freedom he had experienced in the North and was convinced that life in a big city would be more to his liking; and so he chose Atlanta.

Two years later Henry's father died and since he was the only heir, he inherited his daddy's small farm. Not wanting to return to rural living, he rented out the three-room farmhouse to the Davis family who farmed the land for him.

Henry traveled to Macon once each month to check on his property and collect the rent for the house and the produce, which the tenants harvested and sold at the local market.

Mr. Brown had expensive taste and had a hard time holding onto money, he gambled and spent money foolishly on loose women, booze and horses. When he realized he needed more money than his tenant farmer was giving him each month, he was not happy.

He expected more cash returns for the items produced on his land; and because he needed more money in his pockets each month, he convinced himself that his tenants were being dishonest with him. He even accused Mr. Davis of stealing some of the profits, which the man profusely denied.

Mr. Brown was looking for someone to spy on his tenant and he didn't have to look far. He had seen the longing in young Billy's eyes and he recognized his need to escape the dreary and boring life he lived. So, Mr. Henry Brown knew exactly who he would engage to spy on his tenant.

Along with most of the folk in those parts, Henry had heard about Billy's desire to own and play the flute. He knew also that some folks kidded and chided him, just as they did him, when he was a youngster and before he migrated to the big city. Henry saw that Billy, just like himself; never felt as though he belonged on a farm. He never fit in.

Henry was a big kid, his mother died when he was a toddler. His father had ran his own farm and was busy from sun up to sun down, tired and weary at the end of each long day, he had very little time to spend with his son.

Henry had many minders looking after him; he seldom

saw his father and grew up resenting him and the farm which he felt his father loved more than he did his only child.

Being a passionate lover of jazz, Mr. Brown recognized the young man's desire to make music. And because he didn't trust his tenant Mr. Davis, he decided he needed someone close by to be his eyes and ears. Young Billy was the perfect patsy.

"Billy, my boy! My you's a big man now, ain't ya? How old is you, Son?"

"Evenin' Mr. Brown, how you doin'? Next month, I be seventeen.'

"Seventeen! Well, well, you think you grown enough to do a job for me."

"Yes, Sir. What job and how much do it pay?'

"Good man, good man, you do the job right an' I will buy you a bran' new flute. Now, how's that sound?'

"Soun's great so far, but what do ya want me to do?"

"Well, all you got to do is to check on how many times in one month Brother Davis fills up that cart an' mule an' rides it into town."

"How many times they supposed to ride the cart into town?"

"Never mind how many times they 'posed to pack it an' ride it, you just tell me how many times you sees it packed and headed for town."

Billy didn't know he was spying on his neighbor, and if he did know, consciously, chances are he would still have done it anyway. The prize was too great to pass up.

Billy longed to have his own professional flute, so he could not pass up the offer presented to him. He knew that if he owned his own flute, he would be in seventh heaven; the deal was too good to pass up.

Finally owning his very own professional flute; which came

in a mahogany case – he anticipated the euphoria he would experience, he would be in seventh heaven; music was his path to freedom.

The idea made Billy feel dizzy with happiness. He felt whole; he wanted desperately to become somebody and he knew that owning and playing such a beautiful, shining instrument would make him feel whole.

Billy had no idea of the cost; to the farmer and his family until it was too late. The gift was too great to pass up. All he knew, was that he finally had what he wanted, what he had dreamed of having all of his life, or so it seemed.

He had no idea what the final cost was or the extent of damage caused by his obsession. He could only guess when he realized that the Davis family had been evicted from their home just over one month after Henry Brown struck the bargain with Billy.

When Mr. Brown handed Billy his very own musical instrument, he was elated. Finally after years of wishing and dreaming, he was now the proud owner of a real flute.

This was not a handmade one or a hand me down; but a real, store bought, almost brand new flute. He marveled as it sparkled in the sunlight; to say that he was overjoyed, would be an understatement.

His joy overwhelmed him as he ran his fingers over the instrument, he finally had something of value, something he had wanted almost all of his life and he could call his very own.

He was overjoyed with the look and the feel of it and as he ran his fingers over the instrument. Billy closed his eyes, allowing his mind to drift away. He was ecstatic, a dream come true and he could hardly wait to share his good news with his family.

The delight - which made him euphoric - blinded him to the disdain his father held for the instrument and the 'wicked music it would produce'. He rushed home to show and tell his family of his great fortune; because to him it was a fortune, the beginning of a life; a life he could now create for himself.

Immediately, his father wanted to know how he got 'the darn thing'. He demanded to know where he got the money from, to buy it.

When Billy told his father that Mr. Brown gave it to him as payment for a job he did, his father demanded to know what the job was; and in that instant Billy realized the extent of damage his spying did.

Billy began to stutter again, something he thought he had outgrown. His father yelled at him, calling him a 'stupid, dumb, hardheaded, heathen.' He said he was selfish and only thought about his own self.

"That thing you blow into is the devil's work and the devil gon follow you, you mark my words. This was a' evil thing you don don." They ain't got no place to live," he yelled at his son. "Cos of you, they done lost their home and everything."

While his father was screaming at him, Billy could see the muscles in his father's neck swelling and twitching, he could feel his angry spit on his face; then his father stopped suddenly.

And in that instant, Billy was scared; he had never seen his father so angry and he thought he was going to strike him.

"Jim Davis is my friend an' my closest neighbor, he a deacon at my church, an' he got a family to take care of; an' now, cos of you they got no place to live and all on account of you and your, your GET OUT of here, you makes' me sick. Pack up an' go 'fore I beat you to kingdom come."

Billy swallowed hard; and in that moment, just for a brief

second he avoided his father's angry eyes. He wanted to run from his father, his rage was so raw.

Yet, this passionate emotion was something he had never before experienced and in addition to the fear, he experienced a new emotion; he was overcome with a sense of elation.

His father was engaging him for the very first time in his life; eye to eye and shoulder to shoulder and his anger momentarily turned to sadness.

illy had no idea where he would go, but he knew he had to escape his father's mounting wrath, a wrath that exhilarated him and made him feel connected for the very first time; a feeling he now knew he had yearned for all of his life. This exhilaration was masked with a rage he didn't know he had.

His father had never shown an interest in him or paid any attention to him, until now. Both the emptiness and the emotional distance between his father and himself welled up inside of him. His own anger was so raw now, that he feared he might strike his father.

I didn't ask to be born and I didn't deserve to be treated like I was an outcast all of my life, he screamed silently to himself.

He was conscious that he was slouching, something he did automatically, unconsciously whenever his father chastised him. So, before he walked away from his father for the very last time, he took in a deep breath, raised his chest and straightened his shoulders, gaining several inches with each breath.

He looked his father in the eye and said, "I was never here."

While still glaring at his father, he bent down, picked up his hold-all, then turned and walked away from his father and his home for the very last time.

Billy walked away not only from the house he was raised

in, having grown up in an atmosphere of cold indifference and virtually no redeeming parental or sibling contact; at least none that he remembered or valued.

It was no wonder that Billy's outlook on life was devoid of empathy and familial emotion.

29

– FREEDOM –

FEELING ELATED ON TWO COUNTS, BILLY NOW POSSESSED THE instrument he only ever dreamed of owning and he had walked away from the people he once referred to as his family.

Billy felt free and began to whistle. He was the proud owner of the brand new flute that sat inside a small black, leather-bound case with a deep blue, satin lining. The case he was carrying in his hand enriched his swagger as he casually walked away. He walked aimlessly swinging his flute case in one hand and his canvas holdall in the other.

It was a beautiful day, the sun was bright but not too hot, he felt free and as he walked away from his father's house and through the many fields, he smiled then whistled.

"I'm free, I'm free. I'm finally free to be me," he said to himself.

His mind was a million miles away as he walked aimlessly unencumbered by anything and delighted as it began to sink in that at last, he was truly and finally free.

As he walked, he saw himself standing on a real stage

playing his music; and for the first time in his life, he experienced true happiness.

He had no idea how long he'd been walking, smiling and whistling, and daydreaming, so he was startled when he heard his name being called.

A wave of fear or perhaps it was dread or anger, he wasn't sure which emotion washed over him. He stopped instantly, uncertain what to do or say. Anxiously, looking around briefly, he picked up his pace and kept on walking.

When he heard the voice again, he felt his stomach contract, and then almost instantly a huge smile appeared on his face as he recognized the voice.

Billy was so deep in thought and hadn't realized he was walking along the path just above the riverbank. When he looked down, he saw old man Bubba standing with his hands on his hips and had a huge smile on his face. Relieved, Billy smiled from ear-to-ear. Finally, he could share his joy with someone who could understand why he was so happy.

Billy was truly excited to see Bubba and he half ran over to his old friend, who was standing beside a chair, at the water's edge keeping a close eye on his fishing rod. Without saying a word, Billy opened up the case, took out the flute and handed it to Bubba.

"Play me a tune old man and bring them fish swimming to your rod, just like the Pied Piper."

Bubba was delighted to see the lad and he willingly played a tune. Billy was amazed when he heard, for the very first time, the lilting notes escaping from his brand-new instrument.

He had no idea that music could be so sweet and melodious, as it lingered in the air as if held by an invisible string. He hugged the old man then sat down next to him.

It took Billy several attempts to get the hang of his new

instrument and he was astounded at the melody, as it flowed from Bubba's lips. Billy was overjoyed with his new flute, even though it took him several attempts before he felt comfortable with it.

After a few hours of instructions from Bubba, he got the hang of it. He felt relaxed sitting at the river's edge, while Bubba continued to fish. From time to time, the old man gave the boy some more pointers. And the two of them sat by the river's edge for nearly two hours. Billy played and Bubba continued to fish.

The little cabin Bubba now lived in was on the other side of the river. It was a small wooden cabin with two small rooms.

The front room which had a coal burner was a little longer than the bedroom; there was a small window in both rooms. In the area closest to the fireplace, there was a washstand that sat on top of a small cupboard. The bedroom window was smaller than the main room.

There were two other cabins close by, both occupied by two former slaves, who were too old to work. There was an outhouse behind the middle house. Bubba's neighbors also fished for catfish and when they had a good catch they sold it to the working families who did not have time to go fishing.

Behind their cabins was a small patch of green, the occupants planted greens, sweet potatoes, okra and yams. They seemed content with their lives, no more toiling in the hot sun, no more back breaking bending or chopping. Billy had not seen Bubba for several years; he had forgotten where he lived or even if he was still alive.

That evening, Bubba invited Billy to join him for supper. He had just caught four good-sized catfish and before entering the house he stopped at his little garden, picked a bunch of collard greens and a few sweet potatoes.

The old man then washed and baked the veg on the hearth, he grilled some okra and the fish he caught. Billy had no idea he was so hungry, the food smelled and tasted so good, he left nothing for the crows.

The meal was excellent and Billy felt pleasantly at home in the tiny one-bedroom cabin, in return for being made to feel so special, Billy took out his brand-new flute and played it for his host.

Later that evening, they sat outside and played together as the moon replaced the sun in the star-studded sky. Bubba's two neighbors sat outside also. It was a balmy night and they all enjoyed being entertained.

Bubba attempted several times throughout the visit to ask Billy about family, but the right time just never came up; when at last he did make an attempt, the questions just flew over Billy's head. Knowing how unhappy the boy was during his childhood, he made idle chat for a while. But there were long silent pauses, and the mild evening crept into the dark, lonely, night.

Billy observed Bubba yawning; his head nodding from time to time

"I 'speck it's getting close to your bedtime old time," Billy said, yawing, not wanting to move, since he had no idea where he would lay his head that night.

But it also become obvious to Bubba that Billy was sleepy; his eyes had begun to droop plus his head was nodding off and on. Bubba wondered if the boy had finally run away.

"I recon so," the old man replied.

Bubba was old and he had seen a lot in his lifetime, he was very good at reading folks, their emotions, and their pain. He knew that this young man was no different from the little boy he used to watch day after day trying to get attention from his family.

As a small boy, he would wander over to Bubba's old cabin and stay with him till late in the evening, no one ever came looking for him. Bubba often wondered what life was like for Billy as a small boy; and he wondered now, speculating that nothing much had changed.

Bubby didn't have a family, but he had seen a whole lot of happy families. At least the children were happy, most parents paid attention to their children and showed love in lots of different ways. But even as a small boy, Billy didn't seem to fit in.

All of his brothers were so much older than him, working with their parents every evening. They were a happy and industrious family, and if he wasn't in the way being chastised, he was most certainly out of the way.

In the past, whenever the old man would question the boy, he would look sad. Bubba often wondered if Billy belonged to this family because the rest of them seemed to be so close. Sensing that something was wrong, Bubba asked Billy if he wanted to bed down in his cabin.

"There's only one bed son, but I got an old pallet I can put on the floor."

Immediately, Bubba saw the boy's shoulders relax and the tension in his face soften.

So, nothing's changed, he thought, *he still an outsider.*

Over the next few months, Bubba encouraged Billy's playing. He helped him to smooth out the rough edges whenever he played off key.

Initially, Billy resented Bubba's input but as he began to understand his instrument he learned to appreciate Bubba's instructions and after a while Billy was able to hear his own mistakes. Billy stayed with the old man for several months.

Bubba taught his guest as much as he could and in return for the old man's hospitality, Billy did odd jobs around the cabin. He also took pride in planting and gathering the vegetables from the old man's garden.

When Bubba felt his protégée had mastered his instrument well enough, and he thought he was good enough to play in the Honky Tonk club, a few mile away, he spoke to an old friend of his who owned the only juke joint in town.

It just so happened that the owner, Maggie Lou, was considering expanding the live band she had recently hired. She had been thinking adding another player would add a new dimension and 'liven up the joint'.

She thought the piano player and the drummer were good together but she felt a flute or sax player would jazz up the band. So, when Bubba approached her about Billy, she agreed to try him out for one night.

Maggie Lou liked what she heard and her patrons also liked the added sound. At first, Billy played on Friday nights. Then after a couple of weeks, the customers wanted to hear more of his music, so Maggie added Saturday nights.

Billy finally found contentment. He stayed with Bubba off and on for the next dozen years, and the odd girlfriend in between, until Bubba died. Days after he died the cabin was cleaned out, whitewashed inside and out and given to a new family.

It was clear that the customers wanted more of Billy's music but since he had no place to live, he knew he needed to move on. Luckily, Maggie Lou wanted him to stay on. She knew that the locals liked his sound.

Pretty soon, the band was playing four nights a week.

Maggie Lou's tavern was the only tavern for miles around, and the music was jumping from Thursday night to the wee hours of Sunday morning.

Monday through Thursday, he would do odd jobs around the club in exchange for a bed and an evening meal provided by the owner.

Maggie Lou owned the joint; won it in a crap game, he was told. It was a shabby shack, but each weekend it filled to bursting. She said 'it was his playin' that brung the customers in'.

He was a tireless, confident flute player and soon enough a sax player too, no doubt of that and in those parts he was surely appreciated.

Billy loved his sax even more than his old flute. To him, it was as precious as the crown jewel held in some castle in England.

This instrument provided him with a sense of freedom and the opportunity to leave the place and the people he had been destined to co-habit with all of his life.

He also knew that his sax would buy him the freedom he desired to walk away one day; free from all that he detested about the South.

One year later Maggie Lou's little shack had become so well-known that folks from far and wide would spend their weekends hanging out there. As the popularity of her little shack grew, Maggie Lou decided to hire a young guitar player, he was from Memphis.

Billy didn't like the new guy one bit. According to Billy, he thought he was 'it'. All the young girls would swoon over him, trying to get his attention.

"He thinks he's special," Billy told the piano player. "Just cos some o' those young gals calls out his name; *'Buster, Buster'*, he said mocking the young girls as they swooned over the guitar player, "but he ain't that good."

Billy didn't like the way he was always cozying up to Maggie Lou, he could tell she was sweet on him and Billy sensed that he might get pushed out. So, when Maggie Lou told Billy that she needed his room because some family was coming to stay with her for a while; Billy felt suspicions were right, he was on his way out

He resented the guitar player, but he decided it was time for him to move. He was more confident now than ever in his ability to hold his own.

He hadn't a clue as to where he would go but as long as he had his music he knew he could make a living; his expenses were not high so he had been able to save most of his wages. Before leaving, he paid a visit to Bubba's grave.

"Goodbye old friend. I'm on way to some place, not sure where, but I swear it'll be far away from here."

After he packed up what few belongings he had stored in his room, he walked to the bus station; still no plan in mind.

When he heard the announcement that the bus parked at station number three would be leaving for Atlanta in ten minutes, Billy grinned. He remembered that his old friend Henry lived in Atlanta, the man who made it possible for him to fulfill his dream. So that is where he decided to go.

It had been years since they had been in contact with each other. Henry was driving a big convertible Cadillac the last time Billy saw him.

He told Billy that he returned to Macon just once and that was to sell the farm. He had also mentioned to him that Atlanta was jumping, that it was the place to live and to play.

30

– RIDING THE FREIGHT TRAIN NORTH –

Working in the clubs in Atlanta was not much better than Maggie Lou's place; most of the musicians in his opinion were stuck up so he stayed on his own, keeping himself to himself.

Billy moved around a lot, and no matter how hard he tried, he just couldn't settle in any place for long. He stayed in Atlanta for a while but he never did get a permanent gig.

He played in Nashville, New Orleans, and several other major cities but after a while, he finally realized that he was sick of the South and decided he might try his luck in New York City or maybe Harlem.

He'd been traveling throughout the South for several years. Never did catch up with Henry, he figured he must have moved on to someplace else, or that he was riding high in one of those rich suburbs.

'New York, New York, that's the place to be.' He'd heard this statement day and night for years, so after another run in with a piano player; he decided it was time to leave this city.

"Never did like piano players," he mumbled as he let yet another nightclub door slam shut behind him.

Later that night, after he got his pay envelope, he packed his bag and decided to try his luck, up north in the big city.

He had heard many times over the years just how expensive it was to live in New York City. So, Billy decided to jump on a freight train from Atlanta to New York's 'Renaissance City.' That first night on the train, he almost regretted making such a rash decision.

Cold and hungry, Billy had no idea how long the journey would take. He also feared that vagrants might jump in the same box car and rob him, so he fought to stay awake. He had no doubt in his mind, that this was a wise move. He still felt anxious, after all, this was an even bigger move than when he first left home with no real place to go.

Billy tried to get into a more comfortable position on his make-shift bed, which was made of flattened out cardboard boxes which he covered with some brown velvet cloth, might have been window drape.

He had no idea where it came from, it smelled of beer, sweat and God knows what, but it softened the rough ridges on the boxes.

Tired and angry, Billy reflected broodingly not on his father kicking him out with nowhere to go; he was actually grateful and more than ready to put his family behind him. No, his angry thoughts were directed at Buster.

"Things was just fine in Macon till Maggie Lou fell for that fool guitar player. Never did like that dude," he said aloud. "Always tryin' to drown me out or cut me off. I don't know what she saw in him, no how. He was fat and he was loud."

Billy arrived in Harlem one bright sunny morning, New York's 'Renaissance City'. He didn't know a soul in this place, but one thing he did know, he would have to find a job and a place to sleep.

Instantly, he liked the feel of the city and he felt free just walking around, there were lots of cafés and honky-tonk joints. As he walked the streets, he was looking for the cafés that had a 'Help Wanted' sign in the window.

After sizing a place up from across the street, he would go in and order a cup of coffee. If he didn't like the look or feel of the place, he would walk right back out. Billy was also looking for a place where he could sleep in after closing hours. He didn't want to spend his money on a room. On his first day in the city, he walked for hours, familiarizing himself with the cross streets and numbered streets, making mental notes of the different areas.

After it got dark, he would walk over to St. Timothy's Catholic Church and sleep on one of the pews. It was far from comfortable, but it was the safest and cheapest place to lay his head. He always woke up early and was able to exit the church unnoticed.

Before going on his job search, Billy would go into a café, order breakfast then head into the mens room to clean up. If he liked the place, he would inquire about a job.

Three days later, still searching for a clean and pleasant café in which to eat; Billy turned the corner on Howard Street and while looking in the wrong direction, bumped into a man walking in the opposite direction. After apologizing, he asked the man if he knew of a good, clean breakfast cafe. The man introduced himself as Smithy then gave him directions to Watson's café. He told Billy that he knew the owner and that he ate there every day.

Finally, after three days of walking around, he finally found what he needed. As he approached the café, he noticed a sign in the window that read, 'Custodian Wanted'. With his duffle bag in hand, he ordered a black coffee, went into the mens room and cleaned up. When he walked out; looking fresh and feeling clean, Billy asked his waitress if the owner was in.

She nodded and pointed in the direction of a tall, slender man with salt and pepper hair. It was a small café owned by Mr. Watson, a mature man about his age.

After giving the waitress his order, Billy walked over to the owner to speak to him as he was cashing out a few customers. Billy joined the line before his meal was served. Mr. Watson looked up at him before speaking and then introduced himself.

"What brings you to New York, stranger and where are you coming from? I saw you with your duffle bag."

Billy learned Mr. Watson had owned the place for several years; that he opened up his café at 6 am and closed at 11 p.m.

The stranger was right Billy thought.

Mr. Watson told Billy he used to have two waitresses, one middle-aged and one in her mid-twenties. The young one, Vicky used to sleep in the back room before she married one of the regular customers. Mr. Watson said he liked having someone on the premises overnight for security.

Billy explained that he had just arrived in town, that he was a musician looking for a job and a place to stay.

"I was born an' raised in the South; I played in a small club for years. The owner got married," he said, lying smoothly. "She closed up the joint, so I decided to put some distance between me and that place, so I thought I'd try my luck and move up north."

"So how long you plan on stayin', or are you just traveling through?" Mr. Watson asked the stranger.

"Mister; now that I'm away from that evil place, I ain't never goin' back there."

Knowingly; Mr. Watson nodded his head smiling.

"Have you ever worked in a diner?" He asked Billy.

"No Sir but I can learn. I really needs a place to stay, that church bench is mighty hard."

Mr. Watson laughed. Then he said, "I need someone reliable and dependable from closing time to opening time because there's been a bit of vandalism in the area."

Billy really wanted this job, it would be perfect for him so he explained to Mr. Watson that he didn't have a job yet but when he did it would be on the weekends, and possibly at night. He said he would return to the café each night after he played his last set and return to his room.

"Well, let me think about it," Mr. Watson said, "and if no one comes in the next few days, well, I'll see how things can be worked out. So how can I reach you?"

Billy smiled and said, "I been looking for a clean café since I come up here, Mr. you gone see me every day for my breakfast."

Mr. Watson returned the smile and the two men shook hands.

Four days later, when Billy went to pay for his breakfast, when Mr. Watson walked up behind him. "From now on breakfast is on the house," he said then turning to Billy, "When can you move in?"

Smithy, the man who recommended Watson's café to Billy was a regular at this establishment and he rented rooms in the same community.

Late one evening, when he was walking back to his rooming house he heard music being played on a saxophone.

Smithy liked the sound and began to follow the music; he soon realized that it was coming from the café where he ate at each day.

After hearing the sweet melody, every evening for the next week, he asked Mr. Watson if he could meet the musician. He was pleasantly surprised to see it was the man he had recommended the café to, some weeks earlier.

In a few weeks time, Billy was heading for an audition on Smithy's recommendation. This was his tenth audition in as many weeks, or was this number twelve, he wasn't sure but this was the first time he had been called back for a second audition.

Even though Smithy, gave him directions to the club, and suggested he should apply for the vacated spot; he was still anxious, somewhat pessimistic and feeling just a little nervous.

It started to rain as Billy walked from the club back to the cafe restaurant ten blocks away from where he worked and slept.

The job didn't pay much but he ate two good meals every day that he worked and the squeaking cot was a darn site better than the box car floor on the freight train or the pew in St Timothy's Church.

Prior to this second call back, he had started counting the last of his change. Just days before, he realized he might have to give up his dream and do something else for a living. And now, as he followed the music wafting over him like the fragrance of a perfumed rose; it filled his heart with joy and hope.

Billy was, by now, cautiously optimistic. He descended the dark stairs at the back of the Sunset restaurant. Making his way down what seemed like an endless passageway, which was lit only by one, yellow, swinging light bulb, there were no windows and it was dark.

"Follow the passage all the way to the green door, that's where we hangs out," Smithy had told him.

31

– EPILOGUE –

BILLY WALKED UP THE THREE STAIRS TO THE STAGE. THE lights were hot, the room was smoky, and the floor was dark. But he could see the crowd before him. The singer and guitarist were already in place.

Pianist, Eddie was missing and the replacement was late. The crowd was getting impatient, so they'd have to perform the first song without piano.

Billy whispered to the singer, "I can do a solo to get them warmed up?"

The lead singer nodded in agreement. Billy stepped forward and took a deep breath and closed his eyes.

He imagined himself back in Bubba's little home playing for him. Playing for himself. When he imagined this moment, stood on stage playing to a crowd.

Three and a half minutes later, the people burst into applause along with his band members. Off to the side, he noticed a very pretty young woman smiling shyly at him. She was walking up the same steps and on to the stage.

"Who is that?" Billy whispered in awe.

"She's our new pianist, wait till you hear her play," replied the guitarist.

Billy watched as she took her seat behind the piano and thought to himself, *I feel like I've waited my whole life.*

TO BE CONTINUED...

PART II

32

– INNOCENT & IMMATURE –

REV. JEREMIAH WATSON	**ELIZA WATSON (CARTER)**
PAUL MARTIN Son	**MABEL** Daughter

ELIZA CARTER HAD JUST TURNED SIXTEEN, WHEN A MARRIAGE was arranged between herself and Reverend Jeremiah Watson; her mother's minister who was more than twice her age. Reverend Watson was a man of few words, except when he preached on Sunday mornings. His sermons would go on forever or so it seemed to the young folk.

Eliza, as she was affectionately called by her mother was a pretty girl of mixed Indian and African parentage. She was admired by most of the young men in the quarters.

Sadly, her mother, who was dying of consumption wanted to see her daughter taken care of before she passed on.

She truly believed that her pastor could provide a decent home for her only surviving child.

The petite teenager looked younger than her age. Eliza was only fifteen when her mother died. If her mother had not been in such a hurry to find a provider for her lovely daughter; in a year or so there would have been several more suitors available. Jeremiah was the preacher in the compound and respected by most of the slaves, especially the elder members of his congregation.

Eliza's mother died four months after she and her mother's pastor spoke their vows. This was not a happy marriage and there was little, if any love, between the teenage bride and her aging husband who had been a confirmed bachelor for most of his life.

Jeremiah saw himself as 'a man of God' and he devoted himself to doing the 'Lord's work'; and he was bound and determined to lead all sinners to God's alter through 'fire and brimstone' and into His heavenly kingdom.

Sadly for the immature and innocent bride, her husband lacked the sensitivity, sexuality and, the spontaneity of a beguiling passionate lover, having never courted or looked at a woman with passion or desire in his groin. Eliza had never been in love, but she was an obedient girl and she wanted her mother to go to her grave in peace. It goes without saying that her marriage vows and her wedding night lacked the stimulation, passion, and excitement she had been led to expect.

Their first child, a boy, was born less than a year later; her husband baptized him Paul Martin, after Saint Martin de Porres. Paul as he was affectionately known wasn't a big baby, but it was a lengthy and painful birth. That first pregnancy was followed by three miscarriages and a still born child before their second, healthy child, a daughter was born four years later. She was named Mabel after her maternal grandmother.

Eliza was a fragile girl, just out of her teens when her second child, was born. Feeling as weak as she was, she prayed that this infant baby girl, would be her last child. She hated the life she had and the despicable life her children would ultimately live.

Reminiscing on her unhappy childhood, Eliza was determined to raise her children in a peaceful home, where laughter was not frowned upon. She came from a stern home, where her father dominated the family, always scowling and shouting. His threats and his leather belt had always been at the ready.

And so, she did all she could to be the best mother to her children. When she did eventually regain her strength, she did all she could, to bring some joy into their lives.

Life was harsh but she was able to bring laughter into their home; she would tickle them to make them giggle. As often as she could, she would play with them, like hide and seek for an apple or homemade toffee she had hidden from them.

Like many brothers, Paul would tease his little sister a lot. He would pull on her pigtails; tie her jump rope into knots and whenever she found her baby doll face down in the trough, the weeping child knew who had done it.

Frustrated and angry, Mabel would cry and run home to her mother to chastise her brother. After scolding him, their mother would hug him and ruffle his curly hair. Paul loved his mother very much; she could always remove or soften the sting inflicted by his stern father.

Mabel learned from her mother that her father's sense of helplessness and discontent fueled his anger.

"At home," she told her daughter, "your father could rant

and rave; he could give orders and make demands."

At home such as it was, he was in command. The anger, frustration, and sense of powerlessness that consumed his emotions each and every day, often turned him into a demanding monster who ruled the house they lived in.

Her mother said he was too beat down most of his life and never felt as if he ever had control over anything, not even his own miserable life. Which for most of the time, did not belong to him, she thought, but never voiced those thoughts.

As a slave, he had no control over his life or anything in his life; except within his own house; which is where he could rant and rave. With painful reminiscing, Eliza realized, how very much her current life reflected her own miserable childhood. Just like her father, her husband seemed incapable of empathizing or recognizing how miserable the world was for his children, or perhaps being unable to change the situation they were in, he just ignored it. Eliza did all that she could to make life as bearable for their children, as she could.

In the summertime, Eliza made plenty of freshly squeezed lemonade from the lemons she plucked from her garden and sweetened it with a stick of wild sugar cane. Sometimes, as a treat she would boil the sugar cane and make candy for her children or add the liquid to the coarse cornmeal to sweeten the bread.

Saturday evenings were the best night of the week for Eliza and her two children. No work on Sunday meant they could sleep in for an extra two and half hours.

But the best part, was when their father, Reverend Jeremiah Watson, would leave them in the house. When he left for church where he would spend hours preparing for his Sunday sermon.

Finally, the family would relax and Eliza would take her

little mouth organ out of its secret hiding place and blow into it making music. Their mother was still young and girlish and she loved to dance.

The mouth organ was always well hidden and only Eliza knew its whereabouts. She feared her stubborn son would play it just to annoy his father if he knew where it was hidden. It was the best night of their week.

Eliza would dance with her children and turn her tiny house into a lively dance floor while her husband was in church, agonizing over his four-hour sermon for the next morning.

Eliza taught her children how to dance, Mabel enjoyed following her mother's footsteps and they would laugh together. Paul wasn't so keen, and after a while he would say, 'my feet's too big an' besides dancin' is for gals. His mother and sister would tease him all in good fun and he would end up laughing at himself.

Paul and Mabel were Eliza's only surviving children; when sadly, she died giving birth to her final still born child. Her children were devastated, Mabel was twelve, Paul was just sixteen.

They were overcome with grief. After their mother died, Paul would tease his sister less. He saw how hard she had to work and deep down he felt sorry for her.

Mabel loved and admired her big brother, even when he teased her; in her eyes he was strong, sure of himself and often defiant. He walked with a confident swagger, most of the time and seldom hunched his shoulders even when the overseer yelled at him to correct something or to do a task over again. She secretly marveled at her brother's boldness and envied the open disregard he frequently demonstrated towards their overly stern father.

After their mother died, it seemed that every woman in his small congregation, most of them widowed, would rotate having their pastor and his family over for a competitive home cooked Sunday dinner. The siblings resented having to sit and listen attentively, as the harsh sermon continued before the meal was served and would continue throughout the meal and into the benediction. The food which was always delicious was the only enticement for Paul; so much better than Mabel was able to cook. However, they both hated being in the company of their father's female parishioners for Sunday meal.

Each hostess would find something to chastise Mabel about and later at home, her father would reprimand her for the same 'indiscretion'. They had to go or suffer her father's wrath as well as the church elder's condemnation. After an 'unchristian' outburst from Paul, he was no longer invited to dine at any of the parishioners' homes.

The unthinkable incident happened one Sunday, after what seemed like an eternity of sitting at the perfectly dressed table, smelling the rich aromas from the feast before him. Paul's stomach was growling from hunger. Plus, he was forced to listen to his father pontificate, condemning the youth as sinners and heathens' in the community. Ripples of choked up anger, frustration and resentment leaped from his mouth. He jumped up, pushed his plate setting away, then kicked over the chair he had been sitting on.

"I'm sick to death o' hearin' all this mumbo jumbo, first for three hours in church then for another two hours waiting to be fed, then all through the meal. I don't need to have this stuff rammed down my throat week after week. You peoples makes me want to hate church the way you go's on an' on about sin. You act like you was never young, never had hopes or dreams, never could think for yo'self. Well I ain't never comin' back here no more and I'm through wid that old church and your mean preachin'. I'm young an' I wants to live my life, for myself, my way."

Banging his fists on the table, the gravy dish spilled all over the white starched tablecloth; leaving everyone in the room, except the preacher, speechless.

All eyes were on his father, who was now standing, but resting his trembling hands on the edge of the elegantly set table. Then, while shouting and shaking an angry finger at his son, he yelled.

"Get out of here you! Ungrateful sinner, and don't come back in 'till you is ready to get down on your knees, an' pray that God almighty in heaven, will forgive you! You heathen, then you beg these good people for their forgiveness."

In an instant Paul was gone, laughing as he walked out, letting the screen door slam behind him; and leaving everyone sitting around the table in amazed silence.

Paul's father instructed everyone around the table to clasp their hands together, bow their heads and offer up a prayer for the sins of his ungrateful, prodigal son.

Later that day, Paul prepared to leave the place he detested and had resented calling home all of his life, for places unknown, to himself or his family.

As the angry teenager threw his meager possessions into his canvas carry all, his father stood overshadowing the doorway to the shared bedroom; with both hands firmly reaching up to the top of the door frame, his body blocking the opening.

He stared at his son, through eyes full of contempt. "You fool! An' where in God's name you think you goin'?" He yelled at his first-born child.

"Any place away from this hell-hole, an' miles away from

you ol' man". Paul's contempt was as visible as it was verbal.

"Boy don't make me laugh," the minister said, laughing at his defiant son. "You still wet behind the ears." His father chuckled as he blocked the doorway.

Not quite seventeen, Paul was not a big lad but as he looked at his father through eyes filled with contempt and disgust; he seemed to tower over the aging preacher.

He spat as he spoke his reply. "I ain't gona' rot an' die here in the South old man, I'm not like you. I wants my freedom NOW, an' if I dies trying, well at least I'll be up North an' away from this hellhole."

Enraged, frustrated and defiant, Paul pushed passed his father, almost knocking him down, he was that angry.

Several hours later Paul crept back into the house, easing his way in quietly to find his sister but Mabel was not asleep; her mind was filled with mixed emotions, concern for his safety but envious of his freedom and his defiance.

When she saw him standing in her bedroom doorway, her eyes lit up and she opened her mouth to speak. Paul put his index finger to his mouth. Mabel sat up, she was confused.

He walked over to her bed and said, "Let me rest here with you baby sis before I leave; don't know when I'll see you again." She hugged her big brother and sobbed softly, letting her tears flow on his exposed neck.

When Mabel woke up the following morning, she was all alone in her bed. For a moment, she wondered if she had dreamed her brother's late night visit to her room.

When she reached to pull her quilt over her, she felt a piece of paper. She picked it up then moved closer to the window, pulling back the burlap curtain to see it better. It was her brother's note, his goodbye, written in his hand.

Mabel read the note with tears in her eyes; tears that

spilled onto the single handwritten page. It was his farewell note to her, and it read:

I love you lil' sis, when I can, I will come for you. Love, Paul.

In the early hours of the morning, just before dawn, Paul left the tiny shack he had lived in all of his life. With seven dollars in his pocket, a heart full of hope and a head full of dreams, he escaped the south.

Mabel brooded for many months after her brother left home; she worried about him and after months turned into years, she still had no news of him; but she continued to pray to God to keep him safe.

One week before her brother had left home, Mabel had found blood in her underwear for the second time. Having no knowledge as to what it was, she was quite concerned. As she walked out of the privy deep in thought with her eyes down cast; she bumped into her brother who was waiting to go in.

"Wow! Lil' Sis," he said, his forehand which was extended to open the privy door, accidentally touching her right breast. "Sorry baby girl. I thought you were out in the field." Then he grinned, "You ain't gon be my baby' sis for long." He chuckled and entered the privy and closed the door behind him.

Mabel ignored him, not knowing what he meant; but she was curious about the blood. But who to talk to about it! She knew she couldn't talk to her father about anything, but she was concerned that it might be dangerous.

She was unable to talk to any of the women at her father's church because she feared most of them and knew they would tell her father and because she had no idea what caused the blood in her panties, Mabel didn't want to tell anyone until she knew what it was.

The frightened teenager wracked her brain as to what to do or who to speak to in private; she finally decided on the mean looking, old, white woman with the long, silver hair and the pointed nose who owned the general store.

Mabel saw this old woman every other month when she went to pick up supplies. Except for the women who attended her father's church on Sundays, Ms. Sally was the only woman Mabel ever came in contact with. But she was afraid of those women because they followed her father's teachings so strictly.

Mabel was often confused, because from what she could see and hear, the more her father condemned them for their sins, the more they seemed to admire him. Determined to get to the bottom of this problem, Mabel decided to walk the mile and a half to the general store the following Saturday morning. She rehearsed what she would say over and over again.

When she arrived at the store there were several people, mostly women but too many for her to safely approach Ms. Sally. So, Mabel stepped outside of the little general store and decided to take a walk. It had rained the night before and well into the early morning, so the unpaved streets were muddy. As the carriages and buggies rode down the road, mud splashed. Even though she stayed on the elevated wooden sidewalk, mud still splashed onto her clothes. As she attempted to wipe it away with her hand, she smeared her pinafore making it look worse; there was nothing she could do, until she got home.

It was the end of the week anyway and her clothes were due for a wash. The road was short with less than half a dozen shops on either side; the first shop she passed was Miss Kittie's Hat Shop.

It was empty but she stopped to look at the hats displayed in the bay window. While gazing into the shop, Mabel reflected on the many times she and her mother had done the same thing.

She sighed deeply, and as she did, she inhaled the wonderful aroma coming from the bread shop next door, the man who owned that shop was Greek. She smiled when she remembered the fresh taste of his bread; it too was closed for the day.

She assumed he must have sold out early; his bread was very nice. At the end of the block was the blacksmith's shop, Mabel knew Ned and waved when she walked past his open door.

He yelled at her over the noise of steel hammering against steel. "How's your daddy keepin'?"

"Just fine, Mr. Ned." She replied.

"You is growin' to be a fine young lady,' he said and waved his hand at her.

Mabel waved back and smiled at her daddy's friend. "Thank you Mr. Ned." She called back to him and continued to walk.

At the end of the buildings, she crossed the street and walked slowly down the other side of the road. Daisy's dressmaking shop was open; the door was closed but when Mabel peered in through the window, she could see three women and a little girl inside the shop.

She took a deep breath and smiled at the pretty dress and matching parasol displayed in the window. Then she continued her idle walk, all the while worried about what to say to the old, white woman.

Bored with walking aimlessly outside, Mabel returned to the general store, she knew it would be closing soon as it was close to noontime.

Feeling somewhat out of place, she meandered around the

overstocked store while waiting for the remaining customers to leave once they'd been served. She wanted to be sure, before she spoke to the owner, that no one who knew her would be in ear shot or listening to her private conversation.

She was about to walk over to the old woman when another customer entered the store. The owner looked at her suspiciously as Mabel moved away when the new customer walked up.

When that last customer left, the owner said in a harsh voice. "You best get what you want girlie cos I'm 'bout to close, you bin hangin' round here like you lost, you want somit'? Speak up child."

Mabel walked up close to the woman and said, 'I ain't got no mama an' I need to talk to a woman."

"Well, close the door and get over here. It's my lunch time, an' I needs to get off of my feet."

The old woman was actually very sensitive as she responded to Mabel's awkward questions; she looked the child right in the eye and said, "Now, don't you fret non, girlie, what you got is what all us women gets; it just means you no longer a girlie, you be a woman now; some folks call it 'the curse'."

Mabel listened attentively as the toothless, old woman told her about the monthly rhythm and pointed to a shelf to get the material she would need each month.

"Make sure you wash them good an' clean an' keep them in a safe place 'till the next month.

Do you have a bo?" she asked, almost as an afterthought.

"No," said Mabel shocked. "I'm a good girl."

"Well, stay away from boys cos' if you go to the haystack you'll end up with a baby, 'cos, you is a woman now, and that's how women an' young gals get babies."

Mabel thanked the woman, paid for her package and walked home; she was as relieved as she was confused.

"Every month." She repeated all the way home. "An' keep away from the haystack." *Haystack*, she thought, *why would I go up to a haystack?*

Life changed significantly for Mabel after she turned fourteen, she never stopped brooding about her absent brother, even though it meant her burden would be less daunting having to only cook and wash clothes for two now.

Mabel loved Paul and missed him, especially the conversations they shared which helped her keep so many happy memories of their mother alive. She was sorry to see him leave, while at the same time envying him his freedom.

Over the two years since her mother died, Mabel had matured considerably. She learned how to cook and mend, she did all of the laundry by hand, and after months of painful criticism from her father, she learned to starch and iron his 'Sunday go-to meeting shirt' to perfection.

The young teenager had matured in other ways; she was physically very attractive. Her hair was a combination of her mother's very black Indian hair and her father's thick and kinky African hair.

Her skin was as smooth as silk and the color of ripe almonds and her eyes were wide and bright. In each cheek she had a dimple, deeply concealed until she smiled, revealing perfectly even white teeth. She was a very pretty girl.

Her Saturday night routine included taking her weekly bath and washing her hair. While working in the fields, she kept her hair braided all week long; but on the weekend she would unbraid her hair and let it hang loose in long, heavy waves.

Mabel was as lively as she was pretty and so full of life, she loved to dance. Her mother taught her how to move when she was still a little girl; they would dress up on Saturday nights after her father left the house to prepare for his Sunday sermon in his church. She remembered how much fun her mother was; sometimes she would tease Paul into dancing with them. They would sing and dance to the music they listened to on the radio her mother kept hidden. Mabel reflected on how much they would laugh. She missed her brother and her mother most of all.

Without her father's knowledge, she would go to the local tavern to dance on as many Saturday nights that she could slip away from home.

After hearing about the carryings on at the tavern and then later discovering that some teenagers from his congregation were frequent customers, Jeremiah had forbidden all of the children in his congregation to enter 'that sinful place of ill repute'. He truly believed that evil resided there.

The overseer of the plantation they worked on all year long would hire day laborers, young able-bodied men looking for work during planting season and harvest time.

These young men worked hard all week, either gathering crops or planting seeds for the next season, and on the weekend, they danced at the tavern.

Mabel loved the sense of freedom she experienced and was often the life of the party. She had many dance partners, especially in the spring and fall season.

On Sunday morning, the planters would attend her father's church. At the end of each season, the men would leave; many of them leaving behind their own seeds.

33

– HOMELESS, PREGNANT, PENNILESS –

WHENEVER MABEL REMINISCED ABOUT THE EMPTY, BITTER LIFE she experienced while living with her father.

She felt the flow of hot tears escaping from her eyes and flowing down her cheeks, as she reflected on the fact that he never once had a kind word for her.

She had just turned sixteen when her father learned she was pregnant and he immediately disowned her. He kicked her out of the only home she had ever known; calling her a sinful whore and told her she brought shame to his house. He cared less about where she would go; he wanted her out of his sight.

Having thought about the hardships she endured throughout her life; remembering the misery she experienced almost daily; the countless restrictions imposed upon her by her extremely strict father, and the sense of hopelessness that consumed her life.

Mabel was now a homeless, naïve, pregnant teenager, without a husband or guardian to take care of her. However, she swore to do everything in her power to provide a much better life for her baby than she had endured. The mother-to-be made a promise the moment her baby was born, that her child, her precious baby daughter would not end up in the empty, miserable scenario which had been her early life.

Such dreams, far too often, turn out to be just wishful thinking. Especially for those who are destitute, immature, and naïve, as was the situation in which Mabel found herself. It was sheer determination and anger that fueled her survival.

Over the years, Mabel had heard about the woman who took in 'wayward' girls. Desperate for a place to stay, she sought the woman out. Mabel was in need of shelter; and not immune to hard work she tracked down the local midwife.

Mrs. Anderson who then delivered Mabel's baby, realized just how young she was, and that she had no family or home to return to.

And so, she took it upon herself to arrange for Mabel to stay with a retired midwife by the name of Ms. Lester who had trained her long ago.

Ms. Lester was not a religious woman; and she held no disdain for young girls who fell for the sweet lies that flowed from the lips of a pursuing, sexually charged men.

Having never married, she had no children of her own but looked kindly on naïve young mothers who had been abandoned by their family and or the child's father.

Ms. Lester was in her sixties, she was a firm but loving advocate, given to strict house rules. She provided the young mothers with a home for six months and taught the naïve mothers the basic skills of mothering.

She was also instrumental in finding the girls jobs, or families for their infant if they chose not to keep their baby.

After observing Mabel, Ms. Lester was impressed with the strength of purpose she possessed and her willingness to work hard. She demonstrated her determination to keep and care for her baby by learning as many skills as were offered.

Mabel was willing to do more than was required of her. She was a quick and eager learner and was always ready to guide and encourage some of the less mature mothers.

When her beautiful daughter whom she named Maize was six months old, it should have been time for Ms. Lester to find Mabel a good home in which she could work and keep her baby. However, Ms. Lester had grown very fond of Mabel who had proven to be a big help running the house and managing the other young mothers, so she invited Mabel to stay on with her.

The young mother continued to work with Ms. Lester for the next three years. She was extremely grateful and considered herself blessed to be where she and her baby were together.

Hard work was no stranger to the grateful young mother; she was always willing and eager to do more than she was asked to do. Mabel was pleased knowing that her hard work was appreciated. Both of the midwives complimented Mabel's dedication and they showed their appreciation in many ways.

When slipping into a melancholy mood, Mabel often found herself reminiscing on the miserable events that framed her life while living with her strict, self-centered father.

Mabel would reflect with anger, on the back-breaking work she did year-round in the fields. She had to toiled six days a week from morning to evening, reaching home just as the sun was setting. Exhausted, she longed to lie on her worn-out mattress but rest was not to be had.

Mabel often resented seeing her father sitting on the porch at the end of his working day, relaxing and smoking his corn cob pipe.

He would spend his evenings nodding, while going over his sermon, like he was the master. The teenager would be just as tired, but she had to fetch water from the well which was more than a stone's throw away.

That was a job in itself, having to walk quite a distance to the well. She would fill two buckets in order to save herself a second journey. Bone tired at the end of her day, she often went to bed without bathing.

Whenever those feelings of melancholy seeped into her thoughts, she reminded herself not to be too content or take anything for granted. Memories were never from her thoughts of the dilapidated shack, which was a poor excuse for a home in constant need of water. Water to cook the evening meal, water to clean up after dinner, water for everyone to bathe, and water for the weekly laundry, which she alone had to do, by hand 'come rain or shine'.

"My father," said Mabel, as she recounted segments of her life to her daughter many years later "… was a mean-spirited man, incapable of displaying affection toward me, his only daughter.

The only interaction he ever had with me was to reprimand me for errors I'd made while cooking or ironing his Sunday preachin' clothes. He would examine the freshly ironed shirt with a keen eye, ready to snap at me if he saw the slightest crease."

"There were times," she continued, while Maize listened with horror, "when he would wake me up in the wee hours of the morning to fetch water for his bath. It was my job to fetch enough water on Saturday night so that he could take his bath early on the Sabbath day, but sometimes I would forget."

"My daddy never struck us but he was mean-hearted. He would look at me like I was the devil himself. When your

Uncle Paul had been out late on a Saturday, all he wanted to do was sleep in late on Sunday morning, but Daddy would have none of it.

He would light every lantern an' every candle to brighten up the room before sun up, just to wake my brother up. They shared the same bedroom. He would rummage around in that tiny room making as much noise as he could, all on account that Paul had been out all night. My daddy saw everyone as a sinner."

Maize enjoyed the stories her mother shared with her and she always had lots of questions, she wanted to know more about her naughty and mischievous uncle.

"Did your brother get up, then?" Maize would ask, amazed at her young uncle's defiance.

"No, child. He would pull his pillow over his head and bury himself under the patchwork quilt my momma made for him." Mabel smiled, reflecting. "He was a stubborn boy."

The teenage mother had just turned nineteen when the chest cold Ms. Lester had been nursing turned into pneumonia; Mabel took full charge of running the home with the aid of Mrs. Anderson and a nurse who visited daily.

Mabel moved a cot into the main bedroom in order to nurse her benefactor during the night. There were three teenage mothers residing in the home, each with a very young baby when the midwife died. Maize was, by then, three years old.

Ms. Lester's grandson inherited the house and was anxious to move in to it. However, Mabel pleaded with him to postpone moving in, until she could find a home for the three remaining mothers and a job for herself. He agreed, giving her a deadline of two months.

After she found a home for the three young mothers, she

began searching for a job for herself. The midwife who delivered Mabel's daughter came to her rescue once more. It was not difficult finding her a good home in which she could work and keep her baby.

Mabel applied for the job as kitchen maid and was grateful for the excellent reference both benefactors had written for her and the job which included a private room.

Maize never knew her biological father and was never sure if her mother really knew him or his real name; her mother had never mentioned him. In her early years, she was not bothered about not having a father; she was raised with so much love, she had no yearning for a father's affection. From birth, she was a permanent fixture either on her mother's back, in her arms or attached to the hem of her mother's skirt.

Mabel was soon settled in as a cook and laundry maid, it was hard work but she never complained. She was grateful for the roof over her head and her ability to keep her daughter at her side.

A year later, Mabel met a carpenter, his name was Daniel Williams; he was hired to replace the wooden fence that surrounded the house where Mabel worked and lived.

Maize had just turned four and she would sit on the grass in the back yard watching Daniel as he worked. At the end of his day, if Maize was still playing in the yard, he would pick her up and swing her around or give her a piggyback ride. The excited toddler would scream in joy. Sometimes, he would sit on the grass with her and eat his lunch.

Mabel would watch the two of them from the kitchen window or when she was hanging out the laundry to dry; she recognized that he was a good man, hardworking and ambitious.

Daniel told Mabel that he had built his own four-roomed

house, he said he wanted a wife and kids; he said he had planted a vegetable garden in his backyard and was also building a double swing in the fenced back yard.

Like most impoverished, single mothers, Mabel wanted a better life for herself and her daughter; and even though she didn't have a relationship with her daughter's father or any other man for that matter, she sensed tenderness and compassion in Danny the carpenter.

He was a pleasant man with a calm and pleasant demeanor; Mabel was drawn to his warm smile and gentle voice. After several months of courting, Mabel and Danny were married and Maize was very happy to have a daddy.

When Danny learned there was plenty of work for good carpenters in a big city like Macon, he decided to move his family there, shortly after their second child was born. They had clearly outgrown their little house and jobs were not as plentiful there, as they had been in years past.

Danny was a hard worker and he provided well for his family. They rented a small house for the time being, until he could save enough money to buy the raw materials to build a house for his family.

Mabel helped out a lot; doing odd domestic jobs and taking in laundry. Their second son, David had just turned two when they moved into their new home.

Sadly, six months after they moved into their new home, an economic depression slowly devastated the country. Everybody felt the financial strain, especially those at the bottom of the economic ladder.

Almost all of the jobs that Danny had lined up were cancelled. Weak and weary, he got out of bed each and every day before sun-up and walked to town, knocking on doors in search of work or any odd jobs.

Unable to get enough work to pay for the home, her husband had borrowed money to build. He would do any job to earn enough money to put food on the table for his family.

By nightfall he would walk back home, his spirit broken; his body cold and his pockets were often empty. His greatest worry was not having money to feed his family.

To help, Mabel took in washing whenever she could and sold the fruit pies she made. She knew he was weak and needed rest but he insisted on going out in the bitter cold in search of work.

"Today will be a better day, you watch and see." He would tell her this as she fought to keep him home.

In search of a better life, Danny died, less than a year after relocating his family. The doctor said it was pneumonia. But Mabel knew in her heart that her beloved husband died from the pain and shame of poverty.

Unable to provide for his family, plus the shame of defeat; at age forty-two, he had become a broken man. Without work; he could no longer take care of his family; and the painful reality of his failure consumed him, it ultimately devoured him. Danny eventually lost the will to live.

Mabel had to pack up and move again, this time with her three children. There was no work to be had in the town she had happily settled into. Having to walk away from her little house with her small children in tow was both emotional and painfully frightening for the young mother.

Mabel loved her husband; he was a good man, a hardworking man who loved his family. He had so many dreams, but sadly died far too young. Homeless again, this time with three children; Mabel was desperate for a job and desperate for a roof over her little family's head, Mabel searched for a room she could afford to rent.

The struggling young mother did all that she could to pay for the rent on the one room they all shared; she took in washing and she continued to make fruit pies and pecan pies. Over the years, she had improved her cooking skills since living with Mrs. Lester.

The young mother-of-three often made a game of picking up as many apples and pecans as they could, that had fallen off the many trees in the road, from the nearby orchard plus the wild blueberries and blackberries that grew in the backyard. She sold her fruit pies, and pretty soon she had lots of orders.

She was limited in what she could do because her children were still very young. If she got a 'real job', say a factory or on a farm, she would need someone to look after her children; they were too young to leave alone. Desperate, she knew that she had to find more work or her children would surely starve. Most of the money she made from baking was used to rent the room they all shared.

Feeling as though she had the weight of the world on her shoulders, Mabel was seriously considering a desperate move. As much as she hated the thought of living in a big city; she did, out of desperation considered moving her little family to a bigger city, like Atlanta. This desperate mother didn't want to raise her children in a big city; she liked the quiet country life. However, if that was the only alternative she had, to make a better living for herself and her children, she would have to make that move.

Mrs. MacArthur, the woman she rented their room from; who in her youth had been considered 'poor white trash; came from a very large, impoverished family. Her parents were pickers, as were the children once they reached an age. She and her many siblings collected old clothes and bottles from rich people's trash cans to help supplement their parent's wages; every one of them worked to survive.

She knew what it was like to struggle and still have nothing to show for it. Mrs. Mac. as she was fondly referred to, admired Mabel's endless efforts to hold on to her children. She had grown attached to little Maize and she also admired the young mother's determination to keep her children with her, regardless of the many obstacles against she faced each and every day.

Rosie MacArthur and her husband loved Mabel's pies and she let Mabel use her big kitchen oven, so that she could cook more of them at the same time. Mrs. Mac also told her many friends about Mabel and her delicious pies.

Mr. MacArthur overheard the owner of a very large plantation tell the blacksmith that he needed a housekeeper and mentioned this to his wife over dinner one evening. Mrs. Mac. later informed Mabel of a possible job out in the country. She told Mabel that the job was for a widower with a small child.

"I think the position comes with a small house, although the previous housekeeper, who was a white woman, resided in the main house. My husband said the little house has been vacant for many a year."

He had told his wife that 'it may not be habitable'. Even so, Mabel was grateful for the information the woman had shared with her and delighted that the position was in Macon, since she had no love for life in a big city.

Mabel prayed not only that she would get the job but that the small house was livable. While saying a silent prayer, the young widow removed the small suitcase from underneath the bed they all shared and removed the references she had stored in it. She then stuffed what few items of clothing they each had, into it. Before Mrs. Lester had impressed upon her the importance of having as many references as she could get from the people she worked for; Mabel had never heard of a reference. Both Mrs. Anderson and Mrs. Lester explained the value in having personal references from the people she had previously work for. She had made a point of asking for a written reference from each new employer after working six months on the job. She would first ask her employer if they were satisfied with her work and if they were, would they please write her a reference. Not one of them refused.

Mabel worked very hard after having her first baby and so, this now desperate widow and mother of three small children had a collection of five, very impressive references.

34

– MR. ROBERT NEWCOMB, PLANTATION OWNER –

MACON GEORGIA, USA

ISABELLA LOUISA SANDERSON WAS A HAPPY AND VIVACIOUS young woman; she was educated at Vassar University, the all-women's college. Isabella came from an affluent family, she was an only child. Sadly, just half way through her four-year commitment, her parents were killed. Their summer cottage on Nantucket Island caught fire when a gasoline tank exploded. The tank had recently been filled, which provided the family with the fuel needed to gas up their yacht and speedboats.

Apparently, there was a hairline crack in the tank from which gasoline had seeped out, unbeknownst to the owners, their guests, and staff. Three people miraculously escaped the ravaging fire; unfortunately Isabella's parents were among the five, fatal casualties. Young Isabella was devastated and her only living relative was a distant aunt, her father's older sister.

Elizabeth was the only remaining elder of the Sanderson family and because she was in failing health, was unable to attend the funeral.

Mr. and Mrs. Winston Newcomb, who were her parents' neighbors and very close friends, comforted the young orphan in her time of need, they made all the arrangements along with her family's lawyers and they attended the funeral.

Overcome with grief, Isabella took a year off from college. It was during her recovering year that she renewed her old acquaintance with the Newcomb's son.

Robert, who was a few years older than Isabella and already established as a prosperous businessman, as his plantation was ever expanding.

Eventually, Isabella returned to Vassar and continued her education, she majored in music, with a preference for violin and the harp.

Twelve months later, Isabella graduated with honors. The Sanderson family attended her graduation, Isabella was delighted to see them and grateful they honored her with their presence.

Several months after she graduated, Robert Newcomb began courting Isabella and within the year, she accepted his proposal of marriage.

The happy couple honeymooned in Europe visiting ancient ruins, artist galleries, and several Masson-De-modes plus a number of symphonic performances. Isabella developed a keen interest in the piano after attending several Chopin concerts; it soon became apparent that she had a new love in her life.

Also, during their month-long honeymoon in Europe, they developed a taste for the rich, full bodied wines they experienced while traveling and sightseeing on the Continent.

Shortly after the couple returned home to his vast plantation, Robert bought his bride a brand new, Spinet piano.

It was placed in the grand parlor, just under the huge bay

window and as the sun kissed the window panes, the piano also glowed from the daily dusting and bi-weekly polishing by one of the parlor-maid. Thus, adding an exquisite component to their already eloquent atmosphere in their grand sitting-room.

Days later, the newlyweds attended the grand opening of a new winery in Macon. Having enjoyed so many of the fine wines they experienced in Europe, the Newcomb's would occasionally drive the short distance from their plantation up to the new vineyard to taste and purchase the locally grown wines.

Whenever the Oliver Winery introduced a new wine, Monsieur Francoise Oliver, the son of the owners, would sit at the grand piano and play while the customers sampled the newest labels.

Wanting only the very best for his lovely bride, Robert Newcomb walked over to the classically trained pianist when he paused for a break and introduced himself. He explained that his new bride wished to have piano lessons, saying, "Since your good name and reputation preceded you, I would like to engage you."

Francoise explained to Mr. Newcomb that he did not reside in Atlanta but visited every fortnight for a long weekend. He explained that he was in full residence at Juilliard where he taught classical piano to resident students.

Amazed at the depth of disappointment that crossed the man's face, Francoise agreed to find the time during his visits to give his wife a few lessons.

Francoise was not disappointed in his student, and Isabella was delighted at having such an outstanding pianist as her instructor; she was eager to learn. Mrs. Newcomb was graced with long slender fingers and a sensitive ear.

Isabella loved music and was enthusiastic to learn how to play her new piano, professionally. Her husband, the rich tobacco and cotton plantation owner had hired the Belgian pianist to teach his wife on her up-right spinet piano.

Monsieur Oliver was delighted with Isabella's skill, she played beautifully. After only a few lessons; she became his prized student.

She played the piano as if she had practiced for years. Whenever her husband entertained business associates, Isabella would entertain his guests as she played classical music.

When the name and reputation of the Belgian pianist, his talents and skills preceded him, he was soon in great demand.

The wives and daughters of the very rich plantation owners sought out his tutelage. However, none of his many students were anywhere near as gifted as Isabella Newcomb.

After the successful birth to their first child, a healthy baby girl, Mr. Newcomb was extremely happy and wanted the world to know that he was now a proud father.

He gave a party and invited his wife's teacher, Monsieur François Oliver to perform for the evening's celebration. Monsieur Oliver later learned that Isabella's previous three pregnancies had spontaneously aborted.

The happy couple delighted in the birth of their first living child, a healthy daughter, whom they named Louisa. It was obvious to most, that the lovely Isabella was now looking very frail. However, in time she managed to regain most of her strength and she was a devoted mother.

Like most men, especially those who were building an empire or a thriving business; Mr. Newcomb wanted a son and heir to inherit his vastly growing wealth. Isabella was two-and-a-half when her mother became pregnant again.

After many months of confined bed rest because of her fragile condition, her mother gave birth to the much-wanted baby boy. The desired son and heir to his father's vast estate, sadly both mother and baby died in childbirth.

After he buried his wife and son, Mr. Newcomb began to drink heavily. His creditors, household staff and his workers understood his grief and they all empathized with him. It goes without saying that Mr. Newcomb was devastated. He mourned the death of his beloved wife and baby boy for many months.

His grief was so profound that he was seldom seen on his property. Whenever he was visible, which was very rare, he was always drunk, losing his balance and carrying a half empty bottle of whiskey.

He had all but neglected his daughter, his only child. Louisa would cry each night for her daddy to kiss her goodnight, but most nights, he was nowhere to be found and the little girl would cry herself to sleep.

Months later the rumors were confirmed, Mr. Newcomb had most certainly lost all interest in his estate. He failed to meet deadlines and it was alleged that he was in default with his banks and so his estate was in danger of being seized.

However, when mismanagement of the plantation caused rumors to spread about his ever-increasing debt or losing the plantation, his manager had a serious talk with him. He told his boss he had three months to turn things around. If not, all would be lost and that he would be the first to leave and Mr. Newcomb could end up in debtor's prison.

His current live-in housekeeper, an older white working-class woman, found his behavior intolerable. As a devout Christian, she felt she could no longer remain in the house with a drunkard. The woman walked away with a heavy heart but felt she could no longer 'work under the same roof with an uncontrollable alcoholic.'

Eventually the family doctor was called in to help his patient detoxify and in due course, Mr. Newcomb did recover. He was able to pull himself together, taking charge of his estate and his responsibilities to his only child, making Louisa the center of his world.

They were seldom out of each other's sight and even when he had to go out of town on business, he often took his darling Louisa with him.

Louisa adored her daddy and he returned her affection affably. One of the first things he did after several months of turning things around for the better, Mr. Newcomb began the search for a much-needed housekeeper.

35

– THE OLIVER FAMILY –

THE BELGIANS & THE GESTAPO, 1930

In the early 1930's, Madame & Monsieur Oliver, lived through the ravaging corruption and senseless destruction that Adolph Hitler had engendered throughout Europe.

Infighting, oppressive fear and senseless ruin was now concentrated in Belgium. Every Jewish person was now living on tender hooks.

The Oliver family decided to flee their home, their century- old business and their way of life; in order to escape the horrific slaughter by the Nazis.

After seeing what happened to some of their Jewish friends, such unspeakable things, no one knew if or when they too would become targets of the Gestapo. Many of their friends had their home and/or their business confiscated, some even burned to the ground.

The owners of the world-famous Oliver winery feared it was only a matter of time before they too would be harassed and have their business confiscated or possibly worse.

The three-tiered family decided to leave Belgium. This was

not an easy decision to make; they loved their home, their community, their life.

The growing harassment and constant humiliating taunts by young boys in Nazi uniforms; often egged on by their superior offices, was too much. There was overwhelming evidence that Hitler's solid concentration in Belgium, was growing rapidly. Evidence of their continued destruction was becoming more apparent every hour.

So, after much debate, the huge emotional and painful decision was made. It took the family several weeks to work out an escape plan, right after they painfully agreed; they had no option but to leave.

They had to be extra vigilant in order to avoid drawing attention to themselves. Having agreed, that they could not sell any of their valuable possessions; they decided, as a family which items to take. Many of those left behind were priceless antiques that had been in the family for generation.

However, most of their precious items were far too large to take with them undetected. Their main aim was to be anonymous, to appear as though they were going about their daily lives in as normal a way as possible; no suitcases, shopping bags or parcels.

Each day was to appear as normal as any other day. So in order to accomplish this and take as many small priceless items with them, Mrs. Oliver devised a plan to smuggle as many of their valuable belongings as possible; sight unseen.

Madam Collette and her mother-in-law cut up clothes to create camouflaged compartments inside their normal clothes in order to conceal some of the family's jewelry and money.

Some small historic and priceless paintings were removed from the gilt frames and placed inside a silk sleeve which had been sewn inside each pant leg.

Mrs. Oliver was a prominent and highly sought-after piano teacher and it broke her heart, having to abscond from her students; many of who showed so much promise, including her son François.

It took them many days to work out an escape plan, which meant making appointments with various venders. A doctor's appointment for François to have his eyes examined, an appointment with Madam Oliver's coiffeur and a dental appointment for Emilie.

The first to leave was Mr. Oliver Sr. and his seven-year-old granddaughter, Emilie. Together, they walked casually to the bus depot, stopping on their way to buy an ice cream cone from the vendor. "How is the family doing Mr. Oliver?" Joseph asked as he lifted the lid off the ice chest.

"As well as can be expected," was the flat reply.

"And how is business, these days?" Mr. Oliver asked his old friend and chess partner.

"Not bad but it could always be better," he said raising his shoulders, head to one side eyebrows raised.

Mr. Oliver paid for the ice cream cones then he and his granddaughter walked over to the bus stop and stood in line, waiting for their bus to arrive. When they stepped onto the bus, Emilie ran to the back of the bus to a double empty seat. They rode the bus to the end of the line.

From there, they walked through a quaint village. The pair stopped at a little store and bought a bunch of roses and a bag of peppermints for Emile.

They would stop from time to time to check on the map her grandfather kept inside his high woollen sock. It took them almost an hour before they saw the Mid-Zuid train station which was not yet occupied by the Gestapo.

After purchasing two tickets, they boarded the next train to freedom and safely crossed the channel from Zeebrugge to Hull in the north of England. From there they took the train down to London's, St. Pancreas train station in the heart of London.

Two days later, Mr. Oliver and his mother walked to the open market and bought food, then casually strolled over to the park. It was midday, so they sat for a while and enjoyed their leisurely lunch.

About an hour later they took another stroll, this time they walked casually through the park in the direction of the main street, which ultimately led to the train station. And with an atmosphere of casual, nonchalance and many prayers silently prayed, by both, they boarded the train to freedom and safety.

The following day, Madam Colette rang for a taxi to take young Oliver to his doctor's office. An appointment had been made one week earlier, so if any attention was given to them getting into the taxi, clearance had been given several days earlier, to keep the doctor's appointment.

Dr. Cohen's office was just one block away from train station. Madam Oliver and her son François got out of the taxi and walked into the medical building. They took the lift to the third floor, got off, then walked to the back of the building and took the stairs down to the ground floor.

Madam Oliver watched and waited as her son crossed the road, and then he walked down the alley way that led to the back entrance of the train station. Once he was out of sight, his mother proceeded to follow in his footsteps. They had agreed to meet on Platform D for the train to Paris.

Madam Oliver arrived as casually as she could and headed straight for Platform A. But as she proceeded towards Platform D, panic gripped her heart. Oliver was nowhere to be seen.

In fact, the gate for Platform D was closed. Madam Oliver

froze, as fear struck her heart. She could feel herself trembling as she felt the color drain from her face. She feared her knees would buckle under her.

Then she did what she had instructed each member of her absconding family to do; 'take a deep breath and walk into a crowd or a doorway or an open shop to gain composure. Do not panic and, walk casually' she had instructed them, 'in order not to appear conspicuous or nervous; but whatever you do, DO NOT PANIC'.

Madam Colette realized in that moment of panic that it was much easier to give those instructions than it was to act upon them. She was terrified, but eventually took her own advice; she inhaled deeply, hoping at the same time, that she did not reveal her agonizing terror.

She could feel herself getting flushed and, in her anxiety, she opened the top button on her overcoat. She immediately removed her hand for fear of looking suspicious and while taking in as deep a breath as she could without looking conspicuous; she retraced her steps.

She was to meet her son at the entrance or close enough to Platform C but there was no sign of him. Trying desperately to appear calm, she counted with her eyes a, b, c, d. The back stroke on the 'd' was missing, so it looked like a 'c'.

"Oh, thank God," she whispered, and in that instant, she saw him.

He was waiting as inconspicuously as he could, all the while wondering why his mother did not approach him.

He guessed she must have seen someone or something that prevented her from coming forward. His mother walked over to the gate as casually as she could manage, all the while her legs felt like jelly.

François glanced at his mother in amazement, but she just

walked past him. Relieved, he waited a few moments then walked behind her.

Ever cautious, Mrs. Oliver walked past their assigned compartment; she brushed the hem of her coat as she past the one they had been assigned to, indicating that he should get on there.

François chuckled silently at his mother's action, but he obeyed her and once he had reached the top step, he grabbed hold of the two handrails and swung back, following his mother with his eyes to make sure which compartment she entered.

When his mother joined his car at last, she took her reserved seat, which was facing her son three rows ahead of him.

She wiggled her nose when she peeped out over her magazine to see him, he giggled into the comic book he was planning to read. Fortunately, their train journey was uneventful and as planned, they avoided each other on the train.

The entire journey, however, took just over two days before they finally arrive in London. François' father and sister met them at Kings Cross Station in London, England.

After many hugs and kisses, Colette asked anxiously about her husband's parents. He patted her hand and told her that they had met some old friends and were having lunch with them at the Savoy.

The family stayed in England for two months. They loved the country, especially the countryside and for a moment they contemplated staying in England.

After much discussion, the family decided that the distance between where they were now and where they had come from was a mere drop in the bucket compared to the distance from Brussels and America.

They hoped not, but in fact doubted that England would be invaded by Hitler's henchmen. Although, they were not prepared to take that chance.

Their greatest fear was that the insidious onslaught of Jews in Europe would eventually escalate across the Channel and if that did happen, they knew that they would be doomed. And so, it was with a sad heart, they left England and took a steam ship to America. François, his parents, grandparents, and his young sister Emilie all immigrated to America.

The Oliver Winery had customers from all over the world; many had become close and loyal friends. When the invasions began, the family had many invitations from old friends; to relocate to several cities in Europe.

As much as they appreciated the offers, the family thought it wise to put an ocean between themselves and their beloved country. The family anticipated complete ruin. They speculated there would be savage slaughter, which did eventually devastate Europe, including areas in England which sadly annihilated so many of their kinsmen.

They were uncertain as to where they would settle in America, however after much research, their first choice was California; it was a well-known fact that the climate and soil in the north and south of that state were excellent for the production of both white and red grapes.

Soon, it became apparent that there was a growing exodus of disillusioned wine makers from Europe. Hundreds of winery owners were escaping their homelands because of the encroaching Nazi invasions. A large percentage of these owners chose to settle in California.

The Oliver family discussed their options and having done

their research, the family agreed to relocate to Georgia. They knew that the rich soil was perfect to cultivate their red grapes.

They eventually settled in a rural village in Macon, which was in the state of Georgia in the south-east region of the United States of America. They were grateful to have escaped the senseless destruction that continued to escalate.

The Olivers were devastated and outraged to learn of the horrendous slaughter of countless innocent people and the ravaging of their personal property and priceless possessions. Many of whom were known to them personally. The family was deeply depressed, fearing for their friends as more devastation was still to come.

It took several years of hard work and many disappointing results before the Oliver Winery became a success.

The first three years, their grapes failed badly and having invested everything they had; they were disillusioned with each failed crop. However, they were confident with the passing of each new year, that they would achieve success. And eventually they did.

Madam Colette Oliver was a concert pianist in her own country and she passed on her love of classical music to her children.

François and Emilie showed no interest in the growing or harvesting of grapes. However, François, their eldest child showed exceptional talent in the piano.

François was a shy and timid boy but obviously very talented. His mother believed that exposing him to his musical peers would strengthen his persona and reduce, if not eliminates, his shyness.

When he was just twelve-years-old, his mother contacted a very dear friend from her childhood who emigrated to New York a dozen or so years earlier.

Madam Mari Corbin and Madam Colette were contemporaries in Brussels. Madam Corbin was herself a graduate of the esteemed institution in New York.

After corresponding with her friend and the academy, Madam Oliver enrolled François in The Juilliard Academy of Music.

François was extremely homesick for the first few years but after his mother and sister visited him, taking him sightseeing and to several concerts he showed his appreciation and began to settle down.

He was a very gifted and accomplished pianist, and years later he became an instructor at the institution. François was never interested in performing for an audience but he loved to play.

His passion was in teaching and exposing young interested and especially gifted students to the great European pianist and so, for many years he was an instructor at the great academy of Juilliard.

After several years of teaching at the academy, he returned to the winery; his grandparents were becoming frail, they were tired and their health was not as it was just a few years earlier.

François parents wanted him closer to home; they felt that his by-monthly weekend trips sufficed for a while, but eventually this was not enough to satisfy the family's need for unity.

And so, reluctantly, maestro Michael François Oliver returned home to Macon to reside full-time with his family.

The vineyard was small in comparison to what they had in Belgium; but, the seven-thousand bottle yield each season was sufficient for the family to live in comfort, although not as opulently as they had been accustomed to in Europe.

Nevertheless, they were content with their lives, which

were much simpler in America, less socializing and less entertaining. Another plus was that it enabled them to keep the half dozen workers busy almost all year-round.

Maestro Michael François Oliver's love of music and his desire to teach students of all ages, who demonstrated a desire to learn the art and beauty of classical music, continued.

36

– MAIZE'S STORY: A NEW BEGINNING –

MAIZE HAD JUST CELEBRATED HER SEVENTH BIRTHDAY AND WAS proudly wearing the two ribbons her mother made out of an old silk pillowslip she had salvaged from the rubbish bin after the owner discarded it.

Mabel was able to make good use of most of the faded material including the two pretty bows dangling from her daughter's long braids. As poor as they were, her children were happy, Mabel never complained and tried to make light of their situation; she would squeeze and tickle her children, making them giggle in laughter. She also hugged and kissed them often while saying how much she loved her precious trio.

Mabel was delighted when she was offered an interview for the job as cook and housekeeper, for Mr. Robert C. Newcomb.

Mabel prayed a silent prayer with each step she took leading her to the job interview. She prayed for a 'real' job and didn't care how hard the work would be; she could finally feed her children properly and put a solid roof over their heads; if she is offered this job.

She knew that Danny would be proud of her. Mabel often felt the presence of her late husband, and she would smile.

While walking with her mother and little brothers, Maize was in awe as they approached the house which was the color of winter snow.

The house sat at the top of a high sloping path and the white picket fence that enclosed the property seemed to be a mile away from the rough country road.

Mabel opened the gate and the four of them walked hand in hand up the long path, it was wide enough for a big truck to drive on it.

Although they were still a good distance from the house, they could see there were several steep steps that lead up to the front of the house; the top step opened on to a wide veranda, which was the width of the entire front of the house, as far as they could see.

There must have been six or seven seating arrangements spaced at regular conversational intervals, plus two double seated swing seats, one at each end of the porch. Each pair of rocking chairs had a small table placed conveniently in between.

Drawn to the happy squealing of a little girl's delightful laughter; Maize had never heard such gaiety before.

She could see a little girl about her own age running across the veranda into a man's out-stretched arms. Maize reckoned the man must be the little girl's father; as he picked her up, and swung her around and around making the child squeal in delight, and then he kissed her goodbye.

A tall, slender woman wearing a long white cotton coat over an even longer black dress or skirt approached the child. The woman's hair was black and pulled back into a bun, she smiled at the child then took her by the hand and they both disappeared into the house. That was the first time Maize saw Louisa May Newcomb.

As the early morning air collided with the fresh April mist, expelling the sweet fragrance of spring, there was joy in the air. Mabel was happy and she felt confident as she walked hand in hand with her children; she smiled and prayed silently to God.

Maize and her brothers broke loose from their mother and moved ahead of her, while skipping up the long, pebbled path. A path that stretched from the main road up the sloping path that led to the huge whitewashed house and beyond.

There was a bench on either side of the side door and just above was a sign that read DELIVERIES. Mabel's instructions were to sit the children on the benches while she was being interviewed for the job. She then took in a deep breath and pulled on the bell chain. While waiting for the door to open, the single mother offered up a prayer to God, thanking Him for this opportunity. She was feeling hopeful and confident.

Mabel was wearing a huge smile when she returned to her children and she knelt down, opening her arms to embrace all three of them.

Her children laughed gleefully and ran into her arms. Memories of that special day, several years later, the joy that Maize felt as she saw the contented expression on her mother's face, would take her to a special place when faced with the horrors still yet to pierce her very soul.

Mabel was delighted when the owner told her about the little three-room cottage with its own private outhouse. There was a small patch of earth in the front of 'the cottage', as he referred to it, plus a larger area in the back. Before they could move into their 'new home', it had to be cleaned and aired out, it had not been occupied for several years.

Mr. Newcomb gave his new housekeeper the key to the

'cottage' as he called it and said, "You can use any of the cleaning things you need from the pantry in the main house".

He also informed her that there may be some things up in the attic she could use in the cottage. He said he would give her two days to clean and set up the house, but on the third day he expected to have a hearty breakfast cooked and served by her.

The job ahead of her was enormous; there were cobwebs everywhere plus years of dust and peeling paint. Even so, Mabel was so excited she started right away. She instructed the children to play in the back yard while she worked on their new home.

Their mother spent all day disinfected and scrubbed every corner of the tiny house until it was sparkling clean and smelling of sweet lavender.

Mother and daughter shared one bedroom and the two little boys shared the second room. It wasn't a big house, but it was a palace compared to the one room where all four had lived and slept.

The largest room in the house was a combination of a kitchen with a hearth, which in the wintertime heated the tiny house. The remainder of the space was separated by an old threefold screen that Mabel found in the dusty attic to create a separate living space where she and her children could relax.

The furniture in the cabin was old, most of it also came from the attic but Mabel soon brightened up each room with the odds and ends she found discarded. She found left over paint in the cellar and was able to paint the old faded furniture.

As a small child she had enjoyed planting red and yellow roses with her mother. Even as a child she loved to watch the seedlings grow.

In her eagerness while watering the seeds, her mother had to caution her to sprinkle and not pour all of the water in one patch. Mabel soon learned to take as much pride in her flowers as her mother did in the roses she planted and pruned each season.

Over the years, Mabel also developed a significant green thumb. She was able to turn plant cuttings into living things of beauty plus food for her family to eat. She was determined that her children would never go hungry, as long as she could cultivate a vegetable garden all year round.

Mabel also loved bright colors and soon got to work planting some of her favorite flowers. There were daisies, azaleas, daffodils, and tulips.

On either side of the front door, she also planted a red and yellow rose bush, she didn't like the thorns on these pretty flowers but she did love the fragrance and they reminded her of her adoring mother.

Under the main window, she planted her favorite, a lavender bush and the sweet fragrance wafted throughout her tiny home. She had so little to give her children but she prided herself on bringing as much color and brightness to their lives as she could.

In addition to the seasonal vegetables her children helped her plant; they also learned to prune the fruit trees that grew in their back yard.

Their little house was always sparkling clean, Mabel made it as cozy as she could, always looking out for the odds and ends that other people threw away.

She was a proud and honest woman, only taking what she knew had been discarded. Mabel could turn an empty gourd into a thing of beauty. She often wondered what she might have achieved if she had been given the opportunity to get an education.

Several months later when she found out that her boss's daughter Louisa, delighted in playing school with Maize, teaching her how to read Mabel was very happy.

Louisa had a governess and when she learned new lessons, she would play school and proudly share her newfound knowledge with Maize who was eager to learn. She, in turn, would play school with her little brothers and she would scold them for not taking their lessons seriously.

Miss Louisa Newcomb was an only child; Mabel learned that her momma died when Louisa was still a little girl and her daddy paid people to look after her. So she had a nurse, when she was a baby, later a nanny, and then she had a governess and a music instructor. Louisa's mother had been a fine pianist, but Louisa had no interested in the piano.

Prior to Mabel and her family taking the job of housekeeper, Louisa was a very sad little girl, she was often lonely when her daddy went away on business. The previous cook was an older woman; she had no children, at least none that lived with her. She seldom had visitors so it was assumed she had no family.

Maize would often find herself daydreaming while watching Louisa, who could do so many fun things, like play the piano, or read her story books out loud.

Sometimes she would sit on the veranda and paint pictures on the easel with her coloring chalks; and at the end of each day she would watch for her papa as he rode homeward on his horse.

While still a young child, Maize observed the deep love and excitement Louisa expressed each time her father returned home and the infinite joy expressed on her face when she heard her father's carriage approach, or the familiar pattern of Shadow's hoofs, her daddy's stallion.

Every time, Louisa's eyes lit up with the biggest smile on her face and she would stop immediately, whatever she was doing, and run in the direction of the horse's hooves or the carriage wheels. Maize would look on in ore; and wonder.

The excited child would run down the wide steps to greet her daddy and he would pick her up in his arms and swing her around, then; he would sit her on his horse and they would ride all around their huge estate.

Her squeals and laughter would leave an echo of joy long after they were out of sight. Quite often Maize would overhear Louisa say, 'I love you daddy, and later on when it was her bedtime she would say 'read me a bedtime story tonight, Daddy."

On more than one occasion while sitting at her piano right after her music lesson, her daddy would praise her no matter how out of tune she was or frustrated her instructor was. Her daddy would console her.

Occasionally, he stood behind her and brushed her long, auburn hair with the mother of pearl hairbrush that had belonged to her momma.

Even at the tender age of seven, Maize knew what it was like to be doomed to a life without hope; to be alive without really living; what it was like to be considered only half of a person, to be at someone's beck and call twelve, fifteen or more hours each day.

Maize knew of the hardships her mother endured, working as an indentured servant. 'Not quite a slave', Mabel would tell her daughter with pride, refusing to be branded with that marker.

Even though deep down, she knew in her heart, that she

was only half a step away from what her own mother was; and for that matter, most of the Black women in her mother's day and indeed in her own time. Mabel knew what it felt like to be invisible, a servant in a house with no control over your time or even your own body.

Mabel had learned years earlier to purposely 'fatten herself up,' she also cut her hair and kept a rag tied around her head. She still did not escape the pinching of her buttocks or a hand squeezing her breast whenever she waited on his dinner guests.

Maize recognized the stress her mother lived under, and she acknowledged this fact head on when she witnessed just how tired her mother was at the end of each of the six long and exhausting days that she toiled in the big house.

There were days when her mother's work continued into the wee hours of the morning, like when *he* hosted a banquette or a shooting party. During those early days when her children were still quite young, she kept them in the kitchen, while she worked.

She would make a clean safe space for them to play in and lay them down when they got sleepy. She would have to wake them up when her work was finally finished, too exhausted to carry even the youngest one.

On those extra-long nights, they would go straight to bed. Mabel would be so exhausted, by the time she finally returned home she was often too weary to kiss her sleepy children goodnight.

The hard work she endured on those late nights, often made her irritable and short tempered, even with her children who were, it seemed on those days, constantly under foot.

Maize was keenly aware of the sadness her mother carried in her heart, because she was unable to give even a fraction to her daughter what the owner was capable of giving to his child.

Louisa was the same age and size as Mabel's only daughter and she knew her daughter was bright and she ached to give her more than she was capable of providing.

When Louisa had began to share all of her lessons with her daughter, Mabel was delighted. She would do all in her power to see to it that her daughter would learn a skill, to sew or write, so that she could teach other girls when she was of an age. Mabel vowed that her only daughter would not be a domestic for anyone, except for her own husband one day.

Maize felt and understood her mother's deep love for her children and she knew all too well the desire she had for them to learn a trade.

For her twelfth birthday, Louisa asked her daddy for a horse. He bought her a two-year-old mere, it was milky white and she named him Snowy. She and her daddy would often go riding together early in the morning.

There were times when Maize wished she had a daddy too, she would sometimes daydream what that would be like.

There were no other children around so when Miss Louisa wanted to play with Maize; she would go to the kitchen and look for her.

She would just take her by the hand and tell Mabel that she wanted to play with her. If she was busy, Mabel would say, "Not now Louisa, Maize can't play right now she has to finish her chores". Louisa didn't like being told 'no' for anything or by anyone.

37

– THE ATTIC –

MISS LOUISA WOULD NEVER TAKE NO FOR AN ANSWER, SHE always got her own way; and if any of the help told her 'no", she would march out of the kitchen and find her daddy who was usually in his study. "Daddy, Daddy", she would call, "Ms. Mabel won't let Maize play with me".

So, her daddy would stop whatever he was doing and go straight away to the kitchen and ask Mabel, "Can you spare her for a little bit?"

Mabel would always sigh and say, "Yes".

So, when Louisa decided that they were going to play dress-up, she asked permission to raid the old trunks and armoires in the attic. "Maize and I want to play dress up in Grandmama's old-fashioned clothes." She told her father.

"But it is very dirty and dusty up there and lots of spider webs, surely you can find something else to play."

Louisa began to pout and as her tears began to dance on the edge of her big blue eyes; her poppa was crushed. Seeing that his darling daughter was on the verge of weeping, her doting daddy always gave in. Still looking at his precious daughter he said to Mabel, "Maize can go, you don't mind a few mice or cobwebs do you gal?" he said winking at Mabel. Without waiting for a response, he told Mabel, "Show her the staircase, tell her that it's at the very top of the house." He gave Mabel the directions even though Maize was standing next to her momma, like he didn't see her.

Louisa smiled at her father, and the two of them walked out of the kitchen holding each other's hand.

Maize had never been anywhere in the house beyond the kitchen and cellars in all the years that she had lived there.

So as she followed her mother into the grand hallway, she reflected on a time not so long ago when she first laid eyes on this estate; a place she felt would be a happy place to call home. And now, almost seven years later, Maize is privileged to see beyond the scullery for the first time ever.

Mr. Newcomb told Mabel to show her daughter where the staircase was. Maize, like her mother had always entered the house by the side door.

Mabel directed her daughter through the large kitchen then through to a wide passageway. The door at the end of the passage opened into the elegant formal dining room, which was massive.

Her mother told Maize sternly, "Now don't you dilly dally, or touch anything; just walk thought to the dining room, then open the big oak doors, you'll will see the wide staircase on your right, after you reach the hallway.

Remember now, don't stop to look or touch anything, just walk straight for the door; open it, and then cross into the hall. An' don't dally; 'cos you got chores to do my gal when you is finished up there."

"Yes, Mamma." Maize replied.

Upon entering the dining room, Maize barely had time to glance at the beautiful floor to ceiling bay window on the far side of the room; the view from those windows was like a beautiful painting she had seen somewhere, she couldn't recall right at that moment.

She just wanted to remain in that spot and gaze out of the huge picture window. She glanced at the colorful flower beds and the rolling green hills in the distance. The sensation she experienced when she stepped onto the thick, lush red and gold carpet, almost took her breath away; the room was so beautiful.

Maize had no idea that a room could be so lavish. She was in orr and wanted to linger. But hearing her mother's stern voice, she tip-toed across the sensuous carpet, afraid she might mar its beauty.

To reach the stairs, she had to walk through the dining room to the opposite door which opened onto the hallway, leading to the grand staircase.

She walked past the huge sparkling dining-room table, which was flanked by ten red leather chairs, four on either side of the table and a much bigger chair at the bottom and top of the table. Sitting high on the table was a huge silver bowl, it was big enough, Maize thought to bath her little brother in.

Hanging from the center of the ceiling was the most beautiful of all; a chandelier, glistening from the sun's reflection on each of the crystal teardrops.

There must have been a hundred if there was one, she thought.

"So much beauty," she said aloud, then put her hand to her mouth for fear she might be overheard.

Following her mother's directions, Maize left one world to enter the threshold of another one. In awe of what she saw, the housekeeper's daughter instantly wished she had been born into it.

Through admiring eyes, the unsophisticated child continued to move on, as she glanced at such grandeur and opulence she could never have imagined.

Maize continued to be in awe of all the beautiful things she saw, she took a deep breath and wished she could stay, just a little longer to take in some more of the beauty that adorned the room.

Never before, had her eyes beheld such beauty. Then she spotted two huge paintings hanging on the wall on either side of the giant paneled door.

There was something about that huge, carved mahogany door, which made her shiver; in fact, she was quite happy to leave the dining room and be on the other side of it, which was to the right of the door she had entered first entered.

She wasn't sure if she should close the door or leave it open, but to her amazement, she had no time to ponder a decision because the great door began to close of its own accord.

Fear struck her again and she ran toward the magnificent brass railed staircase.

The carpet on the stairs matched the carpet in the dining room. She wondered if she should remove her shoes, but she had not been instructed to do so.

This new world was heavenly to behold. Amazed by this brand new experience, she approached the stairs as if led by an invisible rope; she reached the top stair without ever hearing a sound.

Maize stood for a split second on the top stairs not quite sure which hallway to walk down, then she remembered, her mother said to turn right.

"You will pass four doors on both sides of the hallway, just keep on walkin' and at the end of that hallway, you will see a door facing you, open that door then continue to climb those stairs and that will lead you to the attic door. It's never locked 'cos no one ever goes in there."

She finally made it to the huge wooden door which creaked as she pushed it open; she had no idea what to expect but it was exciting just being in a different part of the house. The room smelled stale and it was quite dark so it took a moment or two to adjust her eyes to the dark and dusty room, then she saw a slither of lingering daylight ease its way through a tattered curtain that covered the only window that she could see.

Although she was eager and excited about the treasure hunt, she was about to embark upon, she had a repressing fear that she might have to brush away giant spider webs and kick squealing mice. Fortunately, however, cobwebs and dust was all that she saw.

Maize felt sad for Louisa because she was missing all the fun, but Mr Newcomb adamantly refused to have his daughter go up to the top of the house. He told her it was very dirty, full of cobwebs with lots of old furniture and foul-smelling boxes and maybe even mice. He didn't want her to get dirty or slip and hurt herself. Maize was disappointed that Louisa could not go with her on this treasure hunt, but her fear and regret evaporated when she walked into that attic room. Mr. Newcomb was correct; it was a very dusty and dirty attic.

However, to Maize, it was a magical place, filled with excitement, childish joy and girlish delight plus a sense of adventure. She immediately started looking for treasures. She saw big trunks and battered boxes with old hats and shoes and all sorts of clothes spilling out, items she and Louisa could play dress up in.

"Oh, what fun we gonna have," she said, moving from one trunk to another.

The atmosphere inside was one of childish excitement with a sense of adventure, so many places to search, two tallboys, three chest of draws and two huge armoire's plus big cardboard boxes and old trunks.

"Oh my, where shall I start?" she said, and then giggled when she realized she was talking out loud to herself.

It was quite dark so she moved toward the window to let in more light. The heavy velvet drapes which had at one time been Forest green were now thick with dust and age, she attempted to push them open to let in more light, but the fabric came apart in her hand. She jumped in amazement at the instant destruction of those once perfectly lovely drapes and she was for a moment saddened by the thought of how beautiful they must have been so many years ago. Maize turned to resume her search and was pleased to see that the room was now a little brighter.

Keenly aware that Louisa was waiting for her to return to play dress up, she quickly began her search. She looked into the big oak chest, but it was full of old smelly pants and riding boots.

Then she saw the big, armoire it had three doors, the middle one, which was a panel, not a door as she first thought, had an oval mirror set in the center, it was thick with dust and practically impossible to see her reflection in it.

This was a stationary mirrored panel with a beautifully carved door on either side. She pulled at the knob on the first door it refused to move, frustrated she looked about to find something that would help her pry it open.

She saw a thin flat stick with markings on it, she thought it might be a measuring stick; she bent to pick it up and got the shock of her life.

In her enthusiasm she was oblivious to sounds, other than the scurrying of mice and her own footsteps on the well-worn wooden floor. So invested was she in her pursuit, she failed to hear footsteps on the stairs or the door opening behind her.

He startled her but she was not afraid. Mr Newcomb stood there with a studied air of nonchalance. Maize glanced over her shoulder.

"I didn't hear you come in," she said, reaching for the latch on an old trunk, while sitting on the pile of old mattresses. "I just got here, did Momma send you to fetch ..."

***

It was when she attempted to move that she felt the pain, as if she had been cut in her private parts. Then she felt the wet, sticky sensation between her legs.

She felt dizzy and had lost all sense of time but she knew that she had been ravaged, and in less time than it took her to drink a glass of water. Afraid to cry out, she nibbled at her bottom lip.

To think that he could watch me play with his precious daughter, the daughter he loved and cherished; the same age as me.

How could he or anyone else see me as different from the child I am; as innocent and as childish as his own beloved daughter? She wanted to scream but she could not find her voice.

Should I have suspected, that the adoring father of my playmate would abuse me so? We were best friends. He abused me in the worst way, robbed me of my innocence.

Maize whimpered softly in the dark as she tried to make

sense of the strange surroundings, momentarily she had lost all sense of where she was and what had happened to her.

Fear and shock consumed her, the instant she realized that *he* had violated her, *he* a full-grown man and she an innocent girl; a friend and close companion to *his* daughter. Maize vomited, involuntarily.

Slowly her eyes began to adjust to the room; there was a musty smell, as if this strange, dark place had not been aired out for years.

In her excitement upon entering this new Aladdin's cave, she hadn't noticed the damp and dusty smell. Then the quiet movement over yonder reminded her where she was, and why she was there; to look for old clothes for herself and his daughter to dress up in. As her eyes moved swiftly around the overcrowded room, she saw *him*, his back towards her, as he adjusted his clothes.

Frantically, she prayed in silence for him to leave for fear he would ravage her again. But he didn't leave. She lay there trembling, her mind in a whirl, were her thoughts conscious or unconscious, she wasn't sure; so, she lay there, petrified as night crept into her soul.

His presence in the room, which took her breath away, weighed heavily, as it lingered undisturbed in the dusty air of that creepy attic. The devastation she experienced silenced her and she used her will to suspend the gush of tears she wanted desperately to flow.

She heard herself whimper softly and she was afraid. Were her eyes open or closed, it was so dark where she was lying. Then she heard what sounded like a light tapping sound. Fear caught her by the throat and she opened her eyes, slowly, in search of the sound.

The room was dark but as her eyes gradually adjusted, she

realized there was enough light streaming through the torn curtain on the only window in that attic room.

The ravaged child felt weary and her eyelids began involuntarily to close. Again, she saw a partial reflection in the murky mirror. She held her breath; it was *him*; she could just make out what was behind her. Afraid to move, she tried to remember what the room looked like when she first entered it.

There was a three-mirrored dressing table, that's what she was looking at now and a pile of old mattresses of various sizes – she suddenly realized that's what she was lying on.

At the other end of the pile was a small chest of drawers and directly behind it stood the imposing eight-foot-three armoire she had planned to ransack.

She could see *his* profiled reflection in the dressing-table mirror on the center panel of the armoire, just behind her head.

Maize realized that the sound she heard was coming from the corn cob pipe as he tapped it against the rim of a glass ashtray that was sitting on the chest. *He* was staring ahead toward the window while tapping the contents of his pipe methodically into a glass amber ashtray. *His* face seemed void of expression as he stared off in space.

Terrified, she was afraid to move and she tried to hold in her breath as she watched him take out a tobacco pouch. He pulled some tobacco from it and filled his pipe.

The frightened child watched *him*, as he pressed the tobacco down into the pipe, while praying he would leave. When *he* struck a match, Maize jumped in fear or shock; and she watched *him* puff several times on the pipe.

He must have sensed her gaze on him or heard her movement because he turned sharply and with ice in his voice, he threatened the already petrified child.

"Speak not a word; do you hear me!" He yelled at the terrified child. "Say one word of this to anyone and I'll kick your mother and your brothers off my plantation and into the streets to beg. Do you hear me?"

She jumped in fear at the anger in his voice. He had the audacity to be angry with her after *he* had violated her in the worst possible way.

Fear gripped her by the throat as fresh tears sat on the edge of each eye, glistening before spilling onto her high cheek bones. She whimpered; afraid to move a muscle.

Suddenly, she felt cold, and shivered uncontrollably in that dark, stuffy attic room. And as much as she wanted, no needed the comfort of her loving mother, she knew she could never tell her.

Terrified, she had a strong urge to scream but she feared her mother would hear her and come running.

It was her deep love for her mother that prevented the petrified child from running to tell her mother what had happened; knowing how deeply she loved and protected her children. Maize truly feared what her mother would do.

"Make sure to bring those dresses with you when you come down," he said. "Louisa will be waiting to play dress up."

And in an instant, *he* was gone; leaving as silently and as swiftly as he had entered, never giving a thought to the evil deed that devastated his victim.

He contented himself with the power to demand her silence; then he turned and walked towards the door, opening then shutting it behind him. Maize realized he must have closed it upon entering.

Still whimpering in the dark, she softly called, "Momma."

After *he* had left, she cleaned herself as best she could with a torn shirt, he must have thrown at her, after he finished violating her.

She sobbed when she saw the blood on the shirt. Still trembling, she wiped her face on the hem of her dress. Moving off the pile of mattresses, she walked over to the armoire but the chest of drawers was in front; preventing her from gaining access to it. Maize began to cry, she felt so helpless and so alone.

She thought she heard her mother calling her and in that instant Maize was determined to move that chest out of the way and get the clothes she was told to collect.

In her determination, she found the strength to push the chest out of the way then she opened the freed door of the armoire. When she finally finished pushing and panting; she was exhausted. She snatched the first two gowns her fingers touched, without even looking at them.

All the joy of the anticipated playtime had vanished; shame and anger consumed her. She hated the dresses and wanted to destroy them. They were the reason she had been violated. She bundled the two dresses up so that she would not trip on them going down the three flights of stairs; one was white, the other one green.

She had been sodomized, victimized, and was now exhausted and petrified. As she finally stepped off the last stair which emptied into the wide hallway; she wanted to scream. She was in pain; but thought about her mother and what she imagined she would do to *him.*

So instead of returning to the kitchen, where she knew her mother was working, she defiantly took the six steps away from the last stair and dropped the bundle she had struggled with onto the black and white tile in the center of the hallway.

Then seething with anger, shame and humiliation, she

defiantly ran to the front door, opened it and ran home.

Maize sobbed all the way home, from the palatial front door to the humble cottage she and her family lived in. Once inside the safety of her tiny home; she wept bitter tears.

She had been violated and ravaged by the man who loved her mother's baking; the man who provided a home for her mother and her little brothers; the man who could turn her whole family out on the street, with nowhere to go.

Her sense of powerlessness and fear of him was as real as the nightmare that would continue to haunt her.

Her fists were clenched in anger, when she realized just how much power *he* had over her entire family. And so, it was in that moment, in the safety of her humble home, when her rational thoughts continued to enrage her.

Maize was cognitive enough to create a convincing story; one she had to create for her mother. Telling the truth could leave them orphaned, or at the least, homeless. And so, the frightened child kept the sinful crime against her in silence.

The sky had clouded over and the shimmering warmth of the day had fled; *he* glanced at his gold pocket watch which was attached to his waistcoat by a long heavy gold chain.

He saw that it was almost noon, but rather than return for his midday meal, he chose instead to ride on, and in no particular direction. After all, *he* didn't have a care in the world.

From that moment on, Maize avoided her attacker like the plague and when her mother asked her to take the laundry or the apple pie *he* had requested up to the big house, she would make a game of the errand and take her little brothers with her.

The strain of this devastating attack weighed heavily on her, and it would continue to plague her for years to come.

38

– MAIZE'S BATH –

TREMBLING IN FEAR AND ANGER, MAIZE COULD HARDLY WAIT
to tear her clothes off and clean her flesh. She took the short
cut home, crossing the forbidden emerald green lawns, which
was just a stone throw away from her house.

Blinded by rage, she ripped off her clothes and stepped
into the tub she and her little brothers had filled less than an
hour earlier. This water was meant to wash the pile of dirty
linens that had come off the beds in the big house. With her
arms cradling her bent legs, she was unaware of the icy cold
water as it bathed her skin. Having been violated, she was now
feeling desolate, angry and afraid.

The trembling child sat immobile in the clean, clear water
as each beat of her heart slowed and her angry tears flowed
uncontrollably.

As her sobs softened and the day crept forward, Maize was
in a quandary as to what she should do; remembering *his*
threat, paralyzed her momentarily. So much depended on
what she told her mother. The frightened child knew that her

mother needed her in the big house. Maize vomited into the aluminium bathtub at the thought of entering that house ever again. Her thoughts drifted as she reflected on the shock of what had happened to her.

She kept squeezing her eyes as if block out the whole devastation, and she berated herself silently as she thought back to her casual conversation when she discovered that *he* had entered the attic.

Should I have been afraid? she thought. *Should I have expected some evil act to happen? But how could I have known he has evil in his heart.*

The last time I saw him, he was so attentive to his daughter and her wish to dress up. We were happy and laughing at the thought of what we might find. Is the line between good and evil truly as thin as a razor's edge?

Maize sobbed some more and berated herself. *For what?'* she thought, *I knew nothing of what he did to me, I am not a woman. How could I, in heavens name, have known he would violate me so.*

And as she gazed wearily around the tidy little room, which was a kitchen and sitting room combined. Her tearful eyes rested on the big black hearth which dwarfed the room by its dominance.

As she caught sight of the cast iron kettle, sitting on the fire rack, she knew instantly what she must do. It was her job, along with her brothers, to replace the water, at the end of the day; water that had been used each morning.

Every evening without fail, they would carry the big cast iron kettle out to the well; lower the brass pitcher, which hung by a thick rope, down into the well. It took three full pitchers to fill the kettle half way. They could only fill it half way because the kettle, when empty was already heavy.

It seemed that the gathering of water was an endless

chore; water to bathe the boys at bedtime, water to cook meals and wash dishes each evening, water to scrub the floors. Plus, water to wash *his* shirts and bed linens. When that kettle was less than half full Maize could not lift it alone, it was so heavy.

And now as she looked around the room she glared at that big black, cast iron kettle; knowing she had to do something. She bit her bottom lip as she recalled all the squealing they did as she and her brother's splash water on each other while pouring water into the empty vessel earlier that day.

On bath night, they would take pans to the well, fill them up with water, and then empty the water into the kettle, filling it half way. Maize knew the kettle was now practically empty since their morning wash and breakfast clean-up.

Mabel always left her kitchen spotless before she walked over to the big house to start her long and laborious day's work.

Once the idea crept into her head, the frightened girl had to act fast. If she hesitated for another moment or allowed her mind to wonder, she feared she would not be able to carry out her plan. This was the only solution she could fathom.

After drying herself off and putting on fresh clothes, she emptied the tub, one pan full at a time until it was light enough for her to drag it outside where she drained the remaining water on the flower beds. Maize re-entered the tiny house resigned to carry out her plan.

While the damp heat of the day hung oppressively in the midday air and the white clouds arched effortlessly away, Maize knew that her mother would soon return to prepare the midday meal.

Having emptied the tub, she now had to refill it, half way. By the time she had replaced the bathwater she had soaked her wretched body in and was exhausted.

"It's now or never." She sobbed.

Then she tried to dismiss all thoughts of the loathing, hatred, and betrayal overwhelming her.

The distraught child walked over to the hearth, stretched out both hands and picked up the kettle. With her eyes wide open she took a deep breath, raised her hands as far as she could and allowed the kettle to fall onto her left foot.

The agonizing pain blinded her momentarily. She instantly lifted both hands to her mouth to stifle her scream and she fell to the floor. She had no idea how much damage she had done to her foot, all she knew was that the pain was excruciating. She began to sob, but on hearing her own loud sobs, she held her breath.

Maize knew that her mother would soon return with her brothers to have lunch. She took a deep breath, and moments later she heard her mother tell the boys to gather some tomatoes.

"Only the red ones now, oh and some string beans, about a handful each, for tonight's dinner."

Upon entering the house, Mabel cried out when she saw her daughter curled up on the floor. Hearing their mother's cry, her sons dropped everything and ran back into the house.

"Momma I had a' accident." Maize lied to her mother for the very first time.

Before helping her daughter to their room and into the bed they shared; Mabel told the boys to carry on what they were doing. They looked surprised, but they obeyed their mother and returned to the garden.

"Momma, I had a' accident ..." Maize repeated, in a much softer voice.

It pained her to lie to her mother but she felt the need to protect her family.

39

– MAIZE'S DILEMMA –

KNOWING HOW PROTECTIVE MABEL WAS OF HER THREE children, Maize was afraid of what her mother would do if she told her of the devastating attack. She imagined her mother taking a knife and slitting his throat while he slept. Maybe she would use poison to put into one of her apple pies *he* loved so much. Or maybe, she would take one of his riffles that he kept in the shed and shoot *him*.

In the silence of her lonely room, confused and fearful, Maize watched through the torn window shade, as rain began to fall. The frightened child, feared not only what her mother would do if she found out, she also feared what would become of her and her little brothers. Maize knew how dependent her family was on *him* for the roof over their head and the food they ate.

Feeling drowsy, she wanted to sleep but fought to remain awake knowing that her mother was in the kitchen preparing lunch.

Maize selflessly decided that she could never tell her

mother what really happened to her as long as they lived under *his* roof.

Maize began to share her story of what happened with the kettle, but her mother interrupted her to send for Lilly, the local nurse who took care of all the Black families in the area. Lilly convinced Mabel that it was not too serious, and the swelling and bruising would go down in a couple of days, but the child must keep off her feet.

The nurse promised to look in on her in a day or so. Maize was feeling weary but was afraid to close her eyes in case she said something in her sleep. She knew she had to keep this deep, dark, and sinful secret to herself. Eventually, she allowed her mind to drift into sleep, but her subconscious mind took her back to church, one year ago. She remembered it was a Christmas Eve service.

In her mind's eye, she could see and hear the people as they walked past the nativity scene. Maize remembered hearing whispers about the three young girls in front of her. They were sisters, and each one had an extended belly. Maize struggled in her sleep as her unconscious mind reflected on that scene.

The two women behind her spoke in whispers; "That poor woman, it's bad enough when one daughter is knocked up by the master, but that dog raped all three of her daughters. All three of them gonna have babies at the same time. The youngest is only twelve."

Maize shot up in her bed and tried to make sense of that conversation. Her mother had not told her much about the 'birds and bees.'

But as she reflected on that day, she remembered the minister talking about the 'virgin birth of Christ.' She knew that the word 'virgin' meant pure because when her mother transplanted her plants, she told the children to dig up some fresh, clean earth.

She explained to them that the new deep earth was virgin because it was clean and had never been used to plant seeds. In her restlessness and inability to sleep, she contemplated all of this stored memory. Although it was not crystal clear, she was afraid.

The following morning, Mabel took breakfast in to her daughter. A bowl of hot, brown sugar oatmeal with chips of cinnamon in it from her garden; plus a slice of toast with her homemade blueberry jam spread on top, and a warm cup of milk.

Maize sat up in the bed and smiled. "Thank you, Momma, I feels much better today. I don't know how I … I must a tripped."

"Never you mind now, you need to rest that foot. Miss Lilly said nothing broke, just bruised real bad on your baby toe. You be up an' about after a few days, so rest. The boys is big enough to pitch in, if I need some help. I'll be fine, so you rest an, get better soon."

Maize burst into tears. Mabel reached over and hugged her daughter. She kissed the top of her head, and squeezed her daughter's hand then walked to the door.

"You rest now, you hear me. You can tell me later, what happened when you is feelin' better. Okay."

"Okay, Momma." Maize replied softly, lowering her eyes. She felt the pain of having to lie to her mother. Then her mother was gone.

The following day when Mabel took Maize her breakfast. She told her, "Things will be light at the house because *he* is goin' away for two weeks an' takin' Louisa with him".

Maize was already feeling so much better from all the

loving attention she was getting, but hearing this news made her smile. "I'm glad Momma, now you won't have so much work to do, it be like you on vacation too."

"Oh, I still got work to do baby but not as much like when they both under foot." Mabel smiled at her daughter. When she reached the door, she stopped short of leaving the room and turning back she said; "While you're laid up, you can sew on them tea towels I showed you."

Relieved, Maize smiled and was quick to agree, even though she hated the idea of sewing for a living.

Maize's relief was twofold, she was happy that her mother's daily work load would be lessened by the absence of the family and also because she could move about without fear of seeing *him.*

Feeling relieved, she began to hum knowing that she would not bump into him. Mabel smiled when she heard her daughter humming while still limping around the house and yard.

By the time Miss Louisa and her father returned, Maize's foot had healed completely.

Knowing when they were due to return, Maize had made a silent vow to avoid ever being in *his* presence alone, she didn't ever want to see his face again and she would do all in her power to avoid him.

40

– LOUISA AT THE PIANO –

AFTER ATTENDING A MOZART CONCERT WITH HER FATHER, FOR her fourteenth birthday, Louisa renewed her interest in playing the piano.

The twenty-or-so-year-old piano that once belonged to Louisa's mother had sat permanently covered in the grand parlor. Her mother had been a gifted pianist and a favorite student of Monsieur Oliver, the local music instructor, who delighted in teaching her before her untimely death.

Louisa's father bought *his* daughter a brand-new Spinet Piano, but because of sentimental memories he didn't have the heart to part with his wife's piano, he had it delivered to the cottage.

Mabel saw no value in the huge wooden box which took up far too much room in their already overcrowded tiny house.

Maize however, was instantly drawn to the ebony and ivory keys having heard so many wonderful sonatas floating from the big house, wafting into her ears, as the Belgian instructors played several short pieces on the new piano.

Maize would listen-from a short, yet unreachable distance, as her abuser's daughter's piano instructor both played and attempted to teach *his* tone-deaf daughter on her brand new piano.

As Maize lay in bed unable to empty her mind, pondering what had happened to her. It was hard for her to believe, after years of running in and out of *his* house; playing peek a boo, hop scotch, and many other childish games, first as a little girl with his young daughter and then as adolescent girls together, that he could see her as anything other than a child still.

That he could regard me, as if seeing me for the first time and think nothing of me, truly amazed me. How callous that he could devour me without a thought or care as to who I am; as innocent as his own daughter.

He has watched me grow as he did his own daughter; I was just as innocent and naive as his precious daughter; just entering into puberty.

The tears, fears, and the pain were of no concern of his lust. He demonstrated indifference and contempt. And with the savage destruction of her innocence, this immature adolescent girl was consumed with a new fear.

No longer was she the little girl who would wander freely, picking the odd wild flower, or climbing a tree to look down on the world as she saw it.

He ravaged her body, when he savagely robbed her, first of her innocence, her dignity, and ultimately her pride. She was no longer a virgin. *He* alone removed her sparkling smile and her ability to sleep peacefully at night.

Several months passed before she could dream soundly or wake refreshed. Now with the loss of her innocence, a strange new maturity took control of her mind; her thoughts were of her mother.

Knowing how vulnerable her family was, she would have

to shield her mother from the devastation she had endured. She knew how much her mother loved her and how she longed to provide a better life for her children than she had experienced herself.

Maize was her mother's firstborn child, her only daughter and she held a special place in her heart. Consumed with rage, shock and humiliation, Maize feared what her mother would do if she was to tell her.

"Oh God!" she whispered what should I do?"

With all this weighing heavily on her adolescent heart, Maize carried the burden of the crime committed against her in silence.

41

– MAIZE AT THE PIANO –

AND SO, IT WAS HER ATTACKER WHO, INADVERTENTLY PROVIDED the therapy she needed to heal, from the despicable shame and humiliating memory of his attack.

Slowly and over time, Maize began to recognize the calming power that music provided, and the more she played, the more cognizant she become of the therapeutic nature of music.

Ironic that the only means she had to overcome the horrific nightmares that *he* created, both sleeping and awake, was music. The creator of her bad dreams was the one who provided her, unknowingly, the therapy she required to help heal her body and mind.

In a very short time, Maize could play all of the pieces Monsieur Oliver was playing and with as much clarity, dexterity, and passion as the master himself. The keys on this piano - considered too old and dilapidated for *his* precious daughter - became the instrument, that helped to minimize the trauma; thus enabling her to heal.

Before fleeing from her home at age fifteen, Maize spent every available minute playing the tunes she heard Louisa play on her brand-new piano.

The music that Maize heard and began to play, took her to another place and time; a place where she and her family were not *his* property; a place that was soft and warm and beautiful, like the clouds on a bright, sunny day moving slowly across the perfect blue sky. Soon she was playing with passion and drive.

One evening, after desperately trying to teach his student the beginning chords of Chopin's Prelude, the frustrated instructor finished the piece himself. His disappointment and aggravation was visible and he left Miss Louisa in tears.

Monsieur Charles Oliver, the most sought-after piano instructor in the district and he left *his* house once more with a heavy heart. He had tried many times to tell the child's father that Louisa had no real desire, let alone talent, when it came to playing the piano.

Oliver recognized that the child wanted to please her papa, but it was clear she did not have her mother's gift. He left the house, after each lesson, feeling frustrated and annoyed.

Annoyed, because of time wasted, he walked down the long pathway to his buggy, shaking his head from side to side. He was so perturbed, while unhitching his horse from the old Oak tree in a hurry, keen to return home and relax.

The Belgian piano instructor, annoyed for having wasted his time, placed his right hand on the rains as he stepped into his two seated carriage.

However, while releasing the horses reigns from the oak tree, he was startled to hear his own rendition of Chopin's Prelude being played, as perfectly as he himself, had played it, just moments before.

He was awe struck at the quality of the rendition; the

timing, the flow and the ease of the player's fingers on the keys. So, without thinking, he began walking in the direction of this wonderful, melodious sound.

It was not until he was standing in front of the shabby little cottage that he realized he had walked right into the yard of the housekeeper. Confused, he started to walk away. "This cannot be," he said out loud.

He looked about him to determine in which direction the music was flowing from, when he heard the beginning chords of Beethoven's piano sonata # 8 in C minor and followed the music.

"Impossible!" he almost screamed. He took another step forward and banged on the door.

The music stopped and Maize opened the door. She sucked in her breath when she saw the little white man standing in front of her. He wore a brown felt hat on his head and a beige raincoat draped over his arm, which almost touched the ground. In the left lapel of his brown velvet jacket, just barely visible, was a white rose in the left boutonnière.

This little man who Maize had never seen before held a pair of brown gloves in his right hand and repeatedly hit his right thigh with them. Maize had never seen a man beat on himself before and thought he must be mad.

And as she had never seen this man before, she felt sick to her stomach, fearing that *he* had sent him to fetch her. Fear crossed her face and she stepped back from the door.

"Where is that music coming from?" He demanded to know as he stretched his neck beyond the girl and looked into the house, seeing Mabel come towards the door now too.

"That be my daughter here Maize," said Mabel from behind her daughter. "I keeps telling her to tone it down or close it up 'cos folks need to sleep. I's sorry for disturb-"

"What! This child, played that music, on this old piano! Who has been teaching her? Oh, this is too much! I need to sit down."

Mr. Oliver pushed past Maize and her mother and walked into the tidy but humble little house. He found a seat and sat down.

"Water please?" he said, as he removed his wide-brimmed hat and began to fan his face with it.

"Sit," he commanded and Maize sat again at the old piano. "Play me something."

Maize lifted her hands, hovering over the keys until she thought of something and began to play.

Finally, he waved his hands for her to stop. "You have no sheet music?"

"No, Sir. I just listen and then play what I hear."

Monsieur Oliver was truly amazed and could not believe that Maize had never had a lesson in her life, formal or otherwise. He told Mabel that her child was a musical genius, a prodigy.

"With the proper training, this talented and gifted child could play on the world's stage."

Maize's mother laughed. 'Mr.," she said, picking up a basket full of laundry, "We can't even pay off our grocery bill each month, so don't make me laugh. Goodnight to you, Sir." She walked away basket in hand, mumbling to herself, "World stage, ha." She left the man sitting in her faded, rocking chair, still fanning himself.

The little man eventually stood up. He walked toward the front door where Maize was standing, her mouth slightly open in disbelief at what she just heard.

"Am I really good Mr.?" she said in a whisper.

"My dear child, you are more than good, your musical

ability is superb almost as pure … as, as, it's … why it's astounding, my dear child. I have taught music to some of the world's … dear me, I am truly amazed, stunned. I must go, but you will hear from me in due course. Yes, you will hear from me."

Before leaving, he turned back, looking around the shabby but spotless little house. "You must have professional training," he said almost breathlessly.

Then he took out a card from his vest pocket and wrote some words on the back of it.

"Think about what I have said, you are gifted and with the right training you will become a brilliant and accomplished pianist, take my word for it. You should be in New York at the Juilliard Academy. If I can arrange it, you will go there.

Hold on to this card and if you ever go to New York, go to the Academy and demand an audition. Mention my name; in the meantime, I will do all that I can to promote you and your genius. Goodnight, dear child."

Maize was still in a dream-like state as she began to shut the door after him; and then he stopped, turned again to face her and placed his hand against the closing door. He looked at her, as no other person had before.

"Tell me dear child; where do you go? I mean, where is your mind? No, no, no. I mean … dear me, I mean what are you thinking about when you play these pieces? Where does your mind take you; do you close your eyes, are you standing or sitting I need … where are you? You don't even read music … so, I need to know."

"Mr." She replied, "I don't ever close my eyes, but I go *far* away to a *safe* place where I can't be hurt no more, by no one. I go up through the clouds. Sometimes, I sink down to the bottom of the lake. I just let the music take me where it wants me to go. I know that sounds daft an' I ain't never said that to no one before," she said, lowering her head shyly.

"Value your gift,' he said, and he was gone.

That, funny talkin' little ol' man, must think I'm cracked, an' he must be cracked too, Maize thought. *Me in New York, now that makes my dream to leave this place real puny.*

Five months later, Maize received her very first letter in the mail. It was from Monsieur Oliver, there were two ten dollar bills, the first she had ever seen, and they were both for her.

My dear child,

As promised, along with this note is a bus ticket to New York and $20 plus an invitation to audition at the world-renowned Juilliard Academy of Music.
The ticket is for one way, because I know that with genius as rare as yours, you will be accepted on a full scholarship. One day you can repay me by sending me tickets to your first professional performance.
May God bless you and guide you on your journey.

Your musical admirer,
Monsieur Charles Oliver

Overwhelmed with both fear and excitement; Maize hid the letter, sharing this great but frightening news with no one. She needed time to allow the excitement of this short correspondence to seep into her soul and absorb it into her mind. At last, she had found a way to be free of *him.* "Maybe now I can be free to be me," she said out loud, and her daydreams took her to a distant shore.

Maize had not told her mother, about *him* having his way,

with her. Partly because of the threat to kick their family out if she told anyone.

Maize knew her mother was trapped and was doing the very best she could under the circumstances for their fatherless family. However, as trapped as they were, Maize feared what the outcome would be, if her mother ever found out, that her boss, the man whose house her family lives in, had raped her only daughter.

Living in fear of him attacking her again was a reality and she would do all in her power to avoid being alone in his presence.

42

– THE SINFUL EVENT REVEALED –

EARLY, ONE FRIDAY EVENING ALMOST TWO YEARS AFTER Maize's nightmare experience, Mabel was in the process of cleaning the oven in the main house after she finished cooking their evening meal.

She was all set to go home when Mr. Newcomb walked into the tidied kitchen, a big grin on his face. "I hope you made one of your apple pies for dessert, Mabel."

The overworked mother of three was tired and agitated, because his request came too late in the day.

She sighed deeply as she bundled up the dirty kitchen linen. "Too late. I can't use the oven because it's covered in the cleaning solution an' as you can see," she said while raising the bundle of dirty laundry, "tonight is laundry night."

"Oh darn, Mabel I had a taste of your apple pie on my mind all the way home.

"Well Sir, I made you a nice bread puddin' just like you likes it with raisins an' cinnamon-"

"But I promised my guest," he cut her off. "You know Mr.

Bill, he is the one who made the request. You know your apple pies are famous," he said with a chuckle.

"Well, then am gon'a have to make them in my oven."

"Good gal; I knew I could count on you. You can send the gal over with them, since I can see this is your big wash night."

Mabel packed up all the ingredients for three pies, two for Mr. and Missy and one for her family and headed to her cottage to make them.

Maize was playing the piano, she felt so free whenever she sat there playing one of her many favorite pieces.

When the pies were taken out of the oven, an hour later, Mabel told Maize to wait about half an hour before taking the pies over to the big house.

"Give one to Timmy to carry an' you carry one."

Maize wanted to beg her mother to take them herself but she was busy washing all the linens from the big house; clothes she washed every Monday evening in her own wooden bathtub.

Her mother had called her from the kitchen where she was ironing *his* shirts and Miss Louisa's petticoats.

"Go wrap them up, your brother can carry one. Walk careful now, so they don't get all smashed up."

They began to get ready, grateful that the evening was still light. The full moon was beginning its decline and the warm air was filled with the fragrance of the two lilac bushes her mother had planted, when she first moved into the tiny house.

Maize and her brother were about to leave the house when there was a knock on the door, Timmy and his sister looked at each other silently, wondering who it could be before Maize opened the front door.

When Maize saw, who was standing on her doorstep, holding a box of chocolates, cold chills ran down her spine.

She looked at Buster, *his* stable hand. He said nothing and handed Maize a note and the box, then he turned and walked away, he never said a word to her.

The note read:

These sweet chocolates are just right for a sweet gal like you.

Maize felt sick in her stomach, she sat the pie down on the piano bench and ran out to the outhouse and threw up; she knew what *he* wanted. Filled with repulsion, anger and fear; she decided it was time to tell her mother why she refused to take over her freshly baked fruit pies.

After hearing her daughter's agonizing account of what *he* did to her innocent child, Mabel let out a deep guttural scream then doubled over in two, as if she had been savagely kicked in the abdomen. When she stood up, she wrapped her arms around herself and wept bitterly.

Maize looked on helplessly and wept with her mother. She wept not just for herself but for the pain she knew this caused her mother. She knew deep down that there was nothing her mother could do to stop *him* from having *his* way with her.

By telling her mother of the ugly nightmare, which had been eating away at her for such a long time, Maize had removed the burden of the despicable secret. Until then she had kept silent, for what seemed forever. She no longer held the key to the terrifying secret in silence.

Having told her mother, she had finally opened the door to the dark and filthy dungeon, she had been forced into. Maize felt sure that by sharing this information with her mother, significant changes would have to be made, not only for herself but for her mother and two young brothers; and she was afraid.

While still crying, her mother, who was now consumed with anger, fear and betrayal, reached out for Maize and she held her by the shoulders and started to shake her. She screamed out through her painful sobs.

"Why didn't you tell me, baby? Why you kept this thing to yourself ? We gon leave this place TONIGHT! You hear me child, we gon leave this place and that nasty devil man."

Her mother picked up one of *his* white shirts from her laundry basket waiting to be ironed; she blew her nose on it, and then she wiped her eyes. She looked at Maize and told her to go to bed.

"I got to think what to do baby an' I needs time to think."

Mabel didn't know what she would do, but she knew she would have to do something. Confronting him would be her daughter's word against his, and she knew he would deny his ugly deed; so, what to do?

"I'll take the darn pies over," she mumbled to herself.

On the pretense that she ran out of laundry soap, she returned to the big house and took the pies with her. She placed them on the kitchen counter and yelled in to him, that she dropped the pies off because she needed to get more soap from the cellar for the laundry.

Her employer and landlord walked out of the dining room and looked askance. She was holding a big bar of lye soap.

"I left this behind when I left out, sorry to disturb, I brought the pies. Goodnight again, Sir," Mabel said, as she held her composure long enough to leave the kitchen. Her stomach was in knots and she vomited on the driveway.

After wiping her mouth on her, jacket sleeve, she mumbled to herself, "My God, will our lives ever be our own?"

Maize was anxious the whole time her mother was gone; which was only a few minutes, but it seemed like an eternity.

She was afraid of what her mother would say or do, she feared her mother would confront *him*. She was afraid her mother and little brothers would lose their home She, at least, had one option.

"Momma," she cried, when her mother returned.

She was relieved, given her mother's anger and outrage when she had left the house. Before walking into the bedroom, she reminded her mother of the little foreign speaking man who was Miss Louisa's piano instructor, and of the night he came to the house.

Before, her mother could respond, Maize walked over to the piano and retrieved the little tin box from its hiding place. Maize had kept it buried at the bottom of the piano bench. With trembling hands, the frightened child produced the letter and handed it to her mother to read. Full of rage and at the same time, very much afraid, the devastated mother read the letter her daughter had kept secret.

Mabel was both afraid and sad at the thought of her young daughter in New York. Genuinely concerned, Maize and mother sat up for hours crying, talking, planning, and hugging each other.

Maize tried to convince her mother, by reiterating, many times that she alone was the victim; that she alone needed to escape the lust of the evil landlord and employer they worked for.

Mabel was weary and she knew her daughter was tired as well, so she sent her to bed again.

"I got's to think on this baby; you go on now an' get some rest."

"Okay, Momma," she said softly, "but where can we go if he throws us out. You and the boys are safe here, it's just me," she whispered.

Her mother sighed deeply. "Go to bed baby, I just got to think on this some more. You get some sleep an' we'll talk in the mornin'.

Maize kissed her mother goodnight then walked with her head down, into the bedroom they had shared for most of her life; but she did not sleep. Her mind was in a whirlwind as she tossed and turned in the bed, the bed that made her feel secure, knowing her mother was always lying next to her while she slept.

She did not want to leave her family; she adored her mother, her brothers, even her home. Maize sobbed into her pillow. Maize sobbed because she was so afraid of her mother's boss, the man who provided a roof over her family's head.

As much as Maize feared leaving her home and her family, she realized that her leaving would be the best solution for herself and her family.

And all the while, she prayed that the letter she had hidden from her mother was not a hoax; that the Belgian piano instructor was indeed sincere.

43

– PLANNING MAIZE'S ESCAPE –

ANGRY AND AFRAID, MABEL RE-READ HER DAUGHTER'S LETTER and after reading it for the fifth time, she wept some more. However, these were not tears of rage; they were tears of sadness.

Mabel did not want her daughter to leave her; to go to such a strange place all alone. She had told Maize when she first read the letter that she was 'way too young to be going so far away to such a big, fast city like New York'.

But Maize had shared her fears with her mother, not so much for herself but for her family. She knew how hard it would be for them to just pick up and leave; they had no relatives who could take them in. They had no money to rent even one room.

After a while, she went to check on her daughter, for what she feared would be the last time. Mabel was consumed with so many emotions sadness, anger and fear, but she was able to control her sobs while her daughter slept.

For now, the broken-hearted mother needed distance from

her first-born child, her one and only daughter, who was very precious to her; she needed space and time in order to think more clearly.

As she turned to leave the room again, her throat closed around her emotions and she struggled to hold back the tears.

Deep down, she knew that the letter her daughter shared with her, was a Godsend. It was the answer to their dilemma.

While her children slept, Mabel's tormented mind, finally settled on a plan to remove her daughter from the wicked clutches of that evil, sinful violator of her daughter's innocence.

It was in the wee hours of the morning when Mabel, tormented and afraid, crept into the tiny bedroom and turned up the gas light. Bending down, she gently shook her daughter to wake her.

"I ain't asleep, Momma," the distraught child said softly. Trying to appear calm, as she wiped her eyes swollen from crying.

"Come baby, we gots to move quick and quiet while it still dark out. I don't want to wake the boys."

Maize sat up in the bed, "Why Momma? What...."

"Hush child," her momma said, putting her index finger to her closed lips.

Maize was puzzled but she obeyed her mother. Mabel fetched a large bag from underneath the bed. Maize opened her mouth to speak but her mother put her finger up to her mouth again.

"Shh." Mabel shooed her confused and precious daughter out of the room. Then she gathered what few clothes her daughter had and put all of her possessions into the only piece of luggage they had ever owned.

After leaving the bedroom, Mabel walked her bewildered

daughter away from the back of the house, through the kitchen area and over to the piano bench.

She sat down, inhaled deeply to conceal her emotions, her anxiety, and her fear, Then with a firm demeanor, she sat by her precious daughter on the piano bench and took her hands firmly.

Mabel resolved to do whatever it took to protect her precious daughter. With an attitude of determined resolution, she cleared her throat. She began to share her cautious plan with her frightened child.

Maize was both terrified and relieved at the same time; she had no idea of what lay ahead for her, but she knew she would be far away from the clutches of the demon who had raped her.

She handed Maize the packed bag, all the while telling her of the plan she came up with to save her before *he* came looking for her again.

Fighting back her own tears, Mabel shared the deep concerns she had for her only daughter moving to such a big and crowded city like New York, all alone. Like so many people in the rural south, stories abound from locals who visited big northern cities, most of them negative.

However, Mabel's deeper concern, her greatest fears were pivotal to where she was right there, where they lived and worked. She felt as helpless as her daughter, having no rights to confront or protest her daughter's abuser.

44

– THE TERRIFYING ESCAPE –

WHILE THE MOON HOVERED IN THE NIGHT SKY, MABEL decided to make their escape. "It will take close to two hours or more to reach the bus station, we'll have to walk fast to reach the end of the property and then we can slow down a pace. Take off your shoes baby; I want you to wear mine."

"But, Momma," Maize said, incredulously, half laughing and elevating her voice, "I can't fit your shoes 'cos they way too big for me."

"Hush baby," her mother said, putting her index finger to her lips. "I know baby," she whispered, "but the road is rough an' we got a long way to go. You can wear two pairs of thick socks to pad your feets. Now, tie your shoelaces together so you can wear them around your neck. Here put this piece of velvet under them an' your coat collar, so the strings don't hurt your neck."

"Thank you, Momma," Maize said, half choking on her words, "but what about you? You gots to walk there an' back again, ain't your feets gon' be sorer than mine?"

"Don't you worry 'bout me baby, ol' man Mosley be drivin' that ol' horse n cart bout the time I be on my way back. Come on now, if we gon' catch that first mornin' bus."

"Momma, what about the boys, they be scared if we both gone when they wakes up?"

"I be back in time; don't you fret none; Momma knows what she doin' baby."

It was past midnight when mother and daughter stole away, in the dead of night. It was pitch black out. Just ahead of them, as they half walked and ran; the crescent moon came out of hiding from behind the winter clouds. Like a heavenly torch; shining just enough light to guide them on their way.

Mabel hoped that they would arrive in time to catch the early morning bus. She also prayed that God would guide her to a safe companion who would direct her daughter to the institute.

Breathlessly running several steps ahead of her daughter; the distraught mother also prayed that she would return home before the boys woke up. They ran along the unpaved road as fast as they could; Maize had a hard time keeping up with her mother who was yards ahead of her.

As they ran, Maize was worried and scared. Scared because she didn't know what to expect in New York and she had no idea how she would find the school.

I'll be there all by myself, she thought, not wanting to worry her mother any more than she was already. *An' I don't know a soul in that big city.*

Maize's head was overflowing with frightening thoughts for herself and for her family she would be leaving behind.

"Come child," her mother whispered, as she beckoned her daughter to catch up. "Not too far now, just a few more steps, then, we can slow down a pace."

Once they passed the open area, they continued their journey in silence, Mabel reached for her daughter's hand and they walked hand in hand along the edge of the fields towards town; both praying all the way that no one would see them or stop them.

The road ahead was very rough under foot, mostly gravel; Maize was grateful for the padding from the extra pair of thick socks.

Feeling the full effect of her mother's sacrifice and eternal love, Maize raised her mother's hand to her lips and kissed it.

As she did, Mabel felt the warmth of her daughter's tears on the back of her hand; instantly, the bereft mother took in a deep breath and held it, in order to hold back her own sobs.

45

– ARRIVAL AT THE BUS STATION –

IT WAS THE WEE HOURS OF THE MORNING WHEN THEY FINALLY reached the bus station and they were both exhausted. Plus, Mabel's feet were in very bad shape. However, they were both grateful that they had arrived unseen.

Immediately, Mabel began scanning the room for two seats. When finally she spotted two unoccupied, she nudged her daughter over to them. She double-checked the one-way ticket to New York was in Maize's bag then followed her daughter to the seats while glancing at the passengers who were seated in the segregated area for New York marked 'Negros Only'.

When she returned to her seat, Mabel engaged her frightened daughter in light conversation while rubbing her child's sore feet. Her own feet were in a far worse condition and she still had to take the same rough trail back home, to her sleeping boys. All of her energy, however, was focused on her daughter.

Maize was clearly wincing in pain but eagerly and selfishly, accepting her mother's care and love, without hesitation. While resting first one foot and then the other in her mother's lap, she began to relax as the pain slowly subsided under the gentle but firm massaging of her momma's hands.

And as she relaxed under her mother's loving hands, Maize began to reflect on the thoughts she had while frantically running away. The excitement and thrill of escape, she experienced while desperately fleeing, from the home she loved. Maize's thoughts were ablaze with sadness, gratitude, and anger and fear.

This new fear, was nowhere near as scary as the nightmare she had experienced over and over when visions of the evil attack emerged. Time had not erased her fear or her self-loathing and she desperately hoped that distance would rectify those emotions.

Maize loved her mother and her two little brothers so she feared for them. *What if?* she thought continuously.

And, as if her mother was reading her thoughts, she started tickling her daughter's feet causing her to curl up in laughter. Mabel felt her daughter's sorrow as her own heart ached. She fought hard to stem the flow of tears destined to fall later.

"We Gon' Be All right," her mother said with emphasis. "A'm gone miss you, Momma."

"I know baby an' am gone miss you more. But the good Lord got us safely out a there an' He will watch over us. We ain't the ones who sinned, so you just empty your head of all that worry.

Now, I gots to find you someone to keep you company on your trip. Now Maize, just in case I can't find a good woman or family for you to sit with who is willin' to see you on your way to that big music school … are you listening Maize?

"Yes Momma!"

"Well I want you to look for a nice, big catholic church, cos they never close they doors not even at night. In the mornin', ask someone how to get to that school. Remember you only gots those two ten dollar notes. You can ride the tramcar to the school but otherwise, save as much as you can."

Mabel's began to scan the waiting-room's passengers sitting in the 'colored area' for the bus to New York. Maize observed her mother as she focused on the people sitting behind them.

Curious, Maize turned her head to see what her mother was so intently looking at behind her.

"Momma, we don't know no one here an' you gots to get back to the boys 'fore they wakes up scared cos' we both gone and left them all alone."

"Hush baby, Momma knows what she's doin'."

"But what is you doin', Momma?"

"Be still baby, Momma gona let you know, when I know. I ain't gone let you go to that big city all by your own self, not if I can help it.

Aha," she said smiling, "I think I found what I'm lookin' for baby, Momma will be right back. A'm, goin' over yonder to talk to that lady with the pretty hat on her head."

"But who is she-"

"Maize girl, just sit still and don't you move. I be right back, baby."

Maize stayed put but certainly not still as she visibly followed her mother walking to the end of the second row. Bewildered, she saw her mother stop in front of the nicely dressed older woman. Maize could just about hear what they were saying.

"Excuse me Ma'am, is you travelin' to New York?" said her mother.

"Yes, I am."

"Well, ma'am my name is Mabel an' my daughter over yonda' is Maize."

"Yes, I see her," said the woman, "do you need help?" Mabel's eyes welled up.

Clearly struck by her tears, the woman looked at her with sympathy. "There, there, now." She patted the seat next to her again. "Please, sit here."

Mabel sat down and wiped her tears with the back of her hand. "I'm sorry, I didn't mean to cry, it's just that I have to get my daughter to a safe place, tonight away from ..."

Her voice dropped too low for Maize to hear the next part but she watched the two women until her mother's voice rose again, fierce with pride.

"My baby play piano an' she has a place at that big music school in New York. But I got two little boys at home, they sleepin, an' I gots to get back 'fore they wakes up."

"My dear, God has guided you to me. My name is Elizabeth Martin, I am the wife of the late Reverend, Doctor Joseph Martin; and I'm the choir director at his church, I teach piano and voice.

I will be happy to take your daughter into New York and I will accompany her on her first interview. Rest assured, your little girl will be safe with me.

I too was raised on a plantation, here in the South and I know of such things. Memories of that time, unspeakable memories, well they may fade with time, but ..." Mrs. Martin sighed deeply.

Then she said to the weeping and desperate mother, "I know of your pain, my dear. Send your daughter over to me and I will take care of her and see to it that she keeps her appointment."

Then after a few moments, Mrs. Martin patted the empty seat on the other side of her.

Mabel was so moved by the woman's compassion, she was unable to silence her sobs.

"Please my dear, rest assured that your daughter will be in my good care all the way to New York and I will make it my business to keep in touch with her. I will take her to church with me every Sunday."

"We couldn't ask you to do that. I have nothing to repay your kindness Mrs. Martin."

"There, there now." Mrs. Martin patted Mabel's hand. "I am more than happy to help her escape the horrors that loom over her."

Tears ran down Mabel's face as she hugged the woman and thanked her profusely.

"There, there. Now, we should get in line early so that we can get a double seat and sit together, and I'm sure your daughter will want to sit by a window. May God be with you on your journey home."

Mabel stood and pulled Maize against her chest tightly. "Oh baby, God is good, an' she a good Christian woman an' she play the piano as well for her church. Go now, so you can get a seat together. I got to get back to the boys."

"Oh Momma, you done good, I be fine now," Maize said, as reassuringly as she could.

She squeezed her daughter again tightly, kissed her then turned and walked away. Mrs. Martin took Maize's hand, she squeezed it gently but firmly, and then they walked hand in hand over to the bus line.

The African American passengers waited patiently while

the driver collected all the tickets from the white passengers. After they were all seated, he placed their luggage into the storage compartment under the bus. Then he proceeded to take the black passengers' tickets. He threw their luggage into the storage area; before allowing them to board the bus.

Maize rushed to the very back of the bus to secure the last seats so that she could sit next to her new friend. She also wanted to look out of the rear window for a final glance of her mother before she hurried home to her two sleeping boys.

The teenager fought back the tears of mixed emotions that swarmed around in her head. When she saw her mother, she smiled a final farewell. Her mother smiled back and waved at her only daughter, and then, she turned away to begin her long and arduous journey homeward.

46

– MABEL'S JOURNEY HOME –

WITH SO MUCH ON HER MIND SHE DIDN'T HAVE TIME TO THINK about her own sore feet. However, after taking just a few steps on the rough concrete road as she made a final farewell to her daughter, Mabel knew she would never make it home, not in the state that her feet were in.

Conscious that her daughter would still be looking out of the window; Mabel waited for the bus to leave before she returned to the bus station.

She was grateful when she saw an empty seat outside the building, the wooden bench was cold and damp with the early morning dew, but she sat down on it anyway.

Then she reached into her jacket pocket and pulled out the pair of thick woollen socks she had loaned to Maize to wear. As she pulled off each one of her shoes, she could see the damage all that walking had done. Both of her shoes were worn out; in fact, they were split clean across the outer soles. Mabel said a silent prayer that she would make it home. The shoes she had given to Maize to wear were in just as bad shape as the ones she was wearing.

Tired and cold, she had no idea her feet were in such bad shape, but she knew she had to keep going to get home before the boys woke up.

So, she started praying as soon as she left the station, she asked God for another miracle. "Please God," she said, "I need just one more miracle, let my feet last 'till I makes it home. "This, the only other miracle I need God, but I needs it bad."

It was dark out and the moon was taking shelter behind the winter clouds. However, fear and caution kept the desperate mother looking back to make sure no one was following her. Mabel was very tired and her feet, she was sure were bleeding by now. As if hearing her own mother's voice, telling her as a child, that there was healing medicine in almost everything that grows in God's earth.

Whenever she had a cut or a scraped knee, her mother would go outside and pick leaves from a tree and place them on the cut. Desperate for help, Mabel stopped at a clearing just at the end of the main road, nothing but farmland and tobacco fields ahead.

She reached into the field and broke off two large tobacco leaves; she also spotted wild aloe vera. After pulling at the plant, she revealed the creamy substance. She squeezed it out and spread it on the large leaves, she then replaced the second pair of socks that Maize had worn as her original socks were now in shreds.

Mabel pulled her thick socks over the leaves and squeezed her feet into the worn-out shoes. She prayed the thick tobacco leaves would work to ease the pain in both of her feet, enabling her to walk the rest of the way home.

As she walked along the deserted lane, Mabel wondered what life would be like in New York for her baby. She was a deeply religious woman and as she walked on the unpaved road, she sent up more prayers for Mrs. Martin, the angel of mercy they had desperately needed.

Suddenly, from out of nowhere a man's voice interrupted her thoughts. "Whoa there; I say, who is dat walkin' out this hour o' da night?"

Startled, Mabel froze at the voice that came from out of nowhere. There were no lights, and she could barely see her surroundings, petrified, she held her breath.

Her first thought was that her boss, the violator of her little girl's innocence, had sent someone to fetch them back.

She stopped dead in her tracks, she wanted to run but she was too exhausted; instead she froze and held her breath. Within minutes, a wagon pulled up alongside of her.

"Do you need help?"

Instantly, she recognized the voice, it was old Mr. Siros Mosley, and the petrified woman wept in relief at seeing him. Siros was an elder in the church she attended regularly, he was a wise old man and highly respected by all who knew him. As he drove Mabel home, she told him of the sorry events that led up to her being in that place at that time of the morning.

"You did right Mrs." It was all he said.

By the time he arrived at her door, he had to wake her up. She apologized for dozing off.

"You is home now, be safe an' be sure you take care of your feets, I'll bring by some wild honey later, 'cos' it's good for cut feet." And he went on his way to work.

The hour was late when she crept into her tiny house. Worried, weary, and exhausted, she overslept. Her sons had to wake her up. They wanted to know why their mother overslept; concerned she might be ailing. They also wanted to know where their sister was.

"Your sister's gone away, she be in a safe place, away from Mr. who was doin' her wrong, now that's all you need to know. Now, fetch me the basin an' one cup of hot water an' one cup of cold water; I need to soak my feets, they swelled up on me. Then bring me some honey butter, gauze, some thick socks, a tea towel, an' six of them rug rags an' my scissors from my mendin' basket."

The boys looked at each other puzzled, but they obeyed their mother without question. After she cleansed and treated her feet, the stinging began to subside and the soreness was slowly dissipating.

Mabel was late going to work, another first for her and because her feet were still tender she took the short cut to the big house; this was another first. As difficult as it was for her to walk, her anger gave her the fury to be defiant. Not once during all the years she had lived on *his* estate did she venture to take this shortcut from her little cabin.

It was just a stone's throw from the big house; separated only by a narrow gravel road and the stately manicured green lawns. This was one of *his* many unspoken rules, but she knew all the same. She smiled inwardly as she trespassed, not only on his lawn but against his implied orders. Treading the narrow gravel drive was very painful. But had she taken her usual route, the rough, graveled road, which extended the length and breadth of those manicured lawns and led directly to the kitchen door; well she knew she would never have made it. She had her sons carry her damaged shoes to the handyman Simon, to fix them for her.

He never once inquired about Maize's absence.

47

– MAIZE ON THE BUS –

STILL GAZING OUT OF THE BUS WINDOW, MAIZE'S HOT SALTY tears continued to flow. She prayed that the pregnant clouds, which seemed to be gloating over her head, would not give birth to the anticipated thunderstorm before her mother returned home.

Maize's fear of leaving, was coupled with the fear she felt for her mother, once he realized that she had left. She was more afraid for them, than she was for herself; not knowing what lay ahead of her in that huge city of New York.

Just as the bus pulled out, Maize asked her new guardian angel to pray for her mother's safe return home and for her two little brothers. Halfway through the prayer, Maize fell asleep. Her new friend and guardian also slept.

When Maize woke up, sometime later, her head was on Mrs. Martin's lap. Not quite conscious of where she was, it took her a minute or two to focus. She jumped up and apologized to the smiling woman.

"I'm so glad you were able to sleep, my dear. Why don't

you stand up and stretch your legs." Maize did as she was asked.

It was a very long journey. When Mrs. Martin woke up from one of her naps, sometime later, she saw her charge looking out of the window. She also saw Maize's tear stained face reflected in the glass. She gently placed her hand on the child's shoulder.

"There, there my dear, I know you must be sad having to leave your loving mother and little brothers, but you are safe now and your mother's mind is at peace."

"I know," said Maize, "but I'm gonna miss my momma, my little brothers, and my home. I was so happy there for half of my life." Maize sighed deeply. "What makes men so evil, are all men evil?" she asked while fresh tears spilled over her cheek.

Mrs. Martin took out a fresh, lace trimmed handkerchief from her handbag and dabbed at Maize's tears.

"No, my dear, not all men are evil, but some men are and for those who are evil, or commit evil deeds, their punishment is yet to come, be it in this world or in the next. And so, my dear, in order to heal, you must rid your mind of those agonizing and humiliating thoughts of the evil act that was committed against you. If you dwell on having been victimized, by that sinful, wicked man, you will succumb to a deep depression that will eventually render you powerless and your mother's sacrifice will have been in vain. So, you must rescue the sweet, innocent, and I understand gifted child that you are."

Still looking very pensive, Maize said, "But what can I do to get rid of the ugly, dirty ..."

"You pinch yourself hard, say a prayer out loud in order to drown out the memory. You sit at the piano and immerse yourself, using the gift that God has bestowed on you. Play until your heart is overflowing with the music you have been gifted."

Maize's heart was overflowing with so many emotions. She wiped away her tears, then hugged Mrs. Martin and as she felt the loving warmth of her benefactor's embrace, the reason for her tears shifted.

"Thank you," Maize said; from the bottom of her heart.

She was as weary as she was sleepy; she had not slept well and was unable to retire her conscious mind. Her eyes were swollen from so much crying; but once more she drifted off to sleep.

When Maize awoke for the second time, it was still very dark outside, but she could see something bright in the distance. "Are they lights down yonder? She asked, "Is we nearly there?

"Yes, child those are the lights in the city but we still have a distance to go before we reach the terminal."

Ten or so minutes later, Maize pulled her face away from the window and asked excitedly. "Are we close yet to New York?"

"Yes child, we will soon arrive at the bus terminal, and we will be under all those distant lights you can just barely see." As she said this, she saw the joy fade from Maize's face.

"Come dear and take your seat. We will arrive soon at the terminal; I will take us home so that you can have a decent sleep in a comfortable bed. Tomorrow morning, I will take you to your school. How does that sound?"

Maize's eyes filled with tears once again. "You are so kind Mrs. Martin, to take such good care of me, a stranger; Momma will be so happy when I tell her how you looked after me, Ma'am.' She sighed deeply.

"So much excitement all in one day, my first bus ride and now my first taxi ride, I will remember this day always." Maize smiled at her guardian angel then settled back and looked ahead at the huge city in awe.

Maize had to be awakened by the time the taxi reached Mrs. Martins apartment building and she stumbled sleepily, more than once as she walked up the long pathway to the huge, red front door.

Mrs. Martin apparently, as a rule, would walk up the two flights of stairs to her apartment, but this time she made the exception and they rode the elevator up to the second floor.

Once they entered the apartment, Maize was led into the guest room. Too tired to open up her bag, she slept in her underwear. And as soon as her head hit the pillow, she was fast asleep.

The next morning Mrs. Martin woke Maize bright and early. Handing her a bar of Lux face soap, still in its wrapper, a soft face cloth, and a thick towel, she then walked the still sleepy child to the bathroom and told her to take a shower.

"I'll have a nice breakfast ready for you when you are finished. Don't take too long, we don't want to be late on your first day."

The soap smelled so heavenly that Maize washed herself repeatedly, until she heard Mrs. Martin knocking on the bathroom door.

"Breakfast is waiting for you and I still have to take my shower. I hope you have left enough hot water for me my dear, just teasing," she said.

When they sat down for breakfast Maize smiled and said, "I smell so good, I never washed like that, I mean standing up and the water just pouring on my body.

At first I didn't know what to do, but then I worked it all

out by myself. I must have washed myself over and over, I love the soap, and oh I love New York."

Mrs. Martin smiled. "Maize, my dear, I enjoy having you here and I hope you will visit me often and spend the night whenever you need to take a break from your school. Now eat up, we must leave soon."

Maize's youthful curiosity about so many things, things she had never before seen, heard or experienced, sent her hostess back momentarily into the realm of fear and caution she had experienced and escaped so many years ago.

Before time and distance healed and eventually helped her cultivate the persona that living in the north facilitated.

"Maize, soon, all that is new for you now will become so familiar to you that your memories of before will just fade in time."

"But I don't want to forget my life before I came here - at least most of it," she said hesitatingly. "We were ... are a very happy family and we love each other; we were poor and I never slept in my own bed, all by myself, I always shared a pallet or a small bed with my momma.

Life was hard at least for Momma, but it was home and we loved each other and laughed at silly little things and made up silly games, but that was all we had; that was all we knew. If I had not left the home and the family I love, I never would have known that life could be so much bigger; better."

She looked around the bright and tidy breakfast-room. "And now that I am here, I want more than anything for my mother and little brothers to leave that evil place and to live in freedom, here in New York City".

Maize smiled and hugged Mrs. Martin, who smiled down at her ward.

"I will ring for a taxi to come in ten minutes, okay," said

the kind woman.

"Okay," Maize said with a big smile on her face.

She reveled in the excitement of riding in the elevator. Mrs. Martin smiled. "So you don't remember riding in the elevator when we arrived?"

"Did we? I must have been half asleep," Maize said, laughing. "I like this," she said. "Another first. I can't wait to tell Momma all about the things I have seen, in just one day. Oh, I know my little brothers will like it here as much as I do already."

When she saw the size of the building, Maize's smile faded and she squeezed Mrs. Martin's hand harder than she realized.

"Oh! My dear," she said, releasing her hand. "That is quite a grip you have." She rubbed her hand with the other to soothe it.

"Now just remember child, you have what they want, your talent and your swift ability to learn. This is a very special school and most of the students come from rich families, the majority of them will be white and their families are paying for their child to be there.

You don't have to pay because Mr. Oliver it seems has informed the academy that you are a prodigy. Just remember my dear they want you and your talent, don't ever forget that."

"I won't," she said hesitantly, "but what is a prodigy, Mrs. Martin?"

"A prodigy my dear is someone who has a God given gift, only a few people are as lucky and as gifted as you.

Just remember in case you start to feel unworthy of being there, that you have every right to be there, to develop the gift that God bestowed on you. He has provided a way out of your misery, for you and eventually your family. Your gift can take you far, my dear."

48

– A BRAND NEW WORLD –

MAIZE WAS FILLED WITH AWE AS SHE WALKED THROUGH THE huge glass doors, having climbed at least twenty white marble steps; then they stepped onto the extensive, white marble floor.

The girl had never seen anything so spectacular and immediately felt out of place. A page in a dark green uniform greeted them and directed them over to the reception area.

In the center of the hall was a magnificent glass, circular reception area and to the right of it stood a breathtaking black marble staircase. She allowed her eyes to move around the enormous space in wonderment; then she saw, not one, but four sparkling grand pianos. One each strategically situated in each of the four corners, of the enormous reception hall. Two pianos were as white as snow and two were, ebony black.

Amazed, the young girl just froze, never had she seen a piano so large, so elegant; far better than Louisa's brand new piano.

Feeling overwhelmed by such elegance and beauty, she said softly; "Mrs. Martin, I don't-"

Placing her index finger to her pursed lips, the minister's widow smiled down at her charge, she squeezed the awestruck child's hand.

"Maize my dear, what did I tell you, this magnificent institution wants you; now let us continue to the receptionist's desk."

After they walked hand in hand over to the reception desk, Mrs. Martin introduced Maize and herself to the young lady, sitting behind the desk.

The receptionist was also wearing a smart, olive-green uniform. She smiled at the two visitors, picked up a phone and spoke to someone on the other end of the line.

The two visitors were guided over to two red velvet armchairs and a matching sofa. They both sat down; Maize tried to relax as they waited.

Within minutes, two gentlemen walked towards the two visitors. Both were wearing long white jackets, and a huge smile.

Mrs. Martin and Maize stood up when the men approached them.

"I'm Dr. Schultz my dear," said the grey-haired man, smiling at Maize with an outstretched hand. "And this is Dr. Quinn."

Dr. Quinn extended his hand and Mrs. Martin shook it and introduced herself. Then she shook Dr. Schultz's hand.

"Fear not my dear, Maize will be in good hands," Dr. Quinn said addressing Mrs. Martin. "We will take excellent care of her and you may visit her as often as you wish, during visiting hours."

Maize looked perplexed as she sat in silence looking from one face to another. "Why do I need a doctor?" she said as she moved closer to Mrs. Martin, "I ain't sick."

"Oh, my dear child," Mrs. Martin said reassuringly, "these gentlemen are not medical doctors, they are doctors of music. This means they have studied for many years and they earned the title of doctor or professor. Do you understand, my dear?"

"Yes," Maize said looking around her hesitatingly, "I think so."

"Everything will be explained my dear," said Dr. Quinn. There are many teachers or instructors here, some of them are senior students, but most of us have a title like professor or doctor.

In time, you will get to know your teachers and their titles. Don't worry, there is no rush and in due time you will become as familiar with this, building as the rest of us are."

Dr. Schultz turned to the receptionist and told her that he would take care of the forms; he then informed Maize and her guardian that each new student is assigned to an older, more senior student who will explain the nuances of the institute.

"This is a very large building and we don't want our prized students to get lost," he said. "Monsieur Charles Oliver notified me of your arrival.

And so I have assigned Frank Lester who is an African American senior student and junior instructor as Maize's guide for the next few months until she feels comfortable enough to move around the facility, on her own and in total confidence."

He also explained that there were only four Negro students and with the exception of Frank, who is an instructor, the Negro students are quite young and relatively new to the institution.

He also mentioned that Frank is also from the south and that his specialty is drums, but his musical talents include several instruments.

Dr. Schultz asked the receptionist to page Mr. Frank Lester

and within minutes he appeared with his hand outstretched and wearing a welcoming smile.

"Hello Maize, and welcome to the finest musical institution in the world." He shook her hand and Mrs. Martin's too, and then he took hold of Maize's hand again.

"Shall we go ladies? It is my privilege and honor to take you on a tour and to show you where your room is located, the many classrooms you will use, and best of all," he said with a chuckle, "where the dining rooms are, etc."

Frank, as he wished to be called, was a charming and witty host who obviously loved the institution and thoroughly enjoyed his duties as the welcoming host. The tour lasted just over an hour; Maize loved riding in the elevators that took them from floor to floor.

Frank was well informed and obviously familiar with the institute and he took great pleasure in guiding them through the maze of classrooms; introducing Maize and her 'guardian angel' to each instructor and any students on their rounds.

Just over an hour later, Frank handed Maize a door key then led her to the room she would share with her Chinese roommate.

Frank knocked on the door and Sue Lee opened it immediately, her violin in one hand, with her door key and a huge book bag in the other. Wearing a huge smile, she bowed as was the custom in her country.

"I am Sue Lee," she said, bowing again. "I am happy to meet you here. I must rush, so glad you come now. I must to leave, I have ..." she looked at her wristwatch, "two minutes before my class begins. I see you this evening. I am happy to have you with me, later I will see you; take you down to eat." Then she rushed out, giving Frank a big smile.

The two roommates got along very well, all though at

times, there were misunderstandings due to their different accents and cultural norms. In time, Maize was able to speak and understand specific words and phrases; Sue Lee did likewise.

They fumbled a lot at first, but in a very short time they were able to understand each other; they also did a lot of laughing at and with each other.

On the first Monday of each month, new students at Juilliard were officially introduced to the student body, all of the instructors and the administrators. Maize was one of the three new students to be officially presented that month to the resident students.

The three new students were seated in the front row of the assembly hall; they were instructed to stand up when their name was called.

A couple of rows behind them sat a noisy, freckled face, red head, with some of her friends, who, upon hearing the name of the third new student; 'Maize', they began to giggle.

Maize knew that the red head's behavior was directed at her, since the other two students; a small boy from California and a blond teenage girl from England were both causation and the redhead had not giggled when they were introduced.

Right after lunch, Maize phoned her friend and surrogate mother, she shared her observation and the discomfort she felt. Mrs. Martin cautioned Maize, she thought it her duty to inform her 'that being removed from the South does not necessarily remove you from the harshness of racism.

"I would venture to guess that the culprit is probably from the South and has been raised to disrespect and disregard African American people as being inferior to her, and all white people.

I know my dear, that this experience was unpleasant but

not unfamiliar to you. However, you are no longer in the south, so your tongue is as free as your spirit.

Freedom from the South, allows you to speak your mind and put an end to having to swallow that nasty, ugly tasting pill. You have the power through your gift to outshine all of those who would keep you in chains."

After six months of immersing herself in the rapturous pleasure and techniques of the various music lessons, she was learning and knew how to play with confidence.

As a young, semi-illiterate girl from the Deep South, Maize was in total awe of everything she saw, heard, and accomplished.

Maize was pleased with the compliments she received from her instructors and she was feeling so much more confident now. She loved everything about the institution, her instructors, her roommate and her weekend visits with Mrs. Martin.

She had thrown herself into her lessons, and with few exceptions was made to feel welcome by the majority of the students who were impressed with her passion, her enthusiasm and her skill, especially when they learned about her background.

Maize was one of only four African American students, but she was the only one who came from an impoverished family and from the racist, Deep South.

There was, however, that group of girls from Georgia; and they did all that they could, to make Maize feel like an inferior, unwelcome outsider.

The main protagonist, Madge Taft, made it known to everyone, on that particular afternoon while sitting in the common room, that her poppa paid a huge amount of money for her to attend this institution.

Then, while flipping her long auburn curls from her shoulder and looking directly at Maize, a sly smirk replaced her smile.

"He also gives lots of money so that the likes of this poor little negro can attend this institution," she said with emphasis, while glaring at Maize.

"So you should be thankful little gal, and beholden to me and my rich daddy."

Maize decided, at the end of that last dig, that she was not going to hold her tongue any longer. And, with her left hand dramatically on her hip, she pointed the fore finger on her right hand directly at the speaker.

"I ain't beholden to nobody!" she said, loud enough for everyone in the common room to hear her. "I'm here because my friend is a professor here, one of your instructors in this institution.

He says I belonged here in this school the very first time he heard me play the prelude to Beethoven's Piano Sonata No 7 on a broken-down piano. An' I ain't never had a piano lesson in my life before I cam here an' I hadn't even read music.

Professor Oliver heard me play on an old piano and was amazed. He made all the arrangements for me to come here. He told me an' my momma that I was a prodigy, so there, miss high and mighty, rich girl."

"Well!" said Madge, breathing on her red finger nail, she had just finished painting. "I expect all the cotton you had to pick just made your fingers stronger than most of us who never had to wash a dish, let along pick cotton all day long."

Madge laughed and turned her head to glance at her friends, most of the girls in the room laughed with her.

Maize was rigid with anger, but she held her composure. She walked over to her antagonist and with her right hand on her hip and the index finger of her left hand pointing and wagging in front of Madge.

She said, "You right; I do have strong fingers but it ain't 'cos I had to pick cotton, my fingers got strong pickin' the lice out of the little white girl's hair, which was the same color as yours. I found out later that lice like rusty hair 'cos they can hide much better, especially in rusty, curly hair like yours, which is why you never see me sit close to you."

Maize picked up her homework bag and headed for the door. She was trembling inside, feeling both anger and fear. But she also felt good about her spontaneous response. And after taking a deep breath, she turned around and said to no one in particular, "I wouldn't sit too close to her if I was you, like I said; head lice like red European hair, especially curly, an' they jumps from head to head."

Maize closed the glass door behind her. Then she peeked in to see all the girls moving a safe distance away from Madge, who looked horrified.

When the prodigy returned to her room, she was still trembling; she feared she had spoken out of turn and expected there might be some retribution for her strong words and accusations. Unable to relax, she rang Mrs. Martin from the pay phone on her floor. She told her what had taken place in the common room. Mrs. Martin put her hand over her mouth to mask her chuckles.

"A strong character cannot be created my dear within the confines of placid, quiet, or fearful tranquility. One has to experience trials of suffering, anxiety, pain and ultimately closure in order to strengthen one's character.

One must 'be inspired' or 'in-spirit' to be creative, ambitious and ultimately successful. Then and only then can success be achieved and appreciated.

And remember my dear, that the lack of kindness hardens the soul. I'm sure the young lady in question has seldom, if ever, experienced the likes of you; a proud, young Black woman who refuses to allow the likes of her, to belittle you.

Well, I for one, am very proud of you and I know your mother will be when you share this event with your family back home."

After two years in the institute, Maize, the semi-illiterate teenager from the unsophisticated rural south, felt as much a part of the academy as the rest of her year.

Her performances were outstanding and she had gained the respect of her classmates. Her professor even suggested she go to London for her final year. He said there were scholarships available for students with her passion and drive.

The idea of going to London to study made her dizzy; she thought she must have been dreaming. *How could so much happen over such a short time to someone like me?* she thought.

Mrs. Martin continued to delight in her young and inspiring friend and on Sunday mornings, she would collect Maize from the institute and take her to church.

Afterwards, they would return to her apartment and have a leisurely lunch. Almost every Sunday, Mrs. Martin had an outing planned so after relaxing for a while, they would take the subway either to the park, a museum, or the zoo.

Maize who, had never been on a holiday but had read or heard other girls talk about what they did while on vacation, knew that this was what it must be like.

After each outing, they would stop at an ice cream shop or café for tea and cakes. Maize loved her new life and she wrote home every week sharing her adventures with her family.

She was so very happy and she longed for the day when

she could bring her family up north to join her and live the life of freedom she now enjoyed.

She missed her family and longed to see them, however, her fear of *him* prevented her from returning home even when she was on summer break.

Maize knew how hard her mother worked, so in the summer months she took on a job working at the church that Mrs. Martin attended.

After the pastor heard her play the piano, he had asked her if she would be interested in giving piano lessons to his daughter and son. Almost all of the money she earned, she sent home to her mother to continue to buy her brothers' schoolbooks and save up, so they could all visit her in New York one day.

This new world that Maize had become accustomed to was so far removed from where she came from, however she never lost sight of the hardships and the struggles her mother and brothers labored with every day.

Maize vowed that one day she would bring them up north. She wanted desperately to see her mother and her brothers. In all of her letters home, she said how much she missed them and wanted to see them. Her mother's response was always the same.

"Not yet baby, I'll let you know when it's safe. An' you never know, maybe we'll come see you before you come back here to visit.
Your brothers and me, been savin' an' one day you gone look up an' we be there in New York. We all love you baby, an' I'm happy 'cos I know you're safe away from here an' him. We love you baby.
- Momma

49

– THE DEVASTATING NEWS –

LATE, ONE WARM SUMMER MORNING IN THE EARLY MONTH OF June, Maize was called into the administrator's office. Although this was not a common occurrence, she had from time to time been summoned to the office, usually to sign new papers for some scholarship or another she had been granted. On this occasion, she would leave the office with a very heavy heart.

The office manager handed the cheerful girl a cable and as the unsuspecting teenager began to read it, the phone rang.

"My you are a popular girl this morning, here dear; this phone call is for you.

The call was from her brother, but when she heard his voice, she realized the cable, she had not yet read must have been sent to convey bad news. Maize heard her brother's somber voice on the other end of the line, his voice choking.

"Did you get the cable from Miss Louisa about Ma? You've to come home now Maize; the doctor toll' Miss Louisa that Ma is failin' fast; please come home Sis? We needs you here."

Maize was devastated and she cried all the way to her room, and with a heavy heart, she began packing immediately. Sue Lee was still in class so she left a note for her explaining where she was going.

Having tasted the pleasures and the freedom that life in the North provided her, Maize was more than reluctant to return to the South, back to that plantation where she was nothing more than a pair of extra hands.

Hands that were now smooth and soft; made to play the piano; to create music for the whole world to hear and appreciate. But return she must, duty called her and she would travel with a heavy heart.

Feeling overwhelmed with the written and verbal news, her mother is very ill!" Could it be a trick she thought to get her back?

Momma was always so strong. No! As much as she wanted the terrifying news to not be true; she knew that was not the case. Her brother's choking voice was sincere and the cable had come from Louisa. Maize prayed to God, that she was not just being selfish.

She truly loved her mother and her little brothers, but she feared returning back there. Maize was also afraid of losing her one and only chance at freedom, not only for herself, but eventually for her entire family. She feared that the life she had come to love was being stripped away from her.

Feeling the weight of the world on her young shoulders she obeyed the call to returned to the one place she knew she hated more than any other place in the wide world.

News that her mother was dying of cancer devastated her, and so it was with a heavy heart that she said goodbye to the life she was initially loathed to adopt but later grew to appreciate and love.

She rang Mrs. Martin with the sad and terrifying news. Mrs. Martin tried to comfort Maize, but she knew deep down, that the pain of losing a close and loving relative is a solitary journey for the devastated survivor; a journey that the survivor must endure and often, in silence.

Maize feared that her dream to graduate, get a job, and bring her family to New York; where they too could live freely and enjoy a good life, where shattered.

She was overcome with the sorrow of her mother's illness while juxtaposed with sadness at having to leave what seemed a perfect life.

Reluctantly and emotionally, she continued to pack her bag, the same one that brought her to this once daunting place, as a steady stream of tears flowed.

She was feeling far too young to have to take on the responsibility of caring for her dying mother and raising her two younger brothers.

But her greatest fear of all, was having to interact with him, while taking over her mother's demanding job. She was truly afraid of *him*, if she didn't have her mother to protect her, she feared what her life would be like back home, living again on his property.

And so it was, with a heavy heart, that she said goodbye to the life she was initially loathed to adopt, but had soon grown to appreciate and love.

Sadly her dream to graduate, get a job, and bring her mother and little brothers up north, where they too could live freely and enjoy a good life, was now shattered.

Maize was overcome with both the painful sorrow of her mother's illness while juxtaposed at having to leave what was for her a perfect life. A life and place she hoped one day that she and her family could enjoy and be free.

Devastated, Maize could not face the pain of saying goodbye - so many goodbyes. But she did call her special friend Frank, the senior who had befriended her when she first arrived

Maize loved him like a big brother and, because he was originally from Georgia, she knew he would understand on a level that she felt her other friends could not.

She asked Frank if he would ride with her to the bus station even though most classes were still in session. He agreed willingly.

"I hate to see you go baby sis," he said looking very sad, "but I know when family duty calls; well, ain't nothing more important than your own family. You be safe baby girl, you take care and stay in touch. I'll see you when you get back here".

"I sure hope so Frank, but right now I don't know what's going to happen, only thing I do know is that I am scared, I just ain't ready for all of this. How I'm gone take care of my little brothers, if Momma dies? An' I just cannot stay in the South no more."

"I be prayin' for ya baby girl, God didn't give you all that talent for nothing. He's got a plan in mind for you, baby girl."

Maize realized Frank was trying to be helpful and supportive and she hugged him.

"I'll see you around, sometime, some place, somehow," he shouted as the doors closed.

Maize tried to return his smile, so that he would not feel so bad, but she knew her false smile would bring on a flood of tears, so she just hugged him goodbye. Frank stayed in the station hoping to give her a final wave goodbye, but she felt so weary and waited down, she flopped heavily into her seat and never once considered looking out of the window.

On the journey back to that dreaded place, Maize prayed that her mother would survive. She prayed deeply as the journey took her closer and closer to the life she both feared and hated.

"She still young, God and she was always very strong and all of my prayers are going up to you God to make my momma well again." Maize travelled with a heavy heart, keeping her eyes closed and her hands clenched tight in prayer as she continued to pray, despairingly; she would doze off periodically.

Overwhelmed by the news of her mother's illness, Maize was in a daze during most of her journey home. Home, that place she loved so much as a child; from where she had to flee from in the middle of the night.

Once, so full of love and happiness, now conflicting with the painful and frightening memories. Her stream of tears flowed freely and frequently during the long bus journey towards the home she once loved but learned to loathed and now, dreading her first encounter with *him*.

It was early morning on the following day when she arrived at the station, too early for the sun to appear on the horizon. There was no one to meet her when she stepped down from the bus, not that she was expecting anyone.

The line to collect luggage was long and as usual, her luggage was among the last to be removed. Maize stooped to reclaim the bag once it was pulled from the belly of the bus.

Once outside the station, she stood for a few moments. Even though she wasn't expecting anyone, she had an urge to breathe in the fresh Georgia air, so void of the pungent fumes which had stifled her on her first encounter in New York City.

After exiting the bus station Maize turned right; taking the same familiar path she and her mother had struggled with more than two year earlier, but this time in reverse.

And, quite sadly, very much alone. Maize hoped she would reach her old home before the noon-day sun scorched the earth.

The roads were still unpaved so she had to keep as close as she could to the overpowering overflowing corn fields were the soil was less harsh on her feet; the corn, which dwarfed her was protruding beyond their assigned boundaries.

Trucks and wagons frequented this road as she well knew so she had to keep her ears peeled, less she be run down by a tardy driver, speeding up to capture lost time, having wasted it no doubt on an extra pint of beer.

But as luck would have it, old Mr. Siros rode by with his cart being pulled by old Fannie, his tireless donkey.

After commiserating with her over her mother's illness, Mr. Silos said he would continue to keep her mother in his prayers. He offered genuine concerns, as he told her to keep her mother's scissors well sharpened and pinned to her apron.

Maize lowered her eyes when she realized that her mother must have told him, why she had to send her daughter away. Maize thought she would throw up, reliving that nightmare memory and she felt her cheeks getting flushed.

She wondered how many people knew what had happened to her. Embarrassed, she lowered her head in shame wishing she could become invisible.

When old Mr. Siros stopped in front of her mother's house; the anger, fear, and humiliation that Maize had experienced while still living in his house, came flooding back to her. All she wanted to do was run and hide. But she couldn't. Maize prayed she would get through this traumatic ordeal without having to see or speak to him.

The imprint of *his* words reverberated in her head, as if they were spoken only earlier that day. Still now, they sent shivers down her spin.

"If you know what's best for your ma and your brothers, speak not a word, murmur not a flutter."

Maize remembered it all so clearly. He turned to walk away, and then suddenly spun on his heels saying with sarcasm in his still angry voice, "Who would believe you anyway a scrawny little negro ..."

"Your daughter is my age ..."

"What did I say?" He had yelled at the trembling child, his cold piercing blue eyes glared at her in rage.

"Speak not a word to ANYONE if you know what's best for you an' your kin. Do you hear me?"

Maize was deathly afraid of seeing *him*, she hoped that he was nowhere around. She prayed he was out of town; that she would never see him ever again. Of course, she knew these were silly thoughts and so she hoped to avoid ever being in his presence alone.

His angry words continued to haunt her still, despite the distance in space and time that she managed to put between herself and her mother's evil employer.

50

– ENTERING THE HOUSE –

THAT TINY HOUSE, WHICH WAS OVERFLOWING WITH HER mother's friends, women from her church, some were carrying dishes of food, and some people were off in a corner praying. Maize had to push her way through the tiny house.

Tired and afraid she finally reached the door to her old bedroom, the room she has shared with her mother for most of her life.

As she placed her hand on the doorknob, Mrs. Jessup placed her hand ever so gently on the distressed girl's shoulder. Startled, Maize turned around abruptly. When she saw it was Mrs. Jessup, the woman who walked with her momma to church on Sundays, she relaxed.

"The doctor is in with your mamma now, baby. He be out soon I reckon."

Just as Maize released her hand from the doorknob, the doctor opened the door; he still had the stethoscope around his neck. He looked Maize in the eye and without any sense of remorse he said, "You too late girlie, am sorry for your loss." His voice was cold and mechanical.

Overwhelmed with grief, she ran past him; into the bedroom. Seeing her mother's lifeless body, she threw her arms around her body and wept.

"Momma, Momma," she cried, "why did you leave us Momma, what am gone do now?"

Her brothers joined her, and fell on their knees, one on each side of their big sister. Maize continued to sob while hugging them as they cried along with her.

After some time, all of the neighbors had left the house, except for Mrs. Jessup. She prepared a meal for the grieving children and then she knocked gently on the bedroom door before opening it. Mrs. Jessup walked over and gently placed a hand on Maize's shoulder. She bent over and told her that everyone had left.

"I fixed some food for you all, but now I gots to get home, if you needs me later send one of the boys for me."

Maize placed her hand on top of Mrs. Jessup's hand and squeezed it. The woman turned and walked out of the bedroom and closed the door behind her.

Two days after the funeral, *he* knocked on the door of her mother's home. Maize opened it just ajar, her two young brothers were standing at her side.

"What are your plans?" he demanded. "You can stay on here as long as you pull your weight, and do the work your mama did, before she took ill. If you decide to stay here, well, I will forget the bills that still need to be paid. What do you say?"

"Right now, I can't think clear," she said, trembling inside and hoping that her fear was not as visible as it felt. "I'll let you know in a day or two."

He reached his hand towards her shoulder; instinctively she cringed and moved away. He pulled back as if moving from the rattle of a snake and walked backwards down the steps.

Fear and anger caused her to close her eyes, she could feel her stomach churning; she had never felt quite so alone as she did on the day that her mother died.

There was further devastation when Maize realized that she was bound to pay off her mother's debt, in addition to having to raise her two younger brothers.

Feeling desperate and alone; she had no one to turn to for assistance or help and she feared the lack of control she would have over her own body.

Her only ally, her benefactor and devoted friend Monsieur Oliver, unfortunately was not available; at the behest of his parents he had returned to Belgium on business. And so, forever cautious, Maize was able to ward of her attacker by keeping her brothers close to her.

Unable to cook, she engaged another domestic, a hardworking, older woman, known in the village for her outstanding cooking, a skill Mabel's daughter never acquired.

Maize made sure she was never alone in the house when *he* was present. She also kept a pair of newly sharpened scissors hanging from the waistband of her apron.

Two weeks after she resumed her mother's job, *his* daughter Louisa returned home from school for the summer and the two young girls resumed their friendship.

Maize's fears eventually evaporated, but she continued to keep the scissors attached to her apron and avoided being alone in his presence.

In the spring of the following year, Monsieur Oliver was set to return soon to Georgia. He had been informed by the director of Juilliard that Maize had returned to Georgia, to bury her mother but had not come back to school.

Monsieur Oliver was genuinely concerned, but unable to leave Belgium for several months, he informed the director that he would pay his charge a visit the moment he returned to America. He made a point to visit her as soon as he was home.

Maize was delighted to see him and she reflected on the past fourteen months as the reasons preventing her from returning to the institute.

Through tears and sobs, she confided in him as she shared the horror she had experienced prior to moving to New York.

Monsieur Oliver was shocked to hear that she had been abused by the wealthy landowner. He immediately rang her abuser; he threatened to expose *his* evil deed if *he* still insisted Maize remain.

More than anything, Monsieur Oliver wanted Maize to return to Juilliard and complete her studies. He knew of her responsibilities and commitment to her brothers, so he offered to have them move into his parents' home and teach them the art of wine making.

He said, "They will be well fed, cared for, and paid a small wage, after they learn each of the many steps involved, from the refinement of the soil, to the planting of the seeds and the final production of the best Georgia wine."

Monsieur Oliver later took Maize and her brothers on a tour of his family's estate, he explained the process of wine making from the treatment of the soil to the care and cultivation of the grape vines. The boys were impressed with the giant vats and cedar crates.

They were also given a tour of the beautiful home Monsieur Oliver and his family lived in, she was delighted to learn that her brothers would share the rooms on the top of the grand house and that they would eat their meals with the family.

Assured that her brothers would be well cared for, Maize said farewell to them and to Monsieur Oliver and his generous family.

She expressed her relief, her happiness, and gratitude with tears of joy; she longed to return to Juilliard, to continue her training.

Maize was finally free from the dreaded nightmare that loomed over her. She was thankful and relieved to be free of the life imposed upon her and her brothers; the responsibility and constant dread of being ravaged by *him*.

Relieved, grateful and eternally happy Maize was free at last; free of her mother's debt, free of the responsibility or obligation to care for her brothers, and supervising their chores, and best of all, she was now free to return to New York.

Free at last, Maize could hardly wait to pick up where she left off; doing what she was born to do. She had escaped the fear and the dread that had all but consumed her.

Her hands, once soft and flexible, were now dry, her fingers stiff; with all the work, she had to do in the big house and the tiny house she and her brothers had lived in.

After the long and traumatic absence, Maize finally returned to New York, to Juilliard and to her dear friend Mrs. Martin. She re-emerged with as much delight as she possessed years earlier, and she was determined to catch up and eventually surpass where she had so tragically and abruptly returned home.

No longer a novice, she dove in full-speed effusively, determined to exceed where she left off. It took some time, however for her to feel as confident and as comfortable as she once was.

During her extended absence there was very little time to sit at the old spinet piano, which of course, was extremely inferior to the baby grand pianos she practiced on at Juilliard.

Maize had not anticipated the negative effects such a long absence would have on her skill and the lack of flexibility that obstructed the suppleness of her once nimble fingers.

This was due, in part, to the harsh wear and tear on her hands keeping the big house spotless and keeping many hand laundered linens in tip top shape.

Her days were so long and energy draining that she scarcely had time to sit down at the end of each long and tiring day.

She was totally frustrated and becoming more disillusioned with her attempts to recapture all that she had learned; she would marvel with envy at the accomplishments of some students almost half her age.

It was obvious to her, that her enthusiasm had waned significantly and it seemed the harder she tried to capture what she once had, the more frustrated she became.

She finally had to admit and accept that the lack of the flexibility in her fingers was now preventing the keys to flow as fluidly as they once did.

When she first entered the academy, she could hardly wait for her long days to begin; she would also practice for hours on Saturdays. Her instructors would often scold her and insist that she take time off for herself.

However, with the premature death of her beloved mother, Maize felt as if the fire of enthusiasm that previously surged through her entire body, had also died and she was no longer able to reignite it.

She had such dreams for her mother and brothers. Dreams she now felt were foolish, girlish and unattainable dreams.

The more disillusioned Maize became with her diminished abilities, the more time she spent visiting with her dear old friend Mrs. Martin, almost every free weekend. Maize missed her mother so much and found a sensitive listener in her surrogate.

Mrs. Martin was still grieving over the death of her beloved husband several years earlier, so she was completely sensitive to Maize's loss and her need to still grieve. Their relationship grew stronger over the coming years.

Maize worked hard but the spirit and the passion, she once possessed, had waned significantly; she failed a major performance and became inconsolable.

Two weeks later, she received a cable from the church secretary informing her that Mrs. Martin had suffered a stroke and was rushed to the local hospital. Maize panicked, she dropped everything and spent every free moment in the hospital, sitting at the elderly woman's bedside.

Three weeks later, Mrs. Martin was out of danger and was released from intensive care. However, before her doctor was willing to release her, he insisted that she could not return home alone.

Her physician strenuously stipulated that she engaged a home help until she was totally capable of taking care of herself.

Well, Maize would hear none of that, she decided to take a voluntary break from Juilliard and take care of her.

Mrs. Martin was delighted to have Maize living with her; however, she insisted that she continued to practice playing piano every day. Maize agreed and their affectionate relationship was reignited.

Within three months, Mrs. Martin was well enough to attend church services on Sundays. Her church was going through a transition and the very pregnant organist had recently requested maternity leave.

The Pastor announced each Sunday, that the church would need a temporary organist to replace Mrs. Johnson who would soon leave to go on maternity leave for six to ten weeks. Auditions were to be held that afternoon if there were any interested members.

On the following Sunday after each sermon, he made the same announcement. He said there was a sign-up sheet at the welcome desk for anyone interested.

Sadly, there were no takers, not a soul had placed their name on the signup sheet. Frustrated, Pastor Stevens announced that the choir would have to sing acappella.

Mrs. Martin was notably upset, so she persuaded Maize to fill in the gap, until the organist returned after her maternity leave.

Maize was quite reluctant; her organ skills were not as polished as her piano skills, and lately she felt even they were in question, but she promised to give it some thought.

The following week when the pastor made the same plea from the pulpit, Mrs. Martin squeezed Maize's hand.

Reluctantly she agreed, more to please her benefactor than personal desire, but she convinced herself it would be a short-term commitment until the new mother and well-respected organist resumed her job.

Maize played the organ and the piano for the next two years, she also taught music to church members who had the desire to learn. The former out-standing Juilliard student had found her niche and she was content with her life once again.

Whenever Maize made a significant change in her life, she felt the presence of her beloved mother guiding her down the right path.

Like when she accepted the position of organist at the church she now attended. Maize relinquished her place at Juilliard and moved in permanently with Mrs. Martin, who was very fond of her adopted daughter, they had many interest in common besides music.

One of their favorite evening pastime pursuits was playing chess; they also enjoyed working on picture and crossword puzzles.

On Sundays after church, weather permitting they would stroll, through Central Park. Mrs. Martin liked to feed the birds; a hobby she developed with her husband, they would package up the breadcrumbs that had collected in the bread box all week, along with any leftover dry bread and take them to the park to feed the birds.

Maize looked forward to their Sunday afternoon strolls in the park; it enabled her to unwind after sitting for three hours playing the organ.

When the weather was right and the nights were long, Maize often took the short stroll from her room to the park.

Occasionally she would get a letter from her brothers, they were doing well and she was relieved that she no longer had to worry about them. They were content in Georgia and loved the work they did for the Oliver winery.

One evening, three weeks after Maize celebrated her twenty-fourth birthday; she woke up suddenly after feeling a strong presence in her room.

Instinctively, she thought it was her mother but she decided to go over to Mrs. Martin's bedroom. There was no response after her second knock, so she turned to return to her own room.

Walking away, she realized how cold it was in the hallway so she decided to make sure her benefactor was covered. Upon entering her room, she saw that Mrs. Martin was sleeping peacefully.

As she turned to leave the room, she felt the softest breeze, startled she glanced at the window to see why it was open given that it was winter and it had snowed all day, off and on.

The window was not open; Maize shivered at the sudden cold then proceeded toward the door which was now closed. *There must have been a window open somewhere,* she thought.

She walked over to her sleeping friend to make sure she was well covered by her quilt. Automatically, she put her hand on the sleeping woman's forehead, it was stone cold.

Startled, Maize jumped back, and then she called her name, even though she knew without wanting to know that this woman, who had been her savior, her benefactor, her surrogate mother and devoted friend was dead. Mrs. Martin had died in her sleep.

Maize knelt at her dear friend's bed and wept uncontrollably. She awoke the next morning still on her knees. Overcome with sadness, she rang the family doctor to inform him that his patient had died during the night, in her sleep.

Two months after her benefactor died, a third cousin and distant nephew who attended the funeral claimed possession of everything that Mrs. Martin owned.

Dozens of church members attended the funeral, including Maize, who was once more alone in the big city of New York.

Pride prevented her from returning to Juilliard and she was determined not to return to the oppressive south. When it was known that Maize would need a place to live, one of the members offered to rent her a room if, she continued attending the church and playing the organ on Sundays.

Over the years, Maize had made several friends within the church. She also taught piano lessons to adults and children upon reflection, Maize realized she was quite happy, living the life she now lived; she also mourned her dear friend for many months.

Three years later, the church held a memorial service for a member who was a local musician, Maize was asked to play the organ throughout the service. And as luck would have it, her old friend Frank from Juilliard was a pallbearer, he was also a close friend of the deceased.

Frank was very impressed with the organ player, and because his deceased friend had been the pianist in Frank's band, he made a request for a specific hymn to be played on the piano.

Maize was happy to oblige. When she walked onto the alter to take her place at the piano, Frank grinned from ear-to-ear.

They could hardly believe their eyes on seeing one another, but they kept their cool as Maize walked solemnly over to the shining piano. The entire church wept as she played the request - *Take My Hand, Precious Lord, Lead me on.*

Frank left a note with the pastor, for her. Two days later, she contacted him by phone.

The following month, she relinquished her job as organist and handed over the position to a seasoned organist from Chicago who had just relocated to New York.

51

– MAIZE'S REFLECTIONS –

As it happened, Maize did not have an easy transition into the band, every one of the men resented her joining them, saying 'females bring bad luck'.

All of the musicians in the band were accomplished, most having trained with professionals or had taken lessons, but Maize and Frank were the only two who were students and or instructors at Juilliard.

They had been working together for years. Frank said they were set in their ways and didn't like changes. He convinced her to accept the job and instructed the band to give her a chance.

It took some time, but eventually she won them over, first with her talent as a pianist, second with her personality, and thirdly with her cooking.

Living with Mrs. Martin, Maize had finally developed a passion for cooking. Mrs. Martin's husband had been a trained chief before he became a minister. He built his own church and had owned a restaurant in the Bronx.

Before his death, he passed on many of his recipes to his wife and she, in turn, taught Maize how to cook.

The patrons loved her as much as the boys in the band finally did. By then, Billy the saxophone player was crazy about her and wanted to take her to bed. Maize was cute; she was lively, friendly, and extremely talented.

He assumed, based on how friendly she was with all the fellers in the band that she must have slept with most, if not all, the other guy. *Why else would they all be so comfortable with her,* he thought.

Billy was also insanely jealous of her popularity. He had been impressed with her immediately, knowing the minute he heard Maize play, that she was a first-class piano player.

He had never heard of a girl playing in a band, he knew that some sang, but never played an instrument in an all man band.

He heard through gossip that Maize and Frank went way back. Billy had no history with her, nothing in common with her other than they both sat on the same stage to play music at a local venue and, that they were both from the Deep South.

Billy felt he was in second place, accusing her of flirting with members of the band. In truth, he was insecure and jealous of her bubbly personality.

Eventually hearing Billy's story, Maize shared with him the reason she fled Georgia; and about the hardships of life on that plantation, that she was raped as a girl.

And also, how she'd come to live in New York and met Mrs. Martin and had come to join the band through Frank.

"We were both at Juilliard, the music academy in New York," she said. "I was a student, just a girl. Frank was a junior instructor at the time." Maize explained to Billy that he was like a big brother to her and that he showed her 'the ropes'.

Billy didn't like Frank simply because the man had known Maize long before he walked into her life, regardless of what she said or did. But then, Billy didn't like most people.

As they became friendlier, Maize tried many times to boost his ego with compliments, but she could do nothing to improve his mood or his confidence.

Billy was a handsome man, tall and slender, but he had poor self-esteem and he seldom smiled. Throughout his life, he felt like he was a 'runner up', never the best, never in first place.

He knew deep down that his music was not first rate; but it was not for the want of trying. It just seemed to him, though he tried to improve his style, he never felt as though measured up.

Billy often resented all of the applause Maize received from the audience when they requested she played solos.

More than half of the other musicians were married, but that did not stop them from flirting with her. Some less insidious than others but she would laugh off their approaches.

Eventually they got the message; she was not interested in fooling around with married men.

Billy silently observed this and gradually he changed his opinion of the only girl in the band. He was older than Maize but he was crazy about her, he just didn't know how to show it. He had never really cared for anyone, except old Bubba, and never before for a woman.

She was a southern gal, but she was very different from the women he messed around with in the South and he had no time for the 'stuck up northern gals'.

If he wanted her in his life, he knew he would have to change his ways if he was ever going to win her over. Plus, he was older than she was. He realized that as the only single man in the band, he was going to have to smarten up.

A year or so later, in the early hours in the morning, after playing for a private party, the band broke up, each going their separate ways.

It was pouring down rain and hail, with newspapers over their heads, obscuring their side view.

Maize and Billy ran to the approaching taxi and while reaching for the handle on the door, they looked up, recognized each other and the ice melted instantly with their mutual smiles. They both got into the taxi and soon enough, a new relationship began.

52

– A MATCH NOT MADE IN HEAVEN –

Marrying Maize was the best thing that had ever happened to Billy. She made him feel as though he had worth, that

he finally counted for something, that he mattered; because he did matter a lot to her. Maize respected his passion for the music he played and the fact that he never tried to flirt with her or trivialize her playing, as most of the other men did, when she first joined the band.

The respect she had for him developed into a deeper friendship, one that left him confused. Having lived a life devoid of love, except for old Bubba, who Billy realized had truly cared for him.

The instant Billy heard Maize play her instrument, he had known he could never reach her standard of accomplishment. However, on hearing her background, he realized they had a similar history and a mutual understanding based on the lives they had lived, lives they had no control over.

He knew that in her eyes it didn't matter that he was not as 'polished' or as accomplished as some of the other musicians in the band. Yet, she was drawn to him and he learned to respect her, as did most of the band.

But why, why did she love him; why did she want him in her life? he thought.

As the years rolled by, this doubt, insecurity and low self-esteem took root. In his mind; she must feel sorry for him. He knew that she understood his painful past, just as he knew and understood hers.

But she could move on with her life because she had a natural gift. For him, the need to play music was the only means he could see of fleeing the horrors of belonging to another person.

More than anything in the world, Billy was determined not to repeat his father's life, as his older brothers had. Playing a musical instrument had been, for Billy, the only avenue of escape, and so he'd taught himself the basics, with the help of Bubba.

Maize was a sensitive and selfless woman. She observed her husband's limited skills, his lack of confidence and diminishing pride.

As a sensitive young woman, she felt his pain. And later, as his wife, Maize recognized that there was nothing more she could do or say to ease his frustration, his lack of confidence which continued to diminish over time.

Billy seemed indifferent, at times, to his limited skill. She learned several months later, in addition to being very insecure, he was also extremely stubborn.

He recognized early on that his skills were mediocre compared to the group's talent, but they were all professionally trained. And more often than not his frustration and anger was expressed in his performances and he was not happy. He also, after some time, resented his wife for being the star.

She noticed that his downward mood swings had become much more frequent lately and almost every time they performed, he would receive more reprimands for playing off key.

Her gentle touch or warning glance no longer forebode him, if anything, he became angry with her. And like so many women at that time, she thought a child would remedy the void that she felt evolving between them.

With his good moods rapidly deteriorating she was unable to tell him when she first found out that she was pregnant. She kept waiting for 'the right time' to share her wonderful news with him; weeks went by and she found it quite difficult to approach him.

This was her first pregnancy, she was over the moon with joy and she wanted to share this very special joy with someone.

If her mother was still alive, she would have told her right after she told her husband. She could share the news with one or two close friends in the band, but she wanted to share it first with her husband, the man she loved, the man who was the father of her unborn child.

He walked in on her in the bathroom, she was only wearing her brassiere and panties. "What's wrong wid you; you getting fat or sumthin?"

Maize smiled coyly and said softly, "Or sumthin".

He walked out of the bathroom and continued to dress in the bedroom. Maize had slipped into a thin dressing gown, watching him through the open door. Billy was reaching for his jacket, the one with the silver stripes down the seams.

"Damn, I hate this thing," he mumbled to himself. "Billy," Maize called softly.

"Yeh."

"Come here baby, we need to talk." "About what?" he said, his back to her.

"Come on baby, I want to see your face. I've got something to tell you."

"What is it Maize, we runnin' late an' I wants to go over that new number before the crowds come in."

"I know baby, but this is really important and won't take but a minute."

"So, tell me now," he said turning to face her. Not wanting to know what he already suspected.

Maize had both her hands on her stomach. "We are going to have a baby. You're going to be a daddy."

"So is this the sumthin' you want to tell me," he said with a scowl. "You having a baby. So, what you want me to do?"

"Do!" she said, shocked. "Well are you happy, are you glad you gone be a daddy?"

"Maize, if I tell you I's happy, I be lyin' in my teeth. What I wan'a baby fo' anyway. I ain't never wanted no kids."

"But honey," Maize pleaded, "This is our baby, yours and mine. We will have someone new to love and to care for; I thought you would be happy. Children complete a marriage, this baby-"

"Did you ask me if a baby gone make me happy? Well I ain't happy, so there." You wan' it, you take care of it."

Maize was beside herself with sadness as his cutting words over-whelmed her. "But I thought you -"

"Well, you thought wrong. You better make a move on or we gone be late." He turned back to the closet and began looking for a tie to match his blue and silver jacket. Being pregnant did the opposite of what his wife had hoped for.

She wanted closeness and yet, he widened both the

emotional and the physical distance between them; she wanted to build his confidence but he became more uncertain, distant and awkward.

What Maize didn't understand, was that, the real inner building of a marriage totally escaped Billy. And as far as being a parent and father, well; this concept totally and completely eluded him.

Billy wanted no part of being a parent or having to be responsible for anyone other than himself. This was due of course, to his very unhappy childhood, feeling like an outsider all of his life; an alien in his own family.

He never, ever wanted a child - not only was the responsibility of being a parent objectionable to him, he was emotionally bankrupt, having never received support or experienced love from his father, his mother, or any of his siblings. The truth was, Billy had nothing to give.

Billy's time or need for love had long dissipated. He lacked the desire and was too rooted in his anger to change now. He detested the whole idea of a child, a baby.

"What I want with a kid?" He would mumble in disgust and anger. Billy just wanted to run away from everyone and hide.

"My life was fine, it was just the way I wanted it, just me and Maize. I know that as long as Maize is in the band, my job is safe, but when she leaves to have that kid, then she gone want to stay home wid it, an' that'll be the end of my job."

Maize was still in the hospital, giving birth to their baby boy; when her husband was fired from the band. Too many wrong notes; too many mean looks; and too many complaints not only from the band members, but also from many of the patrons.

Billy wasn't much of a drinker at the best of times. In the

earlier days, after each set, he would drink a beer while relaxing with the guys in the band. However, after Maize's announcement, not only did his drinking increase but his choice of beverage changed.

When he was child, unwanted he knew for sure, there were rare moments in his life when he had been happy and it was Bubba who provided what little happiness he'd had throughout his life. Billy would spend long hours with Bubba, both as a child and as an adult.

Then, along came Maize. Initially, he resented her being in the band, while secretly envying her talent. In time, however, he had come to admire her and respect her talent, and as cranky as he was, he fell in love with her.

But now, Billy resented her all the more, because in his mind, she deceived him. In his opinion, she destroyed his life, which he felt, at last, was finally content.

All he ever wanted to do was play for his own listening pleasure; however, he knew he would have to work if he wanted to continue living in New York.

In truth, Billy would have been happy just playing for himself. Music for Billy was the only means he knew of that could erase his emotional pain.

Billy was not at all surprised when he got his walking papers. He knew for months that he was treading on thin ice, but his anger got in the way of reason.

He was too stubborn to reflect or analyze where it came from or how deeply it was buried. Having a child, becoming a parent, such thoughts had never previously entered his head.

Children were to be ignored, despised even, and certainly not wanted, just as he was a child. His world had no room for children. All he wanted in his world was Maize and his flute. But she changed all that, she altered his world.

She had no right to up an' get herself pregnant, an' never askin' me 'is it k?' What's she gon' do with a kid, she can't work and I sure ain't gona take care of it.

This is her doin', not mine. We had it good, just the two of us. Well, am gona have to put her in her place. She might be top dog in that little band, but I'm top dog in my house.

His blind revenge did not dissipate. After Maize returned home from the hospital with her smiling baby boy, Billy announced that he was returning to Macon. The shock that registered on his wife's face gave him a small sense of internal satisfaction.

Knowing her husband as she did, Maize did not to try to dissuade him, she knew he had made up his mind; and that he was going whether she accompanied him or not.

She felt certain, that after a few weeks or months of living back in the dreaded, hateful, and racist infected south, the place they both detested, that he would change his mind.

They had a child now; a son, Maize was sure that deep down Billy wanted a better life for his son, than he had had as a child. They were a family and Maize valued family as much as she valued her gift, so she was going to make sure that they would always be together.

Determined to stand by her man, she pulled up stakes and returned to the South, the place that she loathed with every inch of her body and every breath she took.

Deep in her heart, she hoped their tiny baby boy, who gave her so much joy, would melt her husband's stubborn heart. The South is all about family, she thought, so there may be some good that comes out of moving back there.

Billy knew that she understood his painful past, just as he knew and understood hers. Mentally, emotionally or spiritually, she could escape because she had the natural gift of music and a maternal gift.

She adored the baby boy she had named Kenneth. And she came from a devoted and loving family. Something he had never experienced.

As a very young man, Billy's need to play music, this was the only means he could see of fleeing, not only the south, but also the horrors of his childhood and his feelings of never belonging; of feeling less than second best; like an outsider.

He hated the place where he was born and raised; hated it so much he could hardly wait to get away and he even promised himself when he finally left, that he would stay away forever.

As a young man, Billy needed to escape the South and out from under the people who claimed to be his family and he achieved his goal.

He escaped and he was content living his new life in New York. But his anger, jealousy and frustration now drove him back to the place where he always felt inadequate, insecure, and never, ever at peace.

PART III

53

KENNETH'S REFLECTIONS

When Kenneth opened the door to his tiny bedroom, he stood for a brief moment, before crossing the threshold.

He walked over to the faded, sunken, threadbare, upholstered armchair. Feeling both weary and nostalgic, he plopped into the chair that had been in the corner of his bedroom for as long as he could remember. Tired, he gripped the worn, fabric arms of the old chair and breathed deeply.

He hadn't realized, just how long he had been daydreaming or reminiscing or both, until he looked at his watch. In any event, he had been deep in thought for some time.

Kenneth stood up abruptly and began stuffing what few belongings he had into his knapsack, then after taking in another deep breath, he exhaled. He felt his body quiver and heard a momentary cry. As a rule, Kenneth was not given to dramatics, but on this occasion, something stirred inside of him deeply. Unconsciously, he took in another deep breath, as his eyes darted toward the bedroom door.

"I've got to get out of here," he said in a whisper, "and now is the time." He knew he could no longer delay the inevitable.

"What was so difficult?" He asked himself. "It's not as if there was any love between us." Kenneth had kept the promise he made to his beloved mother.

'Stay at least one month with him after I'm gone, who knows son; your father might just change,' she had said to him. Even knowing full well that her husband, now Deacon William Johnson, would never change.

Kenneth knew when he promised his mother, on her death bed, that the month, the intolerable thirty days would make no difference at all. He also knew that his mother knew, there was absolutely no chance of his father changing the way he felt about their only child.

There was no love for him as a child, so why would there be even the remotest change now that his wife was gone. Ken realized years ago that it was his mother and her protective love that made life just bearable for him whenever his father was present.

"When did my father begin to dislike, no, loath me?" he said aloud; and the sound of his own voice interrupted his thoughts momentarily, startling him; and his eyes immediately and instinctively glanced toward the bedroom door.

He shuddered. Kenneth could not remember.

Overcome with that painful realization, he had to admit that he could not in all honesty recall a time when he felt or experienced anything from his father that was even remotely related to affection let alone love.

"It's time to go," he said out loud, looking around his bedroom. "Before I choke on this bile of painful indifference." *This room,* he thought as he put his packed duffel bag and his guitar next to the door of his tiny crowded room *is a child's room.*

As he took one final glance around the tiny space he had occupied for nearly twenty-four-years, he mumbled to himself. "This tiny room is barely big enough to accommodate the single bed I outgrew years ago; and that piece of cardboard replacing the pain of glass I broke, I can't remember when.

Then his eyes rested on the patch of worn out linoleum on the side of his bed.

How many times did I scuff into my shoes in that very spot? He chuckled. *Funny, I hadn't noticed that bald spot before,* he thought.

His eyes then rested on the squeaky rocking chair in the corner and for a moment he was overcome with a deep feeling of grief, as he reached into his childhood memory. So many stories told over so many nights, so many years ago; sitting in her lap on that old squeaky chair.

Kenneth was all too familiar with the overcrowded four-room house, a house that had been his home since he was born.

A house overflowing with love but now, that love was gone. It disappeared with the death of his mother, leaving in its wake the unbearable noxious stench of hate.

"I can't put this off any longer," Ken said, his voice bearably audible. "I might as well not be here for all of the interaction there is between us. God knows I've tried hundreds of times to make conversation with him but he just refuses to talk to me, with me or at me.

I should have left years ago, well now I am truly free to be me, there is nothing to keep me here any longer."

Ken picked up his only possessions, his duffle bag, a briefcase and his guitar, which represented love, life, creativity, hope, and yes freedom.

He walked out of his tiny bedroom, which had been his sanctuary and after taking one last look around the little four room cabin, he opened the creaking front door; his father was already sitting on the porch.

While holding the wilted screen door open, he said, "Dad, I'd like to talk to you".

He walked out of the house and onto the front porch holding his guitar, he let his duffle bag drop to the ground.

Mr. Johnson was sitting on the slightly creaking metal swing, now rusty with age; he was drinking a brew and listening to a ball game on the portable radio.

Billy jumped as the screen door slammed shut after Ken removed his briefcase which was propping it open. He didn't respond to his son. Billy just wanted to be left in peace, to enjoy his Sunday afternoon.

The old man looked up and seeing his son, he quickly averted his eyes. Kenneth took the two steps from the screen door, to the rusting swing and stood directly in front of his father.

Mr. Johnson's gaze was riveted to the floor of that century old porch, where layers of old paint had chipped over time, exposing splinters of decaying discolored wood planks.

Ken's father refused to raise his tired eyes, even though he could see his son was standing in front of him. He could barely see Ken's shoes under the flare of his white cotton pants.

He thought as he looked in total disgust at the wide-legged pants. *'What in God's name did I do wrong in my life to deserve a chil' like dis?'* Then he sucked his teeth, *chich.*

Ken knew this so well. It was the sound his dad always used when he was disgusted. What he didn't know was whether that disgust was directed at him, his pants, or the result of the game.

"Did the Browns make another touchdown, Dad?" he asked his father knowing that he was an ardent fan of the Atlanta Falcons, his one and only favorite team.

Again there was no verbal response, but there was a distinct shift of his body so that he was no longer directly sitting in his son's view. His jaw tightened and he rolled his eyes as he turned away from Ken and crossed his legs.

"Dad, I know you can hear me and I know how important this game is to you, but what I have to say is equally as important to me.

You can always go back to listening to the game and the final score will be on the news tonight or tomorrow night or next week. I'm leaving Dad and I need to talk to you before I walk away."

"Leavin' boy, don't make me laugh; you still wet behind the ear." But when Billy looked up, he saw the look on his son's face and the overstuffed duffle bag. "Hmm," he said, and then he sucked his teeth again. "So, say what you got to say an' go."

"I'm leaving Dad, not because I think I've let you down, or because you believe I've let you down. There is nothing I can do here that will ever persuade you to think of me as a man. You know that as long as I love music and dance, we'll never see eye to eye.

There is no way I can be myself and earn your respect. You have always called me a sissy and a puff; you have never called me a man. But I am a man, Pop. I am blood of your blood, I am not like you, but I am of you. I can never be the man you want me to be.

I am my own man, with my own likes and dislikes; with my own tastes and style, in dress, music, ideas, and with the talents or gifts that God gave me. You, above all people, should be able to understand about the gifts God gives to us, you've said time and time again that it is a sin to ignore the God given gifts or talents He bestows on us. Or, was that just preacher talk?

Last month when Mom died, I knew I would leave. Mom always knew what I wanted; she knew me as her son and respected me as a man, a man with talent. She asked me to stay until she passed on. I told her I would and that I would try to make you understand me. I know you could never love me, not as long as you refuse to understand me."

Mr. Johnson sucked in his breath, raising his chest by inches. "You through?

"No Pop, I'm not finished. I want you to know that I don't want to leave my home, I don't want to leave my church, my town, and my friends; not like this. But as long as I stay here with you, I die a little bit each day. I don't want to drown or die in this misery, Pop.

I want to live, to love, to dance and to perform. As long as I stay here with you Pop, that's not possible. I've got to leave this town, this house, you. I'm going to be the man I am, in the only way I know how. Pop, I have to respect myself for who and what I am. As long as I stay here in this house with you, I never will.

I don't hate you Pop, I just feel sorry for you, but if I stay much longer and stifle who I am, I will hate you."

He turned, hearing a noise. "Oh, here's my taxi." Ken ran down the steps, waving at the driver. "Wait up, man?" The taxi driver gave him the thumbs up.

Ken stepped back up the four weather-worn steps onto the splintered, creaking, ninety-year-old porch and stood once more in front of his father. In his brief absence Mr. Johnson had turned his radio on again and finished his beer.

"Well I'm going Pop, that's my cab."

"Yeh." Came his father's reply.

After a few seconds Ken said, "I'd like to shake your hand, Dad."

"What fo'?" replied his father; his voice sullen with an edge of contempt.

"Well," replied his son, his only child, fighting a slight pang of emotion that caught him off guard. "I may never come back here, never see you again."

Still sitting on the old rusted seat, his father shifted his body to one side while rolling his eyes as his son began to speak. Seeing the quivering lips and hearing the momentary chocking in his voice; Billy shifted his position again and sucked in his teeth.

"Dad, what I'm about to do is a big step -"

"What big-" Billy began, sucking his teeth.

"Don't cut me off Dad, like you always do. Like I said, I'm leaving and I want to say goodbye, and I'd appreciate it if you would just take a few minutes to listen to what I've got to say. Is that okay with you Dad? 'Cos it's important to me."

Chich, his father made the noise again, sucking his teeth. "Well, get on wid it."

Ken ignored his father's mumbled comments. "Dad you and I have never seen eye to eye, I know I haven't turned out to be the kind of man you wanted me to be."

His father twisted in his seat and made a grunting sound. "Man," he said, "heh".

"Five years ago, when I refused to go to the heavyweight boxing match with you in Las Vegas, you called me a sissy because I told you I don't like violence.

And ten years ago when I was just twelve, Dad you got mad at me 'cos I was performing modern jazz in the school play. You said 'that's for girls and puffs'.

And when I was just six, do you remember Dad, that day

when I came home from school cryin' and my shirt was torn. I had a bloody nose an' a swollen eye. Do you remember what you said to me? Well, I do.

You didn't say, 'Come here Son and tell me what happened or who did this to you'. No. All you were concerned about was 'Who saw you crying like a baby girl?' Those were your exact words. 'Ain't you never gone be a man, what's wrong wid you anyway'.

Do you remember that, Pop? Then you told me to go back to the school yard an' fight like I was a man or stay an' be a sissy all the rest of your life. Well, I'm leaving Dad."

There was no response, not that Kenneth was expecting one, still hope springs eternal, he thought and after all, this would be their last opportunity to talk, since Kenneth had no intention to ever return to this God forsaken place.

"I am still blood of your blood Pop and flesh of your flesh and your righteous indignation cannot erase that fact."

Mr. Johnson sat his radio down on the floor in front of his rusty seat, then he stood up and while looking into Ken's hopeful eyes, he spat out his tobacco juice.

Then, he picked up his radio again and with a calculated deliberation in his stride, he walked past his son and into the house. The squeaking screen door slammed shut behind him, with a clanging bang.

And that was the last time they saw each other.

54

ALONE AGAIN

STILL HOLDING HIS LITTLE RADIO, MR. JOHNSON WALKED wearily into his bedroom, which was small and oppressive just like the mood he seemed to be in, perpetually. The full moon, which was hovering over his tiny house, seemed to shine brighter than ever, into his tiny bedroom that night; and as if seeing it for the first time. *This room is small, when did it get so small,* he thought. He began to hum involuntarily, 'Ain't no sunshine when you gone'. Then he sat heavily on his bed; the bed he had shared for so many years with his Maize.

He took in a deep breath and with the little radio in his left hand he lay down on the bed and swung his legs over the side of it, so that his tired old body was completely stretched out. Only then did he allow the radio to rest on the floor before turning over and facing the exterior bare wall.

Through the cracks in the worn out, faded paper blind, it seemed as though it was still light outside. That faded blind, on the only window, which was completely yellowed with age; was pulled all the way down.

The moon light entered his gloomy room. He put his late wife's pillow over his head hoping to make the room dark and that's the way he liked it.

Billy had no idea what time it was when he woke later. It was finally dark in his bedroom, so he reached up and moved the decaying blind to get a sense of the time. If it was light outside, none of it seeped into his dark and silent little room. Reluctantly, he sat up and scooted his body closer to the window and raised the blind, just enough to peer out.

Still unable to see anything he decided to get up and walk to the front door which was still wide open. It was then he realized it was evening; he had slept for several hours.

I guess I was tired, he thought, as he stretched his arms above his head. And while filling his lungs with oxygen, he realized just how chilled the house was, he quickly closed the front door locking and bolting it against the cool night air and went into the house.

Before walking over to the faded leather chair, the chair he had sat in for over twenty year he turned on the floor lamp; the old television was directly opposite to *his* chair and he turned it on before making himself comfortable for the night.

He knew he would be up all night because he had taken such a long nap. He wondered how many hours he had slept.

Anxious to find out the results of the football game he had been interrupted from, he turned channel after channel to find the sports results.

Frustrated at not finding the news on any of the channels, he looked at his watch, he instantly remembered where the watch had come from and in a fit of rage, he tore it off of his wrist, and then threw it across the room.

That watch, a simple inexpensive Timex, had been a gift from his son almost four years ago. It fit his wrist just fine, in fact, it was the only strap that he could wear in perfect comfort and had done so for close to four years.

"Damn," he said out loud as he stood up from his chair and walked into the tiny kitchen to look at the clock on the stove. "Shit! The last news was over long ago. Damn it! 2:30 in the morning, why did I sleep so long?"

He took out a beer from the fridge and walked back into the front room and resumed his seat on the old chair which now embraced his permanent imprint.

Twilight Zone was on the news channel; of course, it was a re-run so he proceeded to switch the channels. He soon discovered that all of the channels played re-runs during that hour of the morning. He got up in a huff.

"Might as well turn in," he said.

Then he realized right after he said it that he was talking to himself.

"Damn fool," he said as he turned off the television. Before turning off the floor lamp, he double checked he had locked the front door. "Damn cold in here," he said.

He was tired, in mind, body, and spirit, but sleep was the perpetual stranger. It loomed close at hand, but seldom crossed the threshold and when it did it was for very short periods of time, which was why he was so amazed when he realized he had slept several hours earlier in the day.

He wasn't sleepy now but he wanted to sleep; he needed to empty his mind, to get rid of those reoccurring thoughts that had haunted him all of his life. But it seemed the more he wanted sleep the stronger his thoughts, those harsh painful memories revisited him, making it harder for him to drift off.

He knew full well that this night would be one of those nights. He lay down on his bed and after pulling the quit over his head, he placed Maize's pillow under his head.

She alone possessed the ability to soothe his anguished mind. She would lie next to him and listen to him breathe. Maize could always tell when those nightmare thoughts engulfed him; his breathing became long and heavy, but she had known what to do.

Nobody told her what to do; it was almost instinctive. On those occasions, his wife had traced her long, cool fingers and while humming an old Negro lullaby, she would smooth his brow.

Sleep was inevitable but not immanent that night. Maize had been the tranquilizer, that quelled the insidious storm which churned in his conscious and subconscious mind; memories that chased and haunted him no matter how hard he tried to put them to rest.

Nightmares come from so many places, especially when they begin in childhood; once those painful or frightening impressions are formed, they are often indelible, particularly when each one feeds into another.

Some nightmares, those repeated bad dreams that wake one up in the night, the ones that refuse to go away; often distorting one's reality. Those nightmares that refuse to fade often become more perpetual with repetition.

AFTERWORD

I would love to know what you thought of *FREE To Be Me*.

You can write a review with your thoughts at:
Amazon
Goodreads - search Mary V. Macauley

Works by Mary V. Macauley:
FREE To Be Me
Pushing 40 Short Stories

Connect with the author:
Twitter: www.twitter.com/MaryVMacauley

ACKNOWLEDGMENTS

My newest novel FREE To Be Me began as a short story in the 80s just for the internet. Now, my international novel crosses oceans, classes, and races.

My thanks to my daughter Julie Williams and my patient editor Kirsten Rees.

ABOUT MARY V. MACAULEY

At eight-three years young at the time of publication, author Mary V. Macauley - who has always been a trailblazer - is the author of two books FREE To Be Me and Pushing 40.

Before settling in the US, Mary was in the forefront of the necessary changes in the UK with the placement of children of color, being placed with appropriate families; reflecting the child's race, religion, and cultural heritage.

Having been one of two women who started the very first domestic violence shelter in California, back in the late seventies - now has truly proven that AGE IS NOTHING BUT A NUMBER! She is also a mother, grandmother, and great grandmother and writing very much runs in the family.

Her first novel 'Pushing Forty' depicts the lives of women of color in the UK. And the second is an exceptional story spanning two-hundred years and two continents with stunningly intertwined stories of those trying to escape only to discover that trouble will follow.

Her incredible, deep, soulful writing has been compared authors such the renowned Dr. Maya Angelou.

Joyce King, Ph.D, Board President, Professor Of Education at Georgia State University after reading the first five pages described it in just two words . . . "Toni Morrison!"

Mary V. Macauley earned her Master's Degree in Social Work in the UK. Before settling in the US, Mary was in the forefront of the necessary changes in the UK (teaching social worker students and staff in universities) about the placement of children of color, being placed with appropriate families; reflecting the child's race, religion, and cultural heritage.

She has also written a beautiful children's book that eloquently teaches how people are merely 'different' in different parts of the world, but in a beautiful, interesting, exciting way - teaching to accept different cultures! This third book will be available in the future.

Made in the USA
Middletown, DE
27 May 2021